THE BOOK CLUB MURDERS

LAUREN DELGARDO

BLACK SWAN
DIGITAL

First published in 2025
Concept created by Black Swan Digital. Developed by Mark Coleman.

PROLOGUE

The body is still now.

It hovers just below the surface, limbs drifting weightlessly in the chlorinated blue. A slow, lazy sway, like a marionette cut loose from its strings. The moon, swollen and silver, turns the water into a sheet of polished glass, broken only by the faintest ripple where a pale wrist floats upward, fingers half-curled, as if still reaching for something. For help. For air.

But there is none. Not anymore.

I stand at the pool's edge, my breath coming fast, ragged. My clothes cling to my skin, heavy with the weight of the water. My dress, whatever color it had been, is darker now, soaked through, clinging in wet folds to my legs. My hair drips in cold rivulets down the back of my neck. The chill has settled deep in my bones, but I don't shiver.

I should leave. I need to leave. And yet, I can't move.

My gaze stays fixed on the water, on the body suspended just beneath it. The streetlights from beyond the fence cast shifting shadows over the pool floor, twisting the shape below into something grotesque, a drowned specter, a nightmare given form. But it's real. *I did this.*

The air is thick with the scent of chlorine, sharp and chemical, clinging to my skin, my hair, my hands. My hands, my fingers had been locked around her wrists, prying her away, pushing her down. I flex them now, feeling phantom resistance, the last feeble kicks, the desperate thrashing before the water had filled her lungs.

The night is so quiet now.

When it happened, there had been noise, the violent splashing, the gasps that turned to gurgles, the useless struggle. But the world hadn't stopped for it. No porch lights had flicked on, no concerned voices had called out. Just the wind, rustling through the trees, whispering against my wet skin.

Now, everything is still. The wind has died. The trees hold their breath. The only sound is the faint, rhythmic drip of water from my clothes, dark droplets forming small, widening circles where they hit the concrete.

Somewhere in the distance, a car passes, headlights sweeping briefly across the wooden fence before vanishing. A door slams. A dog barks.

No one has seen me. No one has heard.

I glance down at my hands again. They are pale in the moonlight, the nails clean, but I know that if I press my fingers to my nose, I will smell her there. Her skin. Her fear.

I should feel something. Guilt. Panic. Horror.

Instead, I feel light.

The weight, the one I had been carrying for so long, has slipped away, sinking to the bottom of that pool along with her. A dark, dragging burden I had grown used to, gone in an instant.

This was inevitable.

I step back, carefully, my bare feet making soft, wet prints against the patio stones. The gate stands open, just as I left it. A breeze stirs now, sending a shiver down my spine. Or maybe that's the adrenaline.

I take one last look at the body in the water.

The moon shifts behind a cloud, and the pool turns black.

By morning, someone will find her.

And by then, I will be home, wrapped in my sheets, eyes closed in the sweetest sleep I've had in years.

And no one will ever know it was me.

1

THE BOOK CLUB

Vanessa Caldwell's home was the crown jewel of Willow Creek. Perched high on a hill, the sprawling colonial mansion overlooked the quiet streets like a queen surveying her kingdom. The driveway wound up past immaculate hedges and flowerbeds blooming with roses so perfect they didn't seem real. Light spilled from the house's many windows, illuminating the grand columns that framed the front entrance. Everything about Vanessa's home radiated wealth, power, and control.

Inside, the house was no less dazzling. The sunken living room, where the book club had gathered, was all cream and gold. Cream-colored couches, golden accents on the walls, and a chandelier that sparkled like a constellation above them. The air was lightly perfumed with Vanessa's signature scent, something expensive and floral. Even the wine glasses they held were delicate crystal, thin enough to shatter with a strong grip.

It had been Vanessa's idea to start the book club four years ago, and like most things in Willow Creek, she had executed it with precision. "To bring us together," she'd said at the time, flashing one of her dazzling smiles. She had pitched it as an escape, a way for the women of the town to bond over literature and wine. But over the years, the group had become less about books and more about power plays, subtle digs, and carefully constructed alliances.

Tonight was no different.

Vanessa, seated on her cream couch, radiated perfection. She was dressed casually, white jeans and a silk blouse that looked effortless on her toned frame, but there was nothing casual about her demeanor. Her blonde hair fell in soft waves around her shoulders, and her makeup was flawless, her lips painted in a shade of pink that looked like it had been designed specifically for her.

She swirled her glass of rosé and leaned back, surveying the women around her. "This month's book," she began, her voice calm but carrying an unmistakable edge, "was certainly... provocative. Wouldn't you agree?"

The others exchanged glances.

Charlotte Davenport, sitting stiffly in an armchair near the window, nodded first. "It was compelling," she said carefully, her hands clasped tightly in her lap. Her dark hair was swept into a sleek bun, and her outfit—a tailored blazer and fitted jeans—was as polished as her demeanor. Charlotte, a top real estate agent in Willow Creek, was always composed, but tonight something about her seemed off. Her smile didn't quite reach her eyes, and her fingers toyed with the stem of her glass.

Vanessa tilted her head, her smile growing sharper. "Compelling," she repeated. "That's an interesting word to describe betrayal and murder. I suppose it does make you wonder about the secrets people keep, doesn't it?"

Charlotte's knuckles tightened around her glass, but she didn't respond.

Miriam Reed, seated on the opposite end of the couch, cleared her throat. "I think the author was exploring how secrets can fester," she said, her voice measured. "How they don't just destroy relationships, they can destroy people."

Miriam was the oldest in the group, a history professor at Willow Creek University. She was dressed in simple cardigan and slacks, her graying hair pulled into a low ponytail. While the others leaned into the glamour of book club nights, Miriam always arrived looking practical and unbothered. She didn't fit the Willow Creek mold, but she had a way of observing the group that made her presence impossible to ignore.

"Exactly, Miriam," Vanessa said, flashing her teeth in what might have been a smile. "Secrets have a way of coming to the surface eventually, don't they?"

Across the room, Erica Miller rolled her eyes. "Okay, let's not get too philosophical. It's just a book. Besides, I thought the whole conspiracy thing was a little obvious."

Erica was curled up on one of the couches, a glass of wine balanced on her knee. She was the youngest in the group, a stay-at-home mom who always seemed slightly out of place in Vanessa's curated world. Her oversized sweater hung loosely off one shoulder, and her messy brown hair looked like she hadn't glanced at a mirror before leaving the house. But Erica didn't care. If anything, she seemed to enjoy making the others uncomfortable.

From the opposite end of the couch, Daniella Cruz let out a sharp laugh.

"Oh, Erica, you'll see a conspiracy in anything!" Her tone was light, but there was steel underneath.

Erica's jaw tightened. She'd been waiting for some kind of barbed comment from Dani.

Daniella, Dani, was a fiercely competitive sports mom of two relatively talentless boys. She treats everything like a competition and lives to win. Even if that means buying a spot on the podium. Just as Erica suspected she had with her son Todd's recent addition to the ball team.

"Well, some of us have better things to do than schmooze little league coaches," Erica shot back smoothly. "Or did your 'donation' to the team just happen to coincide with Todd's sudden spot in the starting lineup?"

Dani's smile didn't falter, but her nails clicked against the stem of her glass. "Some kids earn their positions, Erica. Others just... expect them."

Tiffany Monroe, the former beauty queen turned lifestyle influencer who was lounging in an armchair with one elegantly crossed leg over the other, let out a soft hum of amusement. She tossed back her platinum curls, and pursed her red-painted lips.

"Now, now, ladies. Let's keep the claws in. Besides, if we're talking secrets, I think we can all agree some things, like the husband in the story, are better left buried."

Her words held weight, though she delivered them with the airy confidence of someone who had spent years perfecting the art of appearing effortlessly charming. Tiffany's trailer park childhood was something she never spoke about. That poor girl was long gone, and no one in Willow Creek knew anything about her.

Erica snorted from the corner, swirling the wine in her glass, but saying nothing.

Tiffany forced her small frown into a smile. "I just think it makes for interesting reading, don't you?"

Belinda "Bee" Thompson, sitting slightly apart from the others, nodded enthusiastically, her perfectly neat, mousey fringe bouncing over full eyebrows. A naïve PTA Mom who lived for her kids and looked for the best in everyone, Bee was probably the only member of the book club who believed in the "sisterhood" they'd said they were setting up. She was probably the only one who read every line of every book, too.

"I thought the wife's revenge plot was fascinating! I mean, it was extreme, but you could see why she did it. I..." She caught Erica's amused look and blushed. "I just think it made her really exciting."

"The wife?" Erica smirked. "I loved her. I mean, sure, she was unhinged, but at least she didn't sit around and let her husband walk all over her."

The room went quiet.

Vanessa's smile flickered, reset, and then froze in place.

"Unhinged is one way to describe her," she said, her tone light but cutting. "I think we were meant to see her as a cautionary tale."

"Maybe," Erica said, shrugging. "But sometimes people deserve what's coming to them. Secrets or not."

Charlotte stared down at her glass, her face pale. Pam Hargrove, who had been watching the bickering unfold with her usual lack of interest, coughed. She was a no-nonsense, chain-smoking, wine-guzzling divorcee with the year-round tan of a woman who did well out of the alimony settlement and never has to work again.

"Let me tell you something, ladies," she drawled. "If I could have gotten away with murder, I would have saved a fortune in the divorce court."

"You still did better than the first Mrs Hargrove," Erica quipped. Pam curled her lip, but just about hid it behind her wine glass as she took another swig.

Jilly Lawson, seated in a corner of the room, shifted uncomfortably.

Jilly was the quietest of the group, a single mom who owned the town's independent bookstore. She was dressed simply, in a floral blouse and jeans, her hair pulled back into a loose ponytail. Jilly never spoke much at these meetings, and when she did, her words were usually ignored or overshadowed. But tonight, even Jilly couldn't hide her unease.

"I don't think the wife was supposed to be someone we root for," she said softly, trying to ease the tension.

"Maybe not," Erica said, finishing her wine. "But rooting for her sure made it more fun."

The conversation shifted after that, the women moving on to safer topics, like writing styles, pacing and whether the author had done enough research. The tension eased, but it didn't disappear completely.

Vanessa stood after a while, clapping her hands lightly. "Well, I think that's enough heavy discussion for one evening," she said. "Dessert, anyone? I have crème brûlées."

The group broke apart, some following Vanessa into the kitchen while others lingered in the living room.

Erica leaned toward Jilly as they walked out to the patio. "This group is exhausting sometimes," she said, laughing under her breath. "But don't worry. I've got something that's going to liven things up soon."

Jilly frowned. "What do you mean?"

Erica smirked, her eyes gleaming. "You'll see."

In the kitchen, Charlotte excused herself to the powder room, her face tight and unreadable. Vanessa watched her go, pouring another glass of wine, her smile plastered in place, though there was a flicker of something darker in her eyes.

Miriam lingered on the sidelines, watching it all unfold. She was good at watching. She had learned over the years that people always showed you exactly who they were if you waited long enough.

Vanessa had built the book club as a space for women to come together, but somewhere along the way, it had turned into something else. A battlefield.

Miriam watched as Vanessa displayed the tray of crème

brûlées, their delicate, caramelized tops glistening under the chandelier. She placed them on the coffee table with the grace of someone who never rushed, who never stumbled. Vanessa didn't know the meaning of the word awkward. Every movement seemed deliberate, every smile calibrated to perfection.

"Dessert," she announced, as though unveiling a masterpiece. "And before anyone asks, yes, I made them myself."

Erica raised an eyebrow. "Your chef get a day off, did he?"

Vanessa laughed lightly, the kind of laugh that dismissed the comment as a joke, even if it wasn't. "Don't be silly, Erica. You know I enjoy cooking when I have the time. It's so... grounding, don't you think?" She picked up a spoon and tapped the golden crust of one dessert with satisfaction. "Help yourselves."

"Not for me," Tiffany demurred. I'm watching my waist. Carlos already has me working overtime at the gym."

Erica muttered something under her breath and leaned back into the couch. She'd already drained her glass of wine and was now eyeing the bottle on the sideboard, clearly debating whether it was too soon for another.

"I'll have hers," Pam said, scooping a second dish to Vanessa's clear annoyance.

Jilly, as always, was quick to smooth things over. "They look amazing, Vanessa," she said with a small, genuine smile. "I don't think I've ever seen a dessert this perfect."

"I wish I could bake half as good as you do, Vanessa," Bee added, smiling.

Vanessa's face softened. "Thank you, Jilly, Bee" she said warmly, handing them each one of the dishes. "You're both so kind."

Charlotte, who had just returned from the powder room, took a seat near Vanessa and quietly accepted a dessert. She'd managed to smooth her expression into something neutral, but her earlier tension still lingered in the stiffness of her shoulders.

She avoided Vanessa's gaze, keeping her focus on the untouched crème brûlée in her hands.

Miriam, sitting at the edge of the couch, took the last dessert but made no move to eat it. She glanced around the room, observing the subtle dynamics that always played out in Vanessa's home.

Vanessa had built her life like her house, grand, flawless, and designed to impress. She'd married Simon Caldwell, one of the wealthiest men in Willow Creek, fresh out of college. At twenty-two, Vanessa had been the quintessential Southern belle, her beauty and charm enough to turn Simon's head and secure her a spot in his world of private jets, charity galas, and multi-million-dollar deals.

But that had been twenty years ago. Now, Vanessa was forty-two and still, just about, holding on to her crown with perfectly manicured nails. Her days were filled with yoga classes, society luncheons, and carefully curated, highly visible acts of charity. But behind the scenes, Miriam suspected, things weren't as pristine as Vanessa wanted everyone to believe.

There were whispers in town about Simon's roving eye and wandering hands, about financial trouble no one dared to mention to her face. And though Vanessa smiled and sparkled at every event, there were cracks in the façade if you looked closely enough. Miriam always looked closely.

"So," Vanessa said, her voice cutting through the silence. "How is everyone's week going? Anything new in Willow Creek that I should know about?"

It was the kind of question that pretended to be friendly but was really an invitation to gossip.

"Well," Jilly said hesitantly. "There's been talk that the new couple on Oakwood Ridge is hosting a block party."

Vanessa arched a perfectly sculpted brow. "A block party? How charming." Her tone suggested it was anything but. "I suppose that's what happens when people move here from... wherever they came from."

"They're from New Jersey," Bee offered quietly, immediately regretting it when Vanessa's lips twitched.

"That explains it," Vanessa said, her smile sharp. "Well, I suppose we should all make an effort to welcome them. It's the polite thing to do, after all."

Erica let out a snort of laughter, drawing everyone's attention. "Polite? Is that what you call dropping in unannounced with a bottle of wine and subtly critiquing their landscaping?"

Vanessa's smile didn't falter, but her eyes hardened for a split second. "I'm always happy to offer advice when it's needed," she said sweetly.

"Sure," Erica said, leaning forward to grab the wine bottle and refill her glass. "Because people *love* unsolicited advice."

"Erica," Bee said softly, shooting her a pleading look.

"What?" Erica asked innocently. "I'm just saying, not everyone's trying to win *Best Garden of the Year.* Not everyone can afford a team of gardeners and a pool boy. Some of us are just trying to get through the day."

"Speaking of getting through the day," Pam interjected, steering the conversation away from Vanessa's icy glare. "Jilly, how's the bookstore doing? I heard you're hosting an author event next month."

"Oh, yes," Jilly said, grateful for the change in topic. "It's a local author. She writes historical fiction. I think it'll be a nice event."

Vanessa leaned back, her smile returning as the attention shifted. "That sounds lovely, Jilly. It's wonderful that you're finding the means to keep an independent bookstore alive. Such a rarity these days."

Miriam noticed the faint hint of condescension in her tone, but Jilly smiled anyway. "Thank you, Vanessa. That means a lot."

Charlotte, who had remained silent throughout the exchange, finally spoke up. "Speaking of events, is everyone going to the gala next weekend? The theme sounds... extravagant."

"Oh, you mean the masquerade ball?" Vanessa said, her smile widening.

"I can't wait," Tiffany chimed in. "My outfit is to die for."

"I'm sure it is," Vanessa said. "Simon and *I* will, of course, be attending. It should be quite the evening."

Miriam glanced at Vanessa and noticed something, just the slightest flicker of tension at the mention of Simon's name. It was gone in an instant, replaced by the same confident smile, but Miriam filed it away in her mind.

The room fell quiet for a moment before Erica, as always, broke the silence.

"I'm not sure I'll go," she said, swirling her wine lazily. "I mean, life's too short for all this posturing. But then, maybe one day, someone will say or do something that changes everything. And when that day comes, I sure as dammit want to be there to see it."

Her words hung in the air like a challenge.

Vanessa's smile grew tight. Dani's eyes narrowed. Charlotte stared down at her uneaten dessert while Pam shrugged and took another sip of her wine. Jilly and Bee exchanged a nervous glance before both studiously looking at the floor.

And Miriam, ever the observer, leaned back in her chair and watched.

2

CHARLOTTE

Charlotte Davenport unlocked the front door of her perfectly manicured home, letting herself into the dark, quiet foyer. The house smelled faintly of lemon polish and lavender candles, details she made sure to maintain, even if no one visited anymore. It was important to keep up appearances.

She dropped her keys onto the glossy white console table, the sound echoing in the emptiness. The house was too big, too quiet, too perfect, just like her life.

Charlotte stepped out of her heels, wincing as her toes hit the cool marble floor. Her feet ached from the long day, but the ache in her chest was harder to ignore. The book club had been particularly draining tonight, though she wasn't entirely sure why. Maybe it was Erica, throwing around those veiled comments like grenades, or Vanessa, whose carefully aimed barbs were as sharp as ever.

Pam hadn't helped with her sarcasm, either.

Or maybe it was just her own fraying nerves.

She padded into the kitchen, flipping on the light to reveal a space that looked ripped straight from a home design magazine: white cabinets, gleaming stainless-steel appliances, and a massive marble island that took up the center of the room. It was beautiful, pristine, and utterly soulless. The fridge hummed quietly as she opened it, pulling out a bottle of sauvignon blanc.

Her hand shook slightly as she poured herself a glass.

Charlotte leaned against the counter and exhaled slowly, her mind drifting back to Vanessa's living room. The pointed questions, the passive-aggressive smiles. Secrets have a way of coming to the surface, Vanessa had said, her eyes lingering just a little too long. Charlotte knew it wasn't random. Vanessa always had a way of wielding her words like a knife, cutting in ways that left you bleeding days later.

She knows, Charlotte thought, her stomach twisting. *Or maybe she doesn't. Maybe you're imagining it.*

But she couldn't ignore the way Vanessa's gaze had lingered on her tonight, the subtle shift in her tone. Charlotte had spent years building walls to protect herself, but tonight, it felt like Vanessa had caught a glimpse of the cracks.

Her phone buzzed on the counter, breaking her thoughts. She stared at the screen, her chest tightening when she saw the name. She grabbed the phone quickly, her fingers trembling as she unlocked it.

Him.

"How you doing?"

Her pulse quickened, and she typed out a reply with shaking hands:

"We need to talk. I can't keep waiting like this."

She hit send before she could overthink it, then placed the phone face-down on the counter and picked up her wine glass again.

Charlotte wandered into the living room, the soft glow of a single lamp casting long shadows across the room. The space was immaculate, designed to impress, the cream-colored sofa perfectly fluffed, the glass coffee table spotless. There were no toys scattered across the floor, no clutter, no signs of life.

It wasn't always like this.

Five years ago, this house had been alive with laughter and chaos. Her sons, Ryan and Caleb, had been younger then, loud, messy, always running through the house with sticky hands and endless energy. And Bobby, her husband, had been a different man.

Bobby had once been the golden boy of Willow Creek, a financial consultant who built their lives on big commissions and an even bigger personality. He had a smile that lit up a room, a laugh that made people trust him. But all of that had faded over the years. The commissions slowed. The trust dwindled. And eventually, so did the money.

Now, Bobby spent most of his days in his small rented office, poring over spreadsheets and pretending the walls weren't closing in. He still smiled, still laughed, but only with other people, and even then, it was forced and hollow. Charlotte barely recognized him anymore.

The truth was, they were drowning. The house was mortgaged to the hilt, their savings were gone, their credit cards stretched to their limits. And yet, Charlotte couldn't let anyone know. She couldn't let Willow Creek see the cracks.

She had worked too hard to get where she was and put up with too much.

Charlotte sat on the sofa and stared at the framed photos on the mantle: her family, perfectly posed in front of a beach sunset; her sons holding tennis trophies; her and Bobby at a charity gala, their smiles frozen in place. To anyone looking in, they were the picture of success.

But Charlotte knew better.

Her real estate career, once the envy of Willow Creek, was no longer enough to keep them afloat. She still sold high-end homes, still attended glamorous open houses and charity luncheons, but the market wasn't what it used to be. Clients were harder to come by, commissions thinner. And after Bobby's financial collapse, it had been up to her to hold everything together.

The phone buzzed again.

Her heart jumped as she reached for it, reading the reply.

"You'll have to wait a little longer. It's not the right time."

Her hand curled around the phone. She wanted to scream, to throw the phone across the room. But instead, she composed herself and typed back:

"It's never the right time. Do you even want this anymore?"

She sent the message, then dropped the phone onto the coffee table. She hated how desperate she sounded and how small he made her feel. She couldn't help wanting him, needing him, but she also couldn't keep living like this, waiting, hoping, pretending.

The sound of the garage door opening jolted her back to reality. Bobby was home.

Charlotte quickly wiped the tension off her face, plastering on a neutral expression as Bobby walked in, looking as tired as she felt. He was still handsome in a weathered kind of way, but his shoulders slumped under the weight of whatever had beaten him down that day.

"Hey," he said, setting his briefcase on the floor.

"Hey," Charlotte replied, forcing a smile.

Bobby paused, his eyes lingering on her for a moment. He opened his mouth like he was about to say something, then thought better of it. Instead, he nodded and headed toward his den.

Charlotte sat there for a long time after he left, staring at the untouched glass of wine in her hand.

Her phone buzzed again. This time, the message was short:

"Don't worry. Everything will be fine. Soon."

She read it twice, then set the phone down and closed her eyes.

Soon isn't good enough, she thought, as she went to prepare dinner.

Charlotte stood in the kitchen, staring at the raw chicken breast on the cutting board in front of her. The knife in her hand felt heavier than usual, the weight of the day pressing down on her shoulders. Her hands moved automatically, slicing the chicken into neat strips, but her mind was elsewhere. On the text messages. On Vanessa. On everything she'd worked so hard to build. On everything she stood to lose.

The scent of garlic and rosemary filled the air as she tossed the chicken into the pan, the sizzle loud and sharp in the otherwise quiet kitchen. She glanced at the clock. 6:45 PM. Dinner was late, again.

In the lounge room, she could hear the faint sound of her sons' voices as they arrived home together. Ryan, sixteen, and Caleb, fourteen, were already arguing over something, their tones flat and uninterested, as though even their fights were just going through the motions.

"Mom!" Caleb shouted from the other room. "Do we have any more Coke?"

Charlotte gritted her teeth and forced herself to keep her voice steady. "I'll bring some in with dinner."

"You always forget to buy enough," he muttered, loud enough for her to hear.

She bit back a sharp reply, focusing on stirring the pan instead. The chicken was browning nicely, the herbs clinging to the golden edges. At least something was going according to plan.

Behind her, Bobby emerged from his den. He drifted back

into the kitchen like a ghost, his tie loosened, his shoulders slouched.

"Smells good," he said absently, though his eyes didn't meet hers.

"Thanks," Charlotte replied, her tone clipped. She didn't want to be angry at him, at least, not consciously. But it was hard not to feel resentful when he moved through their house like a shadow of the man he used to be. Bobby had once been her partner, her anchor, the person who made her laugh when things felt impossible. Now, he barely seemed to notice her.

He grabbed a beer from the fridge and leaned against the counter, cracking it open and sipping it slowly as he stared at the floor.

"Could you set the table?" Charlotte asked, glancing at him.

Bobby blinked as though the request surprised him. "Yeah, sure." He set the beer down and wandered toward the dining room.

Charlotte sighed and turned back to the stove. She added a splash of white wine to the pan, watching the steam rise as the liquid hissed and bubbled. She wasn't just cooking dinner; she was performing. The perfectly browned chicken, the roasted vegetables, the fresh bread she'd picked up from the bakery that afternoon, everything was part of the illusion. A family dinner, a happy home.

By the time the food was ready, the table was set, though Bobby had only managed to find mismatched forks and glasses that didn't belong to the same set. Charlotte said nothing as she placed the dishes in the center of the table.

"Dinner's ready!" she called, her voice echoing up the stairs.

Ryan appeared first, earbuds in, his phone in his hand. He didn't look up as he slouched into his chair, the hood of his sweatshirt pulled up over his head. Caleb followed a moment later, already scrolling through his own phone.

"Phones away," Charlotte said sharply, placing her hands on the back of her chair.

Neither of them moved.

"Now," she added, her voice colder.

Ryan sighed dramatically, but shoved his phone into his pocket. Caleb hesitated for a second before tossing his onto the table with an exaggerated groan.

"Why do we even have to sit down here?" Caleb muttered. "It's not like we talk about anything."

"We do talk," Charlotte snapped, sitting down. "And we're a family. Families eat together."

"Whatever," Ryan said under his breath, reaching for the bread.

Charlotte gripped her fork tightly, forcing herself to smile as she served the chicken. "So," she began, her voice unnaturally bright. "How was school today?"

"Fine," Ryan mumbled.

"Same," Caleb added, already picking at his food.

Charlotte glanced at Bobby, hoping he'd jump in, but he was staring at his plate, cutting his chicken into tiny pieces.

"Any homework?" she pressed.

"Nope," Ryan said, not looking up.

Charlotte's patience was wearing thin. "Ryan, I got an email from your math teacher last week. She said you missed an assignment. Did you turn it in?"

Ryan rolled his eyes. "Yeah. It's done. Can you stop, like, micromanaging my life?"

"I wouldn't have to if you actually communicated," Charlotte shot back.

"Here we go," Caleb muttered under his breath.

"What was that?" Charlotte snapped, her voice rising.

"Nothing," Caleb said, holding up his hands defensively.

Charlotte leaned back, pressing her lips together to stop

herself from saying anything else. Her gaze flicked to Bobby, who still hadn't said a word. He looked up at her briefly, his face blank, before going back to his food.

She took a deep breath, willing herself to stay calm. This was how it always went. No matter how much effort she put into making things perfect, it never worked. Her family didn't care about the hours she spent cooking or the energy she poured into holding everything together.

But that didn't matter. Even though she was planning a new life, away from Bobby, she couldn't let this one fall apart completely.

"How's the chicken?" she asked after a long silence, forcing another bright smile.

"Good, I guess," Ryan said with a shrug.

"Yeah," Caleb added. "It's chicken."

Charlotte swallowed hard and picked up her wine glass, draining it in one long sip.

~

After dinner, she stood alone in the kitchen, washing the dishes as the sounds of her family faded into the recesses of their house. Ryan had retreated to his room, Caleb to the basement, and Bobby back to his den. They were all in their own little worlds, leaving her alone with her thoughts.

The text message replayed in her mind: "Don't worry. Everything will be fine. Soon."

But how soon was soon?

The wine bottle on the counter caught her eye, and she reached for it, pouring herself yet another glass. It seemed to be her only comfort right now, but tonight, even the warmth of the alcohol did little to ease the tightness in her chest.

Charlotte stared out the kitchen window into the dark

backyard, her reflection barely visible in the glass. The truth was, she didn't know how much longer she could keep this up. The house, the marriage, the perfect façade, it was all so fragile, and it felt like it could shatter at any moment.

She clenched her jaw, gripping the stem of her glass. *You can't let it fall apart,* she told herself. *You need to protect the boys.*

But deep down, she wasn't sure how much longer she could keep pretending.

The conversation at Vanessa's opulent house had drifted into familiar territory, small talk that veered between polite interest and passive-aggressive barbs between Vanessa, Erica and herself, while Pam looked down her nose at them all, and Jilly and Bee cowered in their corners.

Erica had been hitting the wine even harder than usual, and Charlotte had seen her staring harshly at Vanessa several times. At one point, Erica had leaned back on the sofa and tilted her head toward Vanessa.

"I don't think I even remember how this whole thing started," Erica said, gesturing vaguely around the room. "The book club, I mean. It feels like it's always been there, like the town itself."

Vanessa smiled, a faint flicker of pride in her eyes. "Oh, it wasn't always here. I started it about five years ago. Willow Creek needed something more... cultured, and I thought, why not?"

"Cultured?" Erica repeated with a smirk. "Is that what you'd call that trashy romance novel a few months back?"

The room rippled with laughter, though Vanessa's smile tightened ever so slightly.

"Well," Vanessa said smoothly, "we needed something light after *The Goldfinch*. Not all of us have the stamina for Pulitzer winners every month."

Erica raised her glass in mock salute, her smirk widening. "Touché. I do have stamina, I'll give you that."

Jilly, perched on the edge of her chair with a cup of tea cradled in her hands, glanced around nervously before speaking up. "I joined about four years ago. Vanessa invited me personally. She said it might help get more people into the store."

Vanessa waved a hand, dismissing the sentiment. "Well, of course. Local business is the backbone of this town. Plus, you needed to get out more, Jilly."

Jilly flushed slightly but nodded. "It has been nice. Meeting everyone, I mean. Even if I don't always get through the books."

"It's the highlight of my week. Seriously," said Bee, smiling around at everyone as though seeking affirmation from any one of them that they felt the same way. They did not.

"I was one of the first members," Charlotte interjected, her voice calm but deliberate. She leaned back, her posture effortlessly poised. "Back then, Vanessa practically begged me to join."

Vanessa raised an eyebrow. "Begged is a stretch too far."

"Well," Charlotte continued, ignoring the remark, "I thought it sounded like a good way to meet people. Bobby and I had just moved to Willow Creek, and I didn't know anyone yet. Plus, I've always loved reading. I was one of those kids who brought books to the dinner table."

Pam, who usually didn't share much about her childhood, laughed bitterly. "My mom used to hide my books until I'd finished all the chores."

Charlotte smiled, though it didn't quite reach her eyes. "Anyway, I figured it would be a good way to establish myself in the community. And it worked, didn't it?"

Erica swirled her wine glass, staring into the deep red liquid. "I joined two years ago. Mostly out of boredom."

"Boredom?" Pam asked, raising an eyebrow.

Erica shrugged; her smile wry. "What can I say? Day

drinking can only fill so many hours. And Vanessa made it sound so... elegant." She cast a pointed look at Vanessa, who rolled her eyes.

"You needed something in your sad little life, darling," Vanessa said bluntly.

"And I'm so glad you gave it to me," Erica replied, her tone dripping with sarcasm. "Truly, where would I be without the Caldwells?"

The group chuckled nervously, though the tension between the two women was palpable.

"I joined after Bee," Jilly said, glancing at her friend. "She convinced me it'd be a nice escape."

"It was," Bee said, her voice soft. "When I first came, you all seemed so polished, so... perfect. I felt like such a sad sack. But the more I came, the more I realized we're all just trying to keep it together in our own little ways."

"Some of us more than others," Erica muttered, earning herself yet another sharp look from Vanessa.

"Well," Vanessa said, steering the conversation back on track, "I always thought the book club could be more than just books. A sisterhood. A safe space where we women could connect, learn from each other, and... grow."

Jilly shifted in her seat, her gaze flicking between the other women. "I guess we all joined for different reasons. To meet people, to escape, to... fit in."

"To be seen," Erica added, her tone uncharacteristically serious.

There was a brief silence as the weight of her words settled over the group.

"Maybe," Charlotte said slowly. "Maybe we stayed because we need each other. Even if we don't realize it all the time."

Vanessa's smile returned, softer now. "Exactly. That's what I wanted when I started it. A place where we could all be ourselves and find true friends."

Tiffany, who had been quiet up until this point, finally spoke. "God knows we could all do with good friends."

The group fell silent again, the air heavy with the unspoken truth.

It was Jilly who broke the tension, offering a small, nervous laugh. "And, let's not forget, we've read some good books along the way, right?"

The group chuckled, though it felt forced. And as the conversation shifted back to the night's book discussion, Charlotte couldn't help but feel a pang of sadness.

The book club had brought them together. But their personalities, lives, and choices now looked like it might tear them apart.

3

ERICA

The first thing Erica Miller noticed when she woke up was the familiar relentless pounding behind her eyes. She groaned, rolling onto her side and burying her face in the pillow, trying to escape the morning light streaming through her bedroom window. It wasn't even that bright, a sliver of dusty light seeping through the almost closed curtains to invade her space. It felt like needles stabbing into her skull.

Her mouth tasted like something had died in it. Wine, most likely. Too much of it. Again.

With another groan, she forced herself upright, clutching the duvet as the room spun briefly. She blinked a few times, letting the mess of her bedroom come into focus: clothes thrown haphazardly over the back of a chair, a trail of shoes leading from the door, an empty wine glass perched precariously on her nightstand next to a half-finished bottle.

She sighed. Her room was like her life, cluttered and untidy, full of things she hadn't gotten around to dealing with. She rubbed her temples, willing the headache to fade. It didn't.

Bits of the night before began to surface in her memory: Vanessa's too-perfect house, the wine, the pointed remarks exchanged across the room. Her lips curved into a small, smug smile. She'd managed to rile them up, hadn't she? Erica might not have Vanessa's money or Charlotte's polish, but she knew how to stir the pot, how to get under people's skin. And last night... oh, last night she'd done just that.

But how had it ended?

She frowned, trying to piece it together.

Vanessa had been in her element, of course, holding court from her cream-colored sofa. She had directed the conversation like a conductor, her words sharp and cutting, her smiles disarming. Erica could still hear the faux sweetness in her voice, the way Vanessa had said, *Secrets have a way of coming to the surface.*

Was she talking about me? Or someone else?

Erica's stomach twisted, a mix of nerves and excitement. She'd thrown her own grenade into the room with her comment about having a "twist" to share, enjoying the flicker of tension that passed through the group. Vanessa had tried to mask her irritation, but Erica had seen it, the way her fingers tightened around the stem of her glass.

What had she said after that? What had any of them said?

The night blurred at the edges. She remembered laughing too loudly at something Jilly had said, remembered Charlotte avoiding her gaze, Pam chuckling at her frostier comments even though she'd pretending not to listen. And then there was Dani's comment about the ball game. Erica grimaced. She probably shouldn't have accused Dani of bribing the coach. She could see the shock on poor Bee's face.

Most of all, though she remembered Miriam sitting quietly, observing them all like a chess player calculating her next move.

And then...

Erica shook her head, wincing as the motion sent another

stab of pain through her temple. Then what? She couldn't really remember leaving the party.

The smell of coffee brewing dragged her out of bed. She shuffled downstairs, her oversized T-shirt hanging loosely off one shoulder, her bare feet cold against the hardwood floors. The house was quiet. Too quiet.

Her husband, Brad, was already gone. He'd left for work hours ago, no doubt slipping out of the house before dawn like he always did. She hadn't even heard him leave. Not that it mattered. Their mornings had become a routine of avoidance: Brad would leave for the hospital before she woke up, and she'd pretend she hadn't noticed.

The kitchen was clean, which meant he'd done the dishes before he left. The coffee machine set on a timer to rouse her from her usual hangover. Typical Brad. Always the responsible one. Always cleaning up after her.

She poured herself a cup of coffee, adding a splash of cream and far too much sugar. The sweetness coated her tongue, but it didn't quite chase away the bitterness she felt brewing inside her.

The kitchen window looked out over their backyard, a modest patch of grass with a sagging wooden fence and a trampoline the kids barely used anymore. The garden beds were overgrown, weeds climbing over the edges like a slow invasion. She'd meant to deal with them weeks ago, but there was always something else demanding her attention. Or at least, that's what she told herself.

Oakwood Ridge was the kind of fading development that felt like it was trying too hard to fit into Willow Creek. The houses were nice but unremarkable, the lawns mostly tidy but never manicured, the cars reliable but far from luxury. It was a far cry from Vanessa's sprawling estate or Charlotte's Pinterest-perfect home. Erica's house wasn't shabby, but it wasn't impressive, either.

She leaned against the counter, sipping her coffee as she scrolled through her phone. Her email inbox was overflowing reminders about a bake sale, a follow-up from the PTA president about a meeting she'd skipped, details of the game on Saturday, a promo for a 20% off sale at Target. It all blurred together, meaningless and monotonous.

Her finger hovered over the delete button, but she hesitated when she saw the text she'd sent herself last night. She clicked on it, her stomach flipping as the photo opened.

The blurry screenshot of a text thread stared back at her. Proof.

Her lips curved into a slow, wicked smile.

She didn't even know why she'd done it. Maybe it was the wine. Maybe it was boredom. Maybe it was the thrill of knowing she had something no one else did. Whatever the reason, she didn't regret it.

Not yet.

~

By the time her headache had faded to a dull throb, Erica was dressed and halfway through her second cup of coffee. Her hair was still slightly damp from the shower, curling lazily around her face, and she'd thrown on a pair of jeans and a sweater that hung loosely on her frame.

She moved through the house, picking up the remnants of last night's chaos. An empty wine bottle on the coffee table. A pizza box someone had forgotten to throw out. A lone sock in the corner of the living room.

She wasn't sure if she was cleaning because it needed to be done or because it gave her something to do.

Her thoughts kept circling back to the book club. To Vanessa's perfectly curated house, Charlotte's forced smiles, Pam's acid wit, Jilly's pathetic meekness, Tiffany's fake, well, everything, and the way Miriam's sharp eyes seemed to watch them all, all the time.

Erica knew she didn't fit in with these women, not really, but that was part of the fun.

They were so careful, so guarded, so terrified of anything that might crack their perfect façades. And Erica? Erica thrived on making cracks.

She glanced at her phone again, her thumb hovering over the text thread.

Her grin widened. She needed to get this right if it was going to work. She had one shot at it.

How *it* would work, or even *if* it would work, she didn't know yet. But that was the thing about secrets, they were useless unless you used them.

Erica parked herself on her couch, one leg tucked beneath her, the other bouncing anxiously against the floor. Her phone rested in her palm, cool and smooth, waiting.

She took a deep breath and opened her messages.

Her fingers hesitated over the keyboard, the weight of the decision pressing into her chest. She wasn't stupid, she knew what she was doing. She knew that this wasn't a good idea, that it wasn't *safe.* But knowing better had never gotten in her way before, and she wasn't going to let it now.

Not when something felt *this* good.

Her lips curled as she typed.

"You awake?"

She stared at the words for a moment, then deleted them. Too casual. Too vague. She needed to be direct. She needed them to *know* that she wasn't playing games.

Her fingers moved quickly:

"I need to see you."

Her thumb hovered over the send button. Her heart pounded. She knew they would answer. They always did.

She pressed send and exhaled sharply.

The seconds stretched as she waited. A trickle of doubt seeped into her confidence, but she smothered it. If she'd learned anything in the past year, it was that the waiting was the worst part, the space between action and consequence.

Then, finally, the message appeared.

"Where?"

She smirked as she typed: "Your choice."

The three little dots appeared, then disappeared. Then, finally...

"Same place as last time. 7 PM."

She let the phone rest against her thigh, her pulse quickening. This was reckless. This was *dangerous.* And yet, she had never felt more alive.

~

By the time the sun began to sink below the horizon, Erica was restless and fidgety.

She tried to keep herself busy. She threw a load of laundry in the machine, checked her email, even forced herself to tidy the kitchen again. But nothing could settle the buzzing in her chest, the anticipation curling around her ribs like a secret waiting to be spoken.

She found herself staring at the clock, willing the hours to move faster. The wine bottle from last night was still on the counter, tantalizingly half-full. For a brief second, she considered pouring herself a glass to take the edge off.

No. Not yet.

Instead, she walked to the bathroom and leaned against the sink, looking at herself in the slightly grubby mirror.

Her reflection stared back at her: the mess of curls, the faint shadows beneath her eyes, the flush on her cheeks that had nothing to do with the wine she hadn't touched today. *Actually,* she thought. *I look pretty good.*

She leaned in closer, adjusting the collar of her sweater, running a hand through her hair, making sure everything was just right.

Satisfied, she turned away, grabbed her keys, and left before she could change her mind.

The drive was quiet, the roads nearly empty. Willow Creek was like that at dusk – the picture-perfect town closing in on itself, tucking its secrets away before nightfall.

Erica tapped her fingers against the steering wheel, the tension growing with each mile.

She wasn't even sure what she wanted out of tonight. Power? Control? Maybe just the thrill of knowing she could still shake the ground beneath someone's feet.

As she pulled into the parking lot of the meeting place dark and nearly deserted at this hour, her phone vibrated.

A single message: "You're early."

She smirked and replied: "So are you."

She stepped out of the car, the cool evening air brushing against her skin. The anticipation thrummed inside her.

And then, from the shadows, a figure emerged.

Erica's smile deepened. Game on.

4

MIRIAM

The bell above the door jingled softly as Miriam Reed stepped into *Chapter & Verse*, the neat little independent bookstore in Willow Creek. The scent of aging paper and vanilla candles wrapped around her like a familiar embrace, the way it always did. Somehow today, even the comfort of books couldn't shake the unease tightening in her chest tonight.

She had spent the morning grading essays, the afternoon rearranging her lecture plans, and the last several hours trying, and failing, to push the tense animosity of the book club out of her mind. Something about last night hadn't sat right with her. The tension, the barely veiled barbs, the way Charlotte's hands had shaken ever so slightly as she reached for her glass. And Erica, well, Erica was always reckless, but last night, she had been *too* reckless. Even Pam, who usually doesn't raise an eyebrow either way, seemed disconcerted by it all.

And now, standing behind the worn wooden counter, Jilly Lawson looked worse than Miriam had ever seen her.

Jilly had always been one of those women who made an impression, even more so because she didn't realize it. She wasn't the type who walked into a room and commanded attention, she didn't have Vanessa's effortless poise or Charlotte's sharp-edged confidence, but she had a warmth that drew people towards her and made them want to stay.

She had the kind of delicate features that made her seem younger than she was, small nose, high cheekbones, full lips that always looked slightly chapped. Her blonde hair, usually tucked neatly into a bun or twisted back in a headband, was slipping free in loose strands tonight, framing her pale face in a way that made her look almost breakable.

Her cardigan, a deep green that usually flattered her fair skin, was hanging off one shoulder, and the dark circles beneath her wide blue eyes told Miriam that whatever was weighing on her had been keeping her up at night.

"You look exhausted," Miriam said, setting her bag on the counter.

Jilly flinched slightly, then blinked up at her, eyes wide and guilty. "Oh, hey, Miriam. Sorry, I was..." She trailed off, waving a hand at the register as if it explained everything. "Just another slow day."

Miriam took in the sparsely stocked shelves, the dust settling on books that should have been selling, the faint flicker of panic in Jilly's expression.

"How slow is slow?" Miriam asked, leaning against the counter.

Jilly exhaled, her shoulders sagging. "Too slow. I've had no choice but to take out a... a loan."

Miriam's stomach tightened. She didn't like the way Jilly said it, like the words tasted bad in her mouth.

"From the bank?"

Jilly bit her lip, a nervous habit Miriam had seen since they'd first met three years ago. She'd been new to Willow Creek then, fresh off a messy divorce, trying to build a new life for herself in a town where women like Vanessa and Charlotte ran the social scene. Jilly had never fit into that world, but she never wanted to. She preferred the quiet of books, the scent of freshly brewed tea, the comfort of stories that never asked for anything in return.

Miriam had met her by accident. She had wandered into the shop one afternoon after a particularly frustrating department meeting at the university, needing an escape. Jilly had been behind the counter, barefoot, her cardigan slipping off one shoulder as she stacked books in careful piles, humming softly under her breath.

She had looked up and smiled. A real smile. Not the forced ones Miriam was used to seeing at faculty dinners and town events, or even from the other women in Willow Creek.

And that had been it. The start of something rare. Something real. A genuine friendship. Which was why Miriam knew, without a doubt, that Jilly was hiding something from her right now.

"Look, it doesn't matter. Really. I can handle it," Jilly said, forcing a smile. "It's just... I miscalculated some things. Took on more than I should have. And now..." She let out a humorless laugh, rubbing her forehead. "Now I just need to figure it out before it gets out of hand."

Out of hand? Miriam's fingers curled around the edge of the counter.

"Jilly," she said, slowly. "Who did you borrow from?"

Jilly opened her mouth, then stopped. Something flickered across her face, fear, maybe. But she masked it quickly, shaking her head.

"It's fine," she said, voice softer now. "Forget I mentioned it. I'm handling it."

Miriam wasn't convinced.

Before she could push further, the bell above the door jingled again. Jilly turned sharply, as if grateful for the distraction as an elderly man shuffled in, pausing near the front display before heading toward the back of the store. The man picked up a book and examined the cover, then glanced at the counter.

"Excuse me, miss? Do you have any copies of this in hardcover?"

Jilly tucked a loose strand of hair behind her ear, her movements quick and a little too eager.

"Oh, um, let me check." She turned and disappeared into the back room, leaving Miriam standing there, staring after her.

Miriam turned her gaze toward the customer, watching as he ran his fingers over the book's spine, waiting for Jilly's return. He was older, maybe in his seventies, wearing a wool coat that was too heavy for the mild evening air. His posture was stiff, his movements deliberate.

Jilly reappeared from the back room, clutching a hardcover book to her chest, her hands slightly unsteady as she handed it to the older man. "Here you go. We have just one left."

The man gave her a slow, deliberate smile as he took it from her. "Lucky me," he said.

Miriam didn't like the way he said it. Or the way he watched her hands move over the register. She watched closely as Jilly rang up the sale, the subtle way her shoulders hunched inward, the way she barely made eye contact with the man. If Miriam hadn't already sensed something was wrong, she might have missed it. But now that she was looking, *really* looking, it was obvious that Jilly was nervous.

Who was this guy? Was he some kind of loan shark? Had he come here to threaten her?

Miriam didn't push, though. Not yet. She simply waited as Jilly handed over the man's receipt with a small, polite nod. He lingered for a beat too long before tucking the book under his arm and making his way toward the door. The bell jingled softly as he left, the sound deceptively harmless.

Jilly exhaled the second he was gone, gripping the edge of the counter like she needed to steady herself.

Miriam folded her arms. "Right, missy. You're going to tell me what the hell's going on," she said flatly.

Jilly shook her head too quickly, already reaching for a stack of receipts, pretending to be busy. "Nothing's going on, Miriam."

"Who was that man?"

"Just a customer. He's always coming in," Jilly said. "He just gives me the creeps is all."

"He's not the one you've borrowed money from then?"

Miriam let the silence stretch. Jilly eventually sighed.

"I don't want to talk about it."

Miriam didn't push. She knew Jilly well enough to know she wouldn't get anywhere by pressing her too hard. Instead, she took a different approach. "Alrighty then. Let's talk about last night, instead."

Jilly let out a breathless laugh, finally looking up at her. "Oh God, *what* a disaster!"

Miriam raised an eyebrow. "It was something, wasn't it?"

Jilly reached for her coffee mug on the counter and took a sip, grimacing. It had clearly gone cold. "I swear, every month, I think the book club meetings can't possibly get worse. And then they do."

Miriam smirked. "Erica was really on a roll."

"That woman rolls like a boulder," Jilly muttered. She grabbed a cloth and started wiping down the already clean counter. "It's like she *enjoys* poking the hornet's nest just to see what happens."

"She does."

Jilly sighed. "I don't know why she even comes. She clearly doesn't care about the books. And she definitely doesn't care about keeping the peace."

Miriam leaned against the counter, watching her closely. "You seemed particularly bothered by her last night."

Jilly hesitated, her hand pausing on the counter before she forced another laugh. "I just don't like the way she... *enjoys* making people uncomfortable." She shook her head. Especially Vanessa. And old Pam doesn't help. She acts like she's above the drama, but she *lives* for it. Did you see her stirring it up?"

Miriam smirked. "I did."

Jilly rolled her eyes. "I swear, I've seen more civilized behavior from middle schoolers."

Miriam thought back to the sharp tension in Vanessa's living room, the way Erica had taunted, the way Charlotte had looked physically ill, the way Vanessa had *reigned* over them all. Even Tiffany, who usually seems blissfully unaware of the tensions around her air-filled head seemed keen to steer the conversation away from buried secrets.

"Something definitely felt off last night," Miriam admitted.

Jilly glanced at her. "Because of Erica?"

"Because of *everyone*." Miriam frowned. "You could cut the tension between Erica and Dani with a knife."

"True," said Jilly. But you know how competitive they both are when it comes to the boys' sports teams. And I wouldn't put it past Dani to have bought Todd his spot in the majors."

"Right. But Charlotte barely spoke all night. And when she did, she looked like she wanted to be anywhere but there. Even Bee seemed out of sorts."

Jilly exhaled through her nose. "Something's going on with Charlotte."

Miriam nodded slowly. "Do you think Vanessa knows what it is?"

Jilly let out a humorless laugh. "Vanessa *always* knows."

They stood in silence for a moment before Jilly shook her head. "It feels like it's getting nasty, doesn't it?"

Miriam took a slow sip of coffee. “I think it’s been nasty for a long time.”

Jilly sighed. “Do you ever wonder why we still go?”

“All the time,” Miriam admitted.

Jilly gave her a small, knowing look. “And yet we keep showing up. Like moths to the flame.”

Miriam thought about that for a moment. “Maybe we just like knowing how the story ends.”

Her words resonated with Jilly.

“Maybe you’re right.”

Jilly Lawson had always felt like she was searching for something just out of reach. Born and raised in a small, sleepy town in Maine, she grew up quietly, surrounded by forests and the relentless crash of distant ocean waves. Her parents ran a modest diner, warm and inviting, where regulars gathered each morning for coffee and gossip. Jilly spent her childhood behind the counter, refilling cups, absorbing stories, always the listener, rarely the storyteller.

When she was twenty-two, she married Patrick, a man with a charming smile and an easy laugh, who promised her a life of adventure. But the adventures never came. Instead, their marriage settled into routine, a comfortable sameness that slowly felt suffocating. Patrick dreamed small, content with predictability, while Jilly found herself staring out windows, her imagination wandering beyond the tidy fences of their life together.

Their attempts to start a family were unsuccessful, a silent strain which neither of them addressed directly, but that lingered between them, growing heavier with each passing year. Over time, their quiet conversations turned into silent dinners, their comfortable life becoming increasingly hollow.

At thirty-seven, Jilly made a decision that startled everyone who thought they knew her, she filed for divorce. It wasn't angry or bitter; it was simply a recognition that their paths had diverged, leaving them both lonely, even in each other's company. Patrick stayed behind, content in the life they'd built, while Jilly packed her car and drove away, heading toward uncertainty but, for the first time, feeling free.

She arrived in Willow Creek on a whim, charmed by its picturesque streets and the promise of new beginnings. Using her modest savings and the courage she'd gathered along the way, Jilly opened Chapter & Verse, the town's small independent bookstore. She built a quiet, peaceful life among books, finding comfort and solace in the worlds they offered her.

Though Willow Creek was different from the hometown she'd left behind, with its polished facades and carefully maintained lawns, Jilly found peace in its rhythms. Yet, despite the friendships she built, she carried with her a gentle melancholy, a quiet ache from a life she had once envisioned but never lived. Jilly became known as the kind, soft-spoken woman who listened more than she spoke, who offered a sympathetic ear and a warm smile to anyone who needed it.

And as the years passed, Jilly often wondered if what she'd been searching for all along was simply a place where she could finally stop running from the quiet sadness, she'd carried all her life.

Jilly let out another laugh, but there was no real humor in it.

"Mind you, if last night was any indication," she muttered, "I think we're in for a *very* messy ending."

5

VANESSA

The bell above the bookstore door chimed again, but this time, the energy in the room shifted.

Jilly recognized the scent before she even turned around, expensive vanilla musk with a bite of citrus, a fragrance as polished as the woman who wore it.

Vanessa.

"I do love a quiet bookstore," Vanessa said lightly, stepping inside with the kind of effortless confidence that made it seem like she owned the place. "Such a *rare* thing these days."

Jilly clenched her jaw.

She had been alone in the store since Miriam left, trying to distract herself by rearranging a display table, but now her hands felt suddenly useless. The store was dimly lit, the warm glow from antique sconces flickering against the exposed brick walls. Rows of books stretched from floor to ceiling, their spines neatly aligned, their covers whispering stories of better times, of more exciting lives.

But none of it, not the books, the store, the quiet, felt like enough to protect her now.

She turned, forcing a smile. "Vanessa. What a surprise."

Vanessa smiled back, though hers was sharper, more practiced. She wasn't here to browse, that much was obvious. She was here because she *wanted* something.

She always did.

Jilly wiped her palms against the fabric of her cardigan, trying to ignore the way her pulse had quickened. The store suddenly felt too small, like it couldn't contain both of them.

Vanessa wandered past the shelves, running her manicured fingers over the spines of books she had no intention of reading. Even in this dim light, her golden hair shone, the soft waves cascading over her shoulders in a way that seemed effortless, but Jilly knew wasn't at all. Her white silk blouse tucked neatly into tailored black trousers was crisp and unwrinkled, not a single detail out of place.

By contrast, Jilly felt disheveled. Her deep green cardigan had slipped off one shoulder, her blonde hair was frizzing from the humidity, and the ache in her shoulders told her she hadn't been getting enough sleep. She probably looked exactly like what she was – a woman on the verge of losing everything.

"I assume you haven't forgotten about our little arrangement?" Vanessa said smoothly, finally turning to face her.

Jilly felt her stomach plummet.

No. She hadn't forgotten. Not for a single second.

She swallowed, keeping her voice neutral. "I'm working on it."

Vanessa raised a perfectly sculpted brow. "Working on it?"

Jilly forced a casual shrug. "Business has been slow this month."

Vanessa let out a slow, exaggerated sigh, shaking her head like a disappointed mother. "Jilly, Jilly, Jilly. That's not my problem." She took a step closer, lowering her voice. "*You* came to *me*, remember?"

Jilly felt heat rise to her cheeks.

It had been a mistake. She knew that now. But at the time, she had felt like she had no other choice.

Months ago, when the bookstore was on the verge of shutting down, Jilly had exhausted every option, bank loans, grants, even considering taking on a business partner. Nothing had worked.

And then Vanessa had come along, all effortless grace and silk-wrapped cruelty, with an offer that had felt like a lifeline.

The terms had been *simple.* A private loan, enough to keep the bookstore afloat. No bank paperwork. No middlemen. Just a promise: she would pay Vanessa back, with interest.

Jilly should have known that with Vanessa, there was always more to the story. And now the expiration date had arrived.

Jilly straightened her shoulders, trying to sound more composed and confident than she felt. "I just need a little more time."

Vanessa studied her for a moment, then smiled the kind of smile that meant nothing good was coming.

"I don't think you understand," Vanessa said with saccharine softness. "I'm don't have any more time to give."

Jilly's hands clenched at her sides.

"I—"

"Shh," Vanessa interrupted, holding up a manicured finger. "Let me explain how this works."

She took a slow step forward. Jilly didn't move.

"This bookstore is... adorable," Vanessa said, glancing around. "But you and I both know it doesn't *make* money. Not real money."

Jilly's jaw tightened.

"You're here because you *love* it," Vanessa continued. "Because you love books, and stories, and," she gestured vaguely, "whatever sentimental nonsense people like you care about."

Jilly swallowed hard.

Vanessa smiled again, but her voice hardened. "I don't care about sentiment."

The words were a knife carving through Jilly's composure.

"What I *do* care about," Vanessa continued, "is getting my money back."

She leaned in slightly, her voice lowering to a threatening whisper.

"So, unless you want to wake up one day and find yourself locked out of your store, I suggest you figure out how to repay your debt, and quickly."

Jilly's heart pounded. It wasn't just a threat. It was a real possibility. If she couldn't find the money to start repaying Vanessa, she would lose everything.

Vanessa tapped a finger against her chin, pretending to consider something. "Or, of course..." She trailed off, letting the silence hang between them like a noose.

Jilly exhaled shakily. "Or what?"

Vanessa's smile widened.

"I suppose we could come to a different arrangement."

Jilly's stomach twisted. "What kind of arrangement?"

Vanessa's expression softened into something almost sympathetic, though Jilly knew better than to believe it. "Oh, Jilly. You don't think I'd come all the way down here just to get heavy-handed about money, do you? Like some mobster?"

Jilly's breath hitched.

Vanessa took another step forward, closing the gap between them. "Simon would be mortified if he found out I'd tried to help a friend and been taken for a fool."

Jilly blinked. "Vanessa, I—"

"Can you imagine?" Vanessa continued, her voice airy, as if this were a casual conversation over brunch. "My husband, of all people, learning that I'd given a struggling little shop owner a loan out of kindness, only to be completely taken advantage of?"

Jilly's stomach dropped.

"That would be terribly embarrassing, wouldn't it?" Vanessa mused. "For both of us, really. But especially for me."

Jilly felt her throat tighten.

Vanessa smiled one last time, a smile as delicate as spun glass, as sharp as a knife. "I suppose I'll have to have a little think about what you could do for me, to make up for that kind of embarrassment. I tell you what, I'll let you know."

Jilly said nothing. There was nothing to say.

Vanessa turned back toward the door, her golden hair catching in the light. "I do love a quiet bookstore," she murmured, echoing her earlier words. "Would be an awful shame if something happened to it."

Then, without waiting for a response, she pushed open the door. The bell jingled softly.

Jilly stood frozen in place as Vanessa disappeared down the sidewalk, her heels clicking against the pavement, perfectly composed.

In that moment, Jilly realized she wasn't in control of anything anymore. She was trapped. And Vanessa was holding all the keys.

~

The cool evening air met Vanessa as she stepped out of *Chapter & Verse*, a sharp contrast to the warmth of the bookstore. She pulled her cashmere coat around her, taking one last glance through the window.

Jilly stood frozen behind the counter, gripping the edge as if the solid wood beneath her fingers was the only thing keeping her upright. Pathetic little woman.

Vanessa allowed herself a small, satisfied smile.

People like Jilly didn't understand the power of leverage. But Vanessa did. Money had always been a tool, a means to an end. And if you let people think you were doing them a favor, they hardly noticed what you were doing until the favor turned into a noose.

Jilly was such an easy mark. Sweet, naïve, always looking for the best in people. It was almost too easy. Almost. But right now, Vanessa needed some quick wins.

Outside the bookstore, Willow Creek was winding down for the evening. The picturesque town, nestled in the heart of New England, looked like something pulled from a lifestyle magazine. The streets were lined with manicured trees that bloomed bright in the spring and burned with color in the fall. The sidewalks, paved in brick, led to rows of boutique storefronts, cozy cafés, and upscale restaurants with string lights twinkling over their patios.

It was a town designed for people who had already made it in life. Lawyers, CEOs, real estate moguls, the kind of people who drove SUVs they never actually took off-road and enrolled their kids in private schools with tuition that rivaled college fees.

There were no *big box* stores here, no fast-food chains cluttering the skyline. Everything in Willow Creek was *curated*, designed to maintain its reputation as a place for those who had good taste, deep pockets, and the ability to maintain appearances.

Vanessa had carved out her life here perfectly. She and Simon lived in a sprawling Colonial on a tree-lined street where every house looked as if it had been professionally decorated for a feature in *Architectural Digest*. Their lawn was maintained year-round by a discreet service, their kitchen renovations had cost more than some people's entire homes, and their guest bathrooms were stocked with Jo Malone hand soap that no one was actually supposed to use.

This town, with its perfection and quiet affluence, was exactly where Vanessa belonged.

Which was why she needed to act fast. Jilly wasn't the only pawn in her game. If she was going to punish Simon for what he'd been doing, and *who* he'd been doing it with, she'd need some money of her own. She'd really hoped Jilly would come up with the goods by now, but she had plans to use her another way now.

She pulled her phone from her handbag, perched her oversized sunglasses on the top of her head, even though the sun had almost disappeared beyond the trees. She checked her messages as she made her way toward her car, her perfectly manicured nails tapping against the screen as she keyed in her passcode.

A single notification appeared. A missed call from Erica Miller.

Vanessa sighed dramatically. *Speak of the devil.*

A moment later, the phone buzzed again. Incoming call: Erica.

Vanessa debated letting it ring out, just to be petty, but curiosity got the better of her. She leaned against the hood of her car, raising one heel behind her to press lightly against the tire as she answered.

"Erica," she said smoothly, adjusting the mirror. "To what do I owe the pleasure?"

There was a brief pause. Then Erica's voice, sharp and clipped. "We need to meet."

Vanessa smirked, tossing her handbag into the passenger seat. "Do we? I think I had more than enough of your company last night."

A dry laugh came down the line, but there was no amusement in it. “Cute. But this isn’t about last night.”

Vanessa arched a brow. “Oh?”

A pause.

Vanessa waited. Silence stretched between them like a game of chicken. Just as Vanessa hoped, Erica blinked first.

“I’d rather discuss it in person,” Erica finally said.

Vanessa exhaled through her nose, already irritated. “So dramatic. Can’t you just text me like a normal person?”

“No.” The single syllable was flat, unyielding.

Vanessa’s fingers drummed gently against the cooling metal of her car. “Fine. Coffee, tomorrow morning. That little café on Main Street.”

The Roasted Bean, one of the town’s most popular cafés, was exactly the kind of place that defined Willow Creek. Small but elegant, its patio was shaded by iron lanterns and perfectly arranged potted plants, with white linen tablecloths that suggested wealth but weren’t gaudy about it. The café prided itself on single-origin espresso and hand-crafted pastries, the kind of place where women like Vanessa could sip their lattes and pretend their lives were as perfectly curated as their Instagram feeds.

“Ten o’clock.”

Vanessa’s smirk widened. “My, my. *So* assertive. Have it your way.”

“See you then,” Erica said, killing the call.

Vanessa stared at her phone for a moment, pursing her lips together in thought. There was something off about Erica’s voice. The usual sarcasm was there, but beneath it, something else. Something weighty. Not that Vanessa particularly cared.

Erica was always playing games, stirring the pot, making herself the center of attention. She lived for drama. And Vanessa? She wasn’t about to indulge her theatrics. She had plans for Erica, but they would have to wait. Right now, she had bigger fish to fry.

She glanced at the bookstore window again, at Jilly's hunched form inside. Vanessa smirked as she slid into the driver's seat and gunned the engine.

Before pulling away from the curb, she looked down Willow Creek's immaculate main road, toward the town's centerpiece park where families with perfect lives pushed their children with perfect manners on swings that never squeaked. Just like her life, the town was an illusion. A beautiful one, but Vanessa knew better than anyone that even perfection had rot beneath the surface.

Whatever Erica was scheming, she wasn't worried. She'd made it her business to find a little weakness in all of the book club ladies. And if Erica thought she was any different?

Well. That was just adorable.

6

CHARLOTTE

Charlotte had been walking. She wasn't sure how long, maybe twenty minutes, maybe longer, but she hadn't been able to face the silence of the house. Bobby had shut himself in his den as soon as dinner was over, the boys were glued to their games consoles, and she... she had needed *air.*

Willow Creek at night was different than during the day. The manicured streets, so bright and inviting under the afternoon sun, seemed colder as the evening began to creep in. Strangely elongated shadows stretched on the cobblestones, the expensive houses looming in perfect rows like silent spectators. The air was crisp, tinged with the faint scent of burning wood from distant fireplaces, the quiet hum of luxury SUVs rolling slowly through the streets.

She pulled her coat tighter around herself, noticing the chill settling on her chest. Her mind was still tangled in the comments from the book club, in the way Vanessa had *looked* at her. As if she knew.

She doesn't know anything. The words repeated in her head, over and over, like some kind of desperate mantra.

And then she saw her.

Vanessa was leaning against her sleek black Audi, parked on the curb opposite *Chapter & Verse*, lifting her phone to her ear. Even in the dim glow of the fading sun, she looked perfect. The golden waves of her hair gleamed in the pale light, her cashmere coat draped effortlessly over her shoulders, her posture relaxed, almost bored.

Charlotte was about to cross the street when she heard the name.

"Erica."

She froze. Vanessa's voice was smooth, amused. The kind of voice that wrapped around secrets like silk.

Charlotte took a slow step back into the shadows of an alleyway between two shops. From this vantage point, she could watch Vanessa, but not be seen. The last thing she wanted was to have to speak to her now. She'd be sure to ask where she was going, and Charlotte wasn't sure she had it in her to lie anymore.

Vanessa laughed softly; the sound almost musical. "Do we? I think I had more than enough of your company last night."

Silence. Then, another laugh, this one sharper.

Charlotte flattened herself against the rough brick wall of the alleyway, heart thudding in her chest, watching Vanessa talking animatedly on the phone, one manicured hand slicing the air while the other clutched her device like it owed her money. Her sunglasses were perched high on her head like a tiara.

Charlotte wondered why Erica was calling Vanessa. They had seemed so out of sorts with each other at the book club. And, judging by Vanessa's expression, they weren't busy making up now.

She inched forward slightly to get a better look.

"Seriously?" came a high, amused voice behind her. "Are you hiding?"

Charlotte jumped and spun. Standing just behind her, perfectly posed and Instagram ready, was Tiffany. Of course. Platinum hair, pastel yoga set, phone in hand, and an expression of gleeful disbelief on her glossed lips.

"I'm not hiding," Charlotte said, a little too quickly. "I'm... waiting."

"In an alley?"

"It's shaded. I'm just... cooling down." She winced at herself.

Tiffany took a deliberate step into the alleyway, her smile widening. "You're spying on Vanessa."

Charlotte huffed. "I'm observing. At a safe and respectful distance. Completely different."

Tiffany peered across the street, then back at Charlotte. "With tactical cover."

Charlotte sighed. "I just don't want to talk to her. She's exhausting. Like—like an emotional Dyson."

Tiffany let out a laugh that bounced off the brick walls. "That's actually kind of brilliant. I mean, she did reduce poor Bee to tears just for saying 'Pro-secco' instead of 'Proh-secco.'"

Charlotte peeked out again. Vanessa was still talking. Still dramatic. Still... Vanessa.

"She's on the phone with Erica," Charlotte whispered.

"Carrying on from last night's pleasantries, no doubt." Tiffany said breezily. "Mind you, I don't blame you for hiding. I don't want to talk to her either."

The pounding of feet broke through their hushed conversation.

"Move, move, move!" Dani barreled along the sidewalk with the force of a stampede, dragging a red-faced ten-year-old in full baseball kit behind her. "Can't stop! Running late!"

She called over her shoulder as she galloped past them. "Hi Charlotte, hi Tiff!" Dani called over her shoulder. "Hiding from Vanessa?"

Charlotte froze. Tiffany snorted. And across the street, Vanessa slid into her driver's seat, engine purring to life, and drove off with the kind of slow elegance that felt entirely staged.

As she reached them, Vanessa rolled down the window, just enough to let her voice drift through the cold night air.

"Well, hello ladies. What are you two doing skulking around in alleyways?"

Tiffany turned, raising her hand triumphantly.

"I dropped an earring. Charlotte was helping me find it."

Charlotte could have kissed her.

"Oh, hi Vanessa," she said, feigning surprise as she dusted her hands together. "I didn't see you there."

"Right, gotta run," Tiffany sang as she tottered away on her tall heels. "Thanks Charlotte."

For a moment, Charlotte and Vanessa locked eyes. Vanessa's narrowed suspiciously. Then her lips curled into one of her trademark fake smiles.

"I'd better get going. Simon will be wondering where I've got to. So good to see you again. And Charlotte..."

Charlotte looked her.

"...You take care, now."

Then the car pulled away, the sound of tires against pavement fading into the distance.

Charlotte stood there for a long time after she was gone, staring at the empty street, wondering if that had been a threat or a farewell. The only person she needed to be careful of was Vanessa herself.

Vanessa took the scenic route home, rolling down her window as the cool air drifted in, her fingers lightly tapping the steering wheel. The streets were emptying now, the last of the boutique stores and high-end cafés closing for the evening.

The Caldwell estate sat at the top of Hawthorne Hill, an exclusive neighborhood with sprawling homes set back from the road, their iron gates whispering *you don't belong here* to anyone who wasn't part of Willow Creek's elite.

Vanessa eased the car through the gates, taking her time up the long driveway that wound through their landscaped garden's manicured hedges and pristinely lit walkways. She pulled into the circular courtyard, noticing that Simon's black Mercedes wasn't there. He'd be out, as usual.

She exhaled slowly, shutting off the engine.

The house, a stunning white Colonial with navy shutters, was exactly what people expected from her. Classic, elegant, controlled. There were no out-of-place decorations, no mismatched patio furniture, not even a single crack in the flawless stone pathway leading to the grand front door.

Everything about it screamed perfection. Which was exactly what Vanessa had built her entire life on. She stepped out of the car, the crunch of her heels on the gravel path echoing against the building. As she walked toward the entrance, she glanced briefly at the large bay window in the living room. The house sat in ominous darkness. She would have to talk to someone about getting some timers fitted for the lights, to make it seem more welcoming.

She took her time unlocking the door, slipping off her coat as she entered, relishing the perfect silence that met her. The faint scent of freshly polished wood and jasmine candles lingered in the air, the smell of a house that had never known a single moment of chaos.

Everything was exactly as it should be. And yet, the moment she closed the door behind her, Vanessa felt a flicker of exhaustion. Not the kind that came from a long day. The kind that came from performing. Because that's what Vanessa Caldwell had always done. Performed.

She had been Vanessa Hayes once. A girl from Charleston, South Carolina, raised in a house with too much charm and not enough money. A girl who had grown up watching her mother, a former beauty queen, apply lipstick before answering the door, because no matter how bad things got, you never let people see you unravel.

And Vanessa had learned.

She had learned that a perfect smile could hide almost anything. That good posture made people take you seriously. That you could be drowning, but as long as your lipstick wasn't smudged and your hands stayed still, people would believe you were floating.

She had spent her entire teenage life preparing for a future that didn't involve struggling. Pageants had been the first step. She had been Miss South Carolina by nineteen. But it had just been a step on the road to her perfect socialite life.

People had adored her. The golden girl with the perfect smile, the flawless wave, the answers that were just clever enough to sound charming but never too controversial to make people uncomfortable.

And then she had met Simon.

Simon Caldwell had been everything she had been trained to want in a future husband. A man's man, from old money, someone who carried himself with effortless confidence, someone whose last name meant something in the right circles.

They had met at a charity gala in Manhattan, introduced by a mutual acquaintance, and Vanessa had known, instantly, that he was her ticket to the life she had always envisioned.

She had played the role of charming Southern belle perfectly, and Simon had fallen hard.

They had been married within a year, a wedding that made

the pages of *The New York Times' Society Section*, a honeymoon on the Amalfi Coast, a life that settled into a perfectly rehearsed performance. Vanessa knew how to play the good wife.

She knew when to smile and when to stay silent. She knew which charities to support, which dresses to wear, which friendships to cultivate.

She had built a kingdom, and she had no intention of letting anyone take it from her.

Especially not a low rent bitch like Erica. Or an uptight washout like Charlotte. She may not love Simon anymore, but she wasn't about to be a divorcee.

Shuddering at the thought, she draped her coat over the staircase railing, pausing for a moment before heading into the living room, where Simon's favorite armchair sat empty, whiskey in a crystal decanter on the table beside it unpoured. Not for the first time, she felt a pang of loneliness. But she quickly brushed it away.

She walked over to the marble fireplace, adjusting one of the framed photographs on the mantel—a perfectly staged family portrait, taken during a ski trip to Aspen. She ran her fingers over the edge of the frame, something sharp twisting in her chest.

She wondered where he was right now. Was he with one of them? She felt the pit of her stomach tense at the thought of his easy smile playing on lips fresh from kissing another woman.

Did Charlotte know about Erica? Did Erica know about Charlotte? She didn't care. Neither of them knew that she, his wife, knew all about their sordid little affairs. And neither of them knew that she'd never give him up. His body maybe, but never the man himself.

Smiling to herself now, she thought about her plan to ruin them both. Not long now, until she could start putting it into action.

The signs were there, but no one wanted to see them.

Erica had always been blunt, reckless, and a little too fond of wine, but lately, there was something off, something simmering just beneath the surface.

She wasn't just drinking at book club anymore. She was drinking everywhere.

At the grocery store, she sipped from an insulated tumbler while chatting with Pam about imported cheeses. At the country club, she ordered whiskey at lunch and raised an eyebrow when Vanessa pointed it out. At home, Brad found her in the kitchen some nights, a bottle of red wine nearly empty, her eyes glazed as she mumbled to herself about people keeping secrets.

And yet, no one stopped her. Not really. Because stopping her would mean acknowledging that something was wrong.

Three nights ago, she'd cornered Vanessa at the country club. The two women had always shared a mutual disdain hidden beneath layers of polite smiles and backhanded compliments. That night, however, the mask slipped.

Erica had been drinking steadily for hours, her words slurring around the edges, voice a few notches too loud for the hush of the bar. Vanessa had tried to deflect, tried to excuse herself with that regal, chin-high air she did so well, but Erica wasn't having it.

"You think you're better than me, don't you?" Erica hissed, sloshing her gin and tonic perilously close to Vanessa's blouse. "With your perfect hair and your Pilates and your—your... face."

Vanessa raised a brow, visibly unimpressed. "You're drunk, Erica."

"Well spotted," Erica drawled, tipping her glass in salute. "Bet you can't wait to tell the book club I've lost the plot. Again." She leaned in close, breath wine-sour. "Thing is, Vanessa, everyone *knows* what you are. They're just too scared to say it out loud."

She didn't say what that was, but the implication hung there, sticky and poisonous. Vanessa left in frosty silence, but not before Erica let out a shrill, theatrical laugh that turned several heads.

Two nights ago, it was Tiffany's turn. Erica had arrived late to one of the kid's birthday parties at Dani's house, already a few drinks in, clutching a bottle of rosé like a life raft. She interrupted everyone mid-discussion, demanding to know why no one knew how to party properly anymore, and announced – to no one in particular that they were all being poisoned by influencers, who, she bawled, were "just narcissists with ring lights."

Tiffany, who had made a career out of sharing her ring-lit musings, smiled thinly.

"I suppose we can't all write unhinged Goodreads reviews at two a.m.," she said sweetly. "But we do our best."

Erica laughed, loud and sharp, and accused her of being "a walking filter with no original thoughts and the intellect of a dumpster." Tiffany went stiff. The room went quieter than it should have.

And just last night, at Charlotte's porch drinks – casual, low-key, until Erica had showed up – she'd managed to offend Bee, Jilly, and Pam in the space of five minutes, before mistaking Miriam's long-time partner for "that new cleaner" and then making a joke about "liberals and their rescue dogs."

She'd insulted Dani's parenting style *and* her wine choice, and at some point, poured herself a generous glass of someone else's gin without asking.

By the end of the night, she'd flopped across Charlotte's outdoor loveseat like a collapsed star, muttering something about “at least I say what everyone’s thinking.” No one responded.

Later that night, Erica stumbled through the front door, her shoes dangling from one hand, her coat barely hanging onto her shoulders.

Brad was waiting in the kitchen, his jaw tight, his arms crossed.

“Erica,” he said, his voice heavy with frustration.

She laughed, kicking off her heels. “If this is another lecture, can we skip it? I’m exhausted.”

Brad sighed, rubbing his temples. “You can’t keep doing this.”

Erica rolled her eyes. “Doing what?”

“Drinking. Picking fights. Running around town like you’re looking for trouble.”

She scoffed, pouring herself a glass of wine. “Maybe trouble’s looking for me.”

Brad exhaled loudly. “Dammit, Erica.”

For the first time that night, her bravado cracked just slightly.

She glanced up at him, her expression unreadable. “Do you even care?”

Brad’s shoulders slumped. He ran a hand over his face, suddenly looking exhausted.

“Of course, I care,” he murmured. “You’re my wife.”

Erica stared at him for a moment. Then, to his complete surprise, she stepped forward and pressed a kiss to his cheek.

“I’m sorry,” she whispered.

Brad’s throat tightened. He lifted a hand, about to touch her arm, about to ask if she was okay. But just as quickly as the moment had come, it was gone.

Erica pulled away, picked up her wine glass, and disappeared down the hallway toward the bedroom.

Brad stood in the kitchen, watching her go. He should have followed her. Should have told her he was worried. Should have done something. But instead, he just sighed and turned back to the lounge.

He didn't know it then, but that was the last conversation he would ever have with her.

7

THE TOWN AWAKENS

Willow Creek woke to sirens.

It was a town that thrived on quiet. Mornings were meant for fresh pastries from The Roasted Bean, for joggers winding their way through tree-lined streets, for crisp copies of The New York Times folded neatly on granite countertops beside steaming cups of coffee.

But this morning, none of it felt normal.

The sound of police sirens and flashing blue lights shattered the usual serenity, cutting through the heart of the town like a wound. Erica Miller's house, a sleek, modern structure nestled at the end of Magnolia Lane, had become the center of an unthinkable tragedy.

Neighbors stood behind the white picket fences of their pristine homes, robes hastily tied, slippers sinking into dew-covered grass, as they whispered in hushed voices. Some clutched their phones, already dialing friends, piecing together what little they knew.

Erica had been found floating, unmoving and lifeless, in her own swimming pool.

Erica Miller. Loud, reckless, impossible-to-ignore Erica was gone.

The scene outside her home was chaotic. Yellow police tape fluttered in the morning breeze, cordoning off the backyard where medics and investigators worked under the rising sun. Willow Creek's police department, small but efficient, had arrived in full force, their cruisers lining the street, their radios crackling with urgent conversation.

A team of CSIs moved in coordinated silence, dressed in dark jackets, their gloves snapping into place as they photographed the scene. Their presence was jarring in this neighborhood, where the worst crime in recent years had been a dispute over zoning laws for a new wine bar.

A black body bag lay near the pool, partially obscured by the movement of paramedics who worked with methodical precision.

Detective Sam Whitaker, a man who had spent years investigating financial fraud and the occasional burglary, stood with arms folded near the patio, his expression grim. He wasn't used to cases like this. Nobody in Willow Creek was.

The pool shimmered unnaturally in the morning light. The water, usually pristine, a perfect turquoise oasis framed by white marble tiles, was still. A few fallen leaves floated on the surface, eerily undisturbed. A wine glass lay shattered near the edge, one sharp fragment glinting beneath the sun. An empty bottle lay on its side nearby.

The police murmured to each other, exchanging theories. How had it happened? Was it an accident?

Had Erica fallen? Had she been drinking? Had she slipped somewhere between her last text message and the moment her lungs filled with water?

Or was it something else?

Inside the house, everything had been left untouched. Erica's phone still sat on the kitchen counter; its screen cracked from where she had dropped it one too many times. Another bottle of half-drunk rosé rested beside it; another glass beside it – poured but never finished. The overhead lights in the living room were on, just as Brad had found them this morning, casting a soft golden glow over a coffee table stacked with unread books and an ashtray with a single smudged cigarette.

Nothing looked out of place. No sign of a struggle. Nothing but evidence of continued heavy drinking and a deep sadness.

~

By mid-morning, the news had spread. It moved through Willow Creek faster than wildfire, whispered from one manicured front porch to another, passed over cups of steaming coffee and half-eaten croissants at The Roasted Bean.

"Did you hear?"

"Erica. The pool. Last night."

"God. How awful."

"Do you think she was drinking?"

"She drank a lot, didn't she?"

"Maybe she slipped."

"Maybe she..." The words trailed off, unfinished. Because the truth was, no one knew what to think. And that terrified them.

Near the edge of town, at the Caldwell estate, Vanessa sat in her immaculate kitchen, stirring a spoon through her coffee with slow, deliberate movements. Her phone buzzed against the marble countertop, messages flooding in, but she didn't reach for it.

Instead, she sipped her coffee, for once not bothered by the local gossip mill. She carefully placed her empty coffee cup of the counter and then, slowly, she smiled.

The book club members gathered outside Erica Miller's house, their expressions carefully composed, a delicate mix of shock and curiosity. They stood in small clusters on the sidewalk, whispering behind manicured hands, their eyes flicking between the swarm of police officers and the covered stretcher being lifted into the back of the coroner's van. The air buzzed with low murmurs, half-finished thoughts, and unspoken questions. But not a single one of them was crying, although Bee looked like she might have been at some point that morning.

Vanessa Caldwell stood slightly apart from the others; her arms crossed over the front of her cream-colored cashmere coat. Her expression was unreadable, her perfectly lined lips pursed as she studied the scene. She was the first to break the silence, her voice low but carrying just enough for those closest to her to hear.

"Well," she muttered, adjusting the cuff of her sleeve. "She always was reckless. And these days, usually drunk. She must have slipped and hit her head on the way in."

Charlotte flinched beside her, inhaling sharply as though Vanessa had struck her. A few of the women cast uneasy glances in her direction, but no one contradicted her. Because it was true. Erica had been reckless. Loud, careless, brash. She drank too much. She talked too much. She pushed buttons for the fun of it. But still, this felt different.

Jilly Lawson wrapped her arms around herself, her green cardigan bunched at the elbows. Her fingers dug into her sleeves as though she were bracing against the cold, even though the morning air was mild. She looked pale, her wide blue eyes locked on the house, on the doorway where two officers stood speaking in hushed tones.

"Reckless or not, this is horrible," Jilly whispered. "I mean, God, Vanessa. She's dead."

Vanessa sighed, as if the entire conversation was exhausting. "Oh yes, Jilly It's terrible alright. I'm just saying, let's not pretend it's a shock that she ended up getting herself into trouble."

Jilly turned to face her, something dark flickering behind her eyes. "It's a shock to me," she shot back, her voice tight. "She had kids, Vanessa. A family."

"What about poor Brad?" Bee added. "He looks hollowed out."

And there they were.

On the porch, Brad Miller stood, his arms wrapped tightly around their two children. James, eleven, and Milly, eight, his face pale and drawn. His dark hair was disheveled, his clothes thrown together like he had dressed in a fog, and there was something hollow in his expression. He wasn't speaking. He wasn't moving. He just stood there, holding their children, staring at the police as though he wasn't entirely sure this was real.

James kept his face pressed into his father's sleeve, but Milly, standing on the other side of Brad, lifted her head, scanning the crowd with wide, confused eyes. She was too young to understand what was happening, but she knew enough to know something was terribly wrong.

No one had the courage to meet her gaze.

Miriam cleared her throat beside Jilly, shaking her head slowly. "The poor things," she murmured, her voice edged with something that almost sounded like guilt. "What are they going to do without her?"

No one had an answer for that.

Charlotte stood stiffly, a little distance apart from the group, her fingers clenched into fists at her sides. She hadn't spoken yet, hadn't moved except to glance at Vanessa when she made that cold remark. She looked ill, her skin pale, her lips pressed into a thin line. The wind blew a strand of dark hair into her face, but she didn't brush it away. Miriam caught her eye, and nodded, sensing that Charlotte seemed somehow more affected than the rest.

She was staring at the house, at the flashing lights of the police cruisers, at the covered body as it was loaded into the van, her chest rising and falling in slow, deliberate breaths. Her fingers twitched at her sides, balling into fists and stretching again.

Vanessa caught the movement too, and tilted her head, eyes narrowing. "Are you all right, Charlotte?" she asked, her voice artificially soft.

Charlotte's gaze met hers, something raw flickering behind her usually composed expression. "No, Vanessa," she said, her voice quiet but sharp. "I'm not all right. Far from it. A woman – a friend – is dead. Erica is..." her voice trailed off as Pam stepped over and gave her a pat on the shoulder. Not so much a comfort as a pull-yourself-together.

A beat of silence passed between them.

Vanessa smiled, the edges of it just a little too sharp. "Well, don't fall apart now," she murmured, smoothing the collar of her coat. "I didn't realize you were that... close."

"Besides," Pam said. "We don't even know what happened. Let's just try to keep our heads level."

Charlotte inhaled sharply but said nothing.

The police presence thickened as another detective arrived, a woman with steel-gray hair and a no-nonsense expression. Officers moved in and out of the house, carrying evidence bags, notebooks, camera equipment. Someone unrolled a Forensic Investigation Unit case, setting it down on the lawn beside the pool.

The town of Willow Creek had never seen a crime scene like this before.

The women of the book club just stood there, watching, waiting, saying nothing, taking it all in.

The air outside Erica Miller's house was thick with something that had no name. It wasn't just grief, not exactly. It was shock. Confusion. That strange, uneasy feeling that settled over a town when something happened that wasn't supposed to happen there.

Willow Creek wasn't a place for tragedy. That belonged to other towns. Murders and drownings and things that made headlines only happened in cities where crime was part of the landscape, not here, not in a place where people left their doors unlocked and their children rode their bikes to school without fear.

But this morning, the illusion had cracked.

The book club members stood at the edge of the scene, a cluster of perfectly put-together women who looked out of place against the backdrop of flashing police lights. The chatter of the neighborhood had died down, the initial flurry of gossip swallowed by something heavier.

Dani arrived in her usual high-speed rush, but even she seemed more flustered that usual, more untogether. on her feet, hugging herself. Her sweat top was pulled tightly around her, her fingers gripping the fabric like a lifeline, as if she could somehow keep herself from unraveling. Her face was pale, her blue eyes too bright, and when she spoke, her voice wavered.

"I came as soon as I heard. Did she..." she stopped, shaking her head. "I mean, do they think she fell?"

Vanessa tilted her head slightly, like she was considering it, before sighing, smoothing the front of her coat. "We don't know, Dani. The cops haven't said anything yet. But considering the amount Erica had been drinking recently, it wouldn't surprise me."

Charlotte, who had been standing stiffly beside them, turned to Vanessa with a look so sharp it could have sliced through glass. "You need to stop," she whispered. Her voice wasn't loud, but it was shaking.

Vanessa arched a perfectly sculpted brow. "Excuse me?"

Charlotte's hands clenched into fists at her sides. "This isn't the time for *that*," she hissed. "She's dead, Vanessa. Have a little respect."

Vanessa let out a slow breath, as if she were holding on to the last thread of her patience. She didn't argue, but she didn't apologize either. Instead, she turned her attention back to the house, where police officers moved in and out, their radios crackling with coded conversations.

Tiffany was making a poor show of being subtle, snapping photographs of the house, of Brad and the kids, of the police cars and the tape, and of course, of herself in front of all of it.

Pam, who never had much time for Tiffany's online musings, looked fit to slap the phone right out of her hand. "This is someone's life, Tiffany," she said angrily. "Not a way to win fans."

"Nonsense," said Tiffany breezily. "It's completely in the public interest."

Miriam, ever the quiet observer, stepped closer to Jilly and placed a gentle hand on her arm. "We should go," she murmured. "Standing here isn't helping anyone."

But no one moved. Because this all felt unfinished.

The community had gathered in pockets, standing at their porches, lining the sidewalk, their faces painted with expressions of disbelief. A woman from down the street had tears in her eyes, dabbing at them with a tissue. Miriam wondered if she'd known Erica well. Or, for that matter, if any of them really had.

Most of them had just about tolerated her at book club and in PTA meetings and at charity events where she drank too much and laughed too loudly. But had any of them really *known* her?

The guilt settled in like a dull ache.

Vanessa's phone buzzed in her pocket. She pulled it out, barely glancing at the screen before sighing and shoving it back in her coat. "Simon's wondering what's going on."

"Did you tell him?" Jilly asked.

Vanessa let out a humorless laugh. "Of course I did. His response? 'That's unfortunate.'"

Dani's lips parted slightly, like she wanted to say something, but no words came.

Then, just as Charlotte turned away, something caught her attention. Miriam heard it too.

Two CSI officers, walking back out of the house carrying full Forensic Investigation kit, were talking quietly to each other, their voices low, their backs turned to the crowd. But Charlotte was close enough to hear. Close enough to catch the murmured words...

"—doesn't look like an accident."

Her stomach lurched.

The other officer grunted, rubbing a hand over his jaw. "Drowning's one thing, but that wound."

Charlotte took a step back, her breath catching in her throat.

What wound?

She turned to the others, but no one else had heard. Jilly was still hugging herself. Tiffany was engrossed in her phone. Dani was chatting to one of the local officers. Pam and Bee were talking to one of the PTA Moms. Miriam was staring at the house with quiet intensity, and Vanessa was watching Charlotte.

"You okay?" Vanessa asked, tilting her head. "You look even worse than you did a minute ago."

Charlotte opened her mouth, then closed it. She shook her head. "I just, I need to go."

She barely registered their reactions as she turned and walked away, her heartbeat loud in her ears.

Because suddenly, this tragedy wasn't an accident anymore. Suddenly, there was something rotten in Willow Creek. But who, and why?

It felt like the answer might be closer than any of them wanted to believe.

8

THE BOOK CLUB RECONVENES

Miriam's house smelled of fresh coffee and something faintly sweet, like cinnamon lingering in the air. Normally, her home was a place of warmth, bookshelves filled to bursting, soft lighting, carefully chosen artwork that made people feel welcome without trying too hard. But today, there was no warmth.

The book club members sat in the living room, each clutching a cup of coffee, each processing their own version of shock. No one had called this an official meeting. Miriam had merely texted them all after leaving Erica's house, suggesting they come by, and one by one, they had all agreed.

No one said it out loud, but the unspoken reason for being there hung in the air.

They didn't know what else to do.

Jilly sat curled into the corner of the couch, her hands wrapped around her mug like it might steady her. Charlotte perched stiffly on the armrest, not drinking at all, her gaze distant. Dani had brought scones, which sat untouched on a tray. Bee was cradling her cup like it might anchor her. Tiffany had cried when she came in and was now scrolling her phone in silence.

Vanessa arrived last, of course. She swept in like a storm pretending to be a breeze, all black cashmere, sunglasses she didn't take off, and a faint perfume that made Miriam's eyes sting. The conversation faltered as she entered. Only Tiffany stood to greet her, that polished smile pinned on like jewelry.

"Vanessa," she said softly. "We weren't sure you'd come."

Vanessa slipped the glasses off. Her eyes were red-rimmed, but dry. "Of course I came. We were *friends.*"

A small, sharp sound came from Pam – something between a cough and a scoff. She didn't say anything, just adjusted the throw pillow behind her a little too forcefully.

Tiffany looked up from the couch. "Does anyone know any more? We still don't know what happened, right?"

"An accident," Dani said too quickly. "That's what they said. She must have slipped in while she was drunk."

Charlotte glanced toward the window, saying nothing.

Silence hung.

Vanessa, of course, claimed the best chair in the room, and sat now, one leg crossed elegantly over the other.

"God, this feels weird," Jilly finally muttered. "Sitting here. Like we're," she trailed off, shaking her head.

"Like we're what?" Vanessa asked, lifting a perfectly shaped brow. "Mourning her? We're not her family. There's nothing we can do."

"I was going to say... like we're about to talk about a book plot. But..."

"What does it matter if we're family," Dani cut in, her voice sharper than usual. "This is *Erica*. We were only with her two nights ago. She was drinking too much, laughing too loudly, making comments that pissed everyone off. And now..."

"She's gone," Jilly finished softly.

The room lapsed into silence.

It felt unnatural, talking about Erica in the past tense. She had been so *alive*. The kind of person who took up space, who filled a room, who didn't let people ignore her even if they wanted to.

"I keep thinking about the last message she sent me," Miriam murmured, stirring her coffee even though she wasn't going to drink it. "She sent me something random after the book club. Something about how she always ruined things for herself."

Charlotte blinked. "What?"

Miriam shrugged. "I didn't think much of it at the time. I figured she was just being dramatic."

"She *was* dramatic," Pam interjected, smiling ruefully.

"And," agreed Vanessa. "She made everything about her. Every conversation, every event, every *meeting*. She thrived on chaos." She leaned back, shaking her head. "Honestly, if she was going to go, it makes perfect sense it would be something messy like this."

Jilly shot her a horrified look. "Jesus, Vanessa."

"What? I'm just saying," Vanessa said, taking a delicate sip of coffee before placing the cup back down. "We're sitting here acting like she was some saint, but she wasn't. She was messy. She *liked* being messy."

"Messy doesn't translate to dead," Charlotte snapped.

"Oh, for God's sake," Vanessa sighed, shifting in her chair. "Listen to us. We sound like a bunch of ghouls, dissecting her life like it's some mystery novel."

Miriam hesitated, her fingers tightening around her spoon. "Maybe it is a mystery."

Charlotte stilled.

Vanessa rolled her eyes. "Oh, please."

"No, listen," Miriam said, setting down her cup. "Before I left this morning, I overheard two of the officers talking. They said something about it not looking like an accident."

The words settled over the room like a fog.

Charlotte's grip on her own cup tightened. Jilly paled, curling in on herself.

Vanessa, however, didn't flinch. She merely exhaled slowly and shook her head. "You misheard them."

"I don't think I did," Miriam said carefully.

"No, she didn't. I heard them say that too," Charlotte said.

"Oh, come on," Tiffany scoffed. "If there were foul play, we wouldn't be sitting here. The police would have said something officially."

"Unlikely," Pam said, her voice barely above a whisper. "They'd still be gathering evidence though."

No one responded.

For the first time, the reality of it settled in.

Erica wasn't just gone. She had drowned in her own backyard, in her own pool, on a perfectly ordinary night in a perfectly safe town. A place where nothing ever happened. And now, maybe, something had.

Miriam cleared her throat. "They mentioned something about a mark."

Charlotte blinked. "A mark?"

Miriam nodded. "They didn't say what. But it was enough to make them suspicious."

The tension in the room became suffocating.

Jilly's breathing hitched. "No," she whispered, shaking her head. "No, that's *crazy*. Erica was... reckless, sure, but she didn't have enemies."

Vanessa let out a short, humorless laugh. "Are you sure about that?"

No one answered. Because suddenly, none of them were so sure.

Then Charlotte said, calm as dusk, "Do you know what's strange? She told me last week that she was working on something. Said it was going to *blow the roof off this neighborhood.*"

Pam blinked. "She told me that too."

"She told all of us that," said Bee.

"And now she's dead," murmured Tiffany.

The women looked around at one another. Somewhere outside, a siren wailed.

Charlotte sipped her tea. Her eyes were dry. Her hands didn't tremble. Vanessa crossed her arms and turned away from the group, her face unreadable. Dani picked up a scone, and put it down again, frowning.

No one spoke.

Finally, Jilly exhaled shakily, gripping the fabric of her cardigan. "I don't want to be part of this," she murmured. "I don't want to sit here and talk about murder."

Bee softened. "I don't either."

"Then why are we?"

Silence.

"Because," Miriam whispered, staring down into her untouched coffee. "If it was murder... then maybe someone we know did it."

The words knocked the air out of the room. No one said anything more after that.

And then, in a flurry of excuses, they all left. Jilly mumbled something about needing to get to the store. Bee scattered with her. Dani said she needed to get the kids from the mall, and Tiffany asked to ride with her. Pam finished her coffee, grabbed a couple of the scones "For later" and made her exit.

Charlotte stayed long enough to gather herself before heading out as well. Only Vanessa lingered, standing near the fireplace, watching the flames flicker behind the glass screen.

"Don't get carried away with this," she murmured, her back to Miriam.

Miriam frowned. "What?"

Vanessa turned, her expression unreadable. "You heard me. I know what you're like, Miriam. Don't go digging into things that don't concern you."

Miriam felt something cold coil in her stomach.

Vanessa gave her a long, knowing look before grabbing her bag and heading for the door. She paused in the entryway, tilting her head slightly.

"It would be such a shame," she mused, her voice as smooth as ever. "If you started asking the wrong questions and turned up more than you could handle."

Then, just like that, she was gone.

Miriam stood in the silence of her living room, staring at the door, at the half-drunk coffee cups, at the place where Vanessa had just stood.

For the first time, she felt something she hadn't yet allowed herself to acknowledge. Fear.

~

Miriam stood by the window, watching the other women leave. Bee was almost at the end of the block, walking fast – too fast – her cardigan pulled tightly around her small frame like she was trying to disappear into it. She didn't look back as she hurried down the sidewalk, her head ducked, her arms locked around herself.

Charlotte, on the other hand, moved slower, more deliberate. She had excused herself with a quiet murmur, something about needing to get home, but she hadn't rushed the way Jilly had. Instead, she had lingered for just a second too long, her fingers tightening around the strap of her purse before she finally turned to go.

But what struck Miriam the most was her expression.

Charlotte hadn't looked heartbroken. She hadn't looked sad. She had looked nervous.

Miriam replayed the moment in her head, Charlotte's sharp reaction to Vanessa's flippant remarks, the way her hands had clenched when the conversation had turned toward foul play.

Miriam exhaled, stepping back from the window. The living room felt different now, thicker with something unnamed, as if the space had absorbed the tension that had settled between them.

And then there was Vanessa. Vanessa had not been shaken. She had not been surprised. She had simply watched, her expression unreadable, her tone clipped but indifferent. She had done what she always did, kept herself one step ahead, kept control, never let the mask slip.

Even when Miriam had mentioned what she overheard, when the words "It doesn't look like an accident" had been spoken into the air like a ghost waiting to be acknowledged Vanessa had barely reacted. Until she'd warned Miriam not to go digging. Now, why would she do that if she didn't have something to hide?

Miriam lowered herself onto the couch, her hands folded in her lap.

The silence in the house was deafening.

She let herself sit there for a long time after the others left, staring at the coffee table where the half-empty mugs sat cooling. The smell of coffee still lingered in the air, but it had lost its warmth.

She thought of Erica.

The way she used to laugh too loudly, the way she rolled her eyes when Vanessa made one of her signature remarks, the way she never backed down from a fight, even when she should have.

Miriam had always liked her. She hadn't always understood her, but she had liked her. At least she'd always said what she thought. Hell, she'd often said what everyone else was thinking but were too afraid to say.

And now she was gone.

She thought about what Charlotte had said, too.

"If it was murder... then maybe someone we know did it."

The words wouldn't leave her. Because she knew, just knew, that Charlotte wasn't just making a passing remark.

Was Charlotte scared? Tiffany certainly seemed edgier than usual, and Dani had been uncommonly quiet.

And Vanessa? Vanessa hadn't seemed scared at all. She'd seemed annoyed, if anything.

Miriam ran a hand over her face, something cold crept over her skin.

This wasn't just grief settling into their town. This was something else entirely. And for the first time, Miriam realized she wasn't just afraid of what had happened to Erica. She was afraid of who might be responsible.

~

Jilly sat in her parked car around the corner from Miriam's house for a while, gripping the steering wheel with both hands, willing herself to breathe normally. The world felt different now. Everything outside the windshield, the perfectly trimmed hedges, the brick-paved sidewalks, the gentle sway of the maple trees lining the street, looked the same. But it wasn't.

Erica was gone.

Her fingers twitched as she thought about what Miriam had said. It doesn't look like an accident. The words sat in her chest like a stone. Jilly had always believed that life in Willow Creek was a script – one that played out predictably, book club meetings, charity galas, holiday brunches, whispered gossip over wine. But this? This wasn't part of the script.

She swallowed and pressed her forehead against the steering wheel. She had to stop thinking about it.

But then, a memory slipped in, uninvited.

Erica, a few years ago, before the wine became a crutch.

Jilly had been setting up for a local book fair, back when the bookstore still had hope, when it was still something vibrant instead of something she was desperately trying to hold together. She had been sweating in the summer heat, lugging heavy boxes of books onto a rickety folding table, trying to keep the wind from blowing away her flyers.

And then, out of nowhere, Erica had appeared.

Jilly barely knew her back then. She was still new to town, still unsure of how she fit into Willow Creek's perfectly curated social circle. Erica had shown up in a sundress and flip-flops, her hair in a messy bun, looking so effortlessly unbothered that Jilly had immediately felt embarrassed about how disheveled she must have appeared.

"You look like you need an extra set of hands," Erica had said, already picking up one of the heavier boxes without waiting for permission.

Jilly had blinked. "Oh, I, I don't want to make you work."

"Work?" Erica had laughed, shaking her head as she dropped the box onto the table. "Please. If I stay home any longer, I'll end up reorganizing my kitchen again, and Brad will have an aneurysm if I move the spice rack one more time."

Jilly had smiled at that, but she had still been nervous, unsure of how to respond. It had been her first taste of Erica's presence, loud, unfiltered, a little reckless, but entirely genuine.

They had spent the rest of the afternoon setting up together, laughing over ridiculous book titles, making fun of the stuffy men from the town council who insisted on only reading historical non-fiction. At one point, Erica had bought an entire stack of poetry books, even though she had openly admitted she probably wouldn't read them.

"It's not about the reading," she had said, flashing that carefree, mischievous grin. "It's about supporting a friend."

Jilly had never forgotten that moment.

Because back then, Erica had been different.

Before the wine. Before the self-destruction. Before the nights where she slurred her words and picked fights just to feel something.

Jilly exhaled, her fingers tightening around the steering wheel.

When had it changed? When had Erica stopped being the woman who bought poetry books she wouldn't read and started being the woman who drank too much at every event, who threw her head back laughing too loudly, who made a game out of making people uncomfortable?

Jilly had never asked what was going on with her. None of them had.

Instead, they had just let it happen, whispering about her from a safe distance, wondering amongst themselves if she was spiraling or if she just wanted attention.

"I wonder if she was happy?" Jilly whispered, even though there was no one to answer her.

She wasn't sure she wanted the answer anyway.

She closed her eyes, forcing the memory away. It didn't matter now. Erica was gone. And Jilly had a horrible feeling they didn't even know the half of it.

9

A TOWN IN SHOCK

Two days had passed since Erica Miller had been pulled from her swimming pool, and Willow Creek already no longer felt like the town it had been before.

Tiffany had told the group that a friend on the force had told her in confidence that Erica hadn't simply drowned. There had been injuries. Ones that suggested something *more*. Something deliberate. Something that had changed everything.

Erica Miller was murdered.

Of course, that wasn't a secret Tiffany was going to keep for long. Within hours of it reaching her ears, the news had spread like wildfire, passed from neighbor to neighbor, whispered across front porches, through text messages, over steaming cups of coffee at The Roasted Bean. It was all anyone in town could talk about.

"This kind of thing doesn't happen here," murmured one longtime resident, her voice hushed as she stood in line for coffee. "I mean, drownings, sure, accidents, absolutely. But murder?"

"I knew it would turn out to be murder," another woman

whispered. "I knew as soon as I heard. They said she had marks on her."

"Marks? What kind of marks?"

"They won't say. But if they're investigating it as a homicide, it must be bad."

The conversations were all the same, filled with questions no one had answers to, speculations that grew wilder with each retelling.

By that afternoon, the news crews had arrived. Their vans parked along Main Street, reporters in tailored blazers stood outside Chapter & Verse and The Roasted Bean, filming carefully rehearsed segments about how Willow Creek, a town known for its charm, its wealth, its safety, had been *shaken* by the brutal, untimely death of one of its residents.

The police had given a brief statement.

"The investigation into Mrs Miller's death is ongoing," said Detective Sam Whitaker, his voice steady, his expression unreadable. "At this time, we are treating this as a homicide and pursuing all possible leads. We encourage anyone with any information to come forward."

It wasn't much. But it was enough. Because someone in Willow Creek had killed Erica Miller.

Vanessa Caldwell watched the coverage from her living room, sipping her morning coffee as if this were just another Thursday.

The large flat screen on the wall switched from Main Street to showing footage of the crime scene, Erica's house, the flashing lights, the tape, the growing number of officers moving in and out. She had seen it all in person, of course, but there was something strangely theatrical about watching it unfold on the news.

She barely blinked as Detective Whitaker spoke, his voice cool and measured.

The news anchor, a polished brunette with wide, serious eyes, lowered her voice, as if speaking any louder would shatter the town completely.

"*Sources close to the investigation have revealed that Mrs. Miller sustained injuries that suggest possible foul play. While police have not disclosed details regarding the nature of these injuries, they have confirmed that the case is now classified as a homicide and are appealing for any information which could lead to an arrest.*"

Vanessa exhaled slowly, setting her cup down.

So. It was official now.

She reached for her phone, scrolling through her messages. The group chat for the book club had exploded, unread notifications piling up by the second.

Jilly: *Did you see the news?*

Bee: *I can't believe this. I feel sick.*

Dani: *They're officially calling it a homicide now. Jesus.*

Pam: *Strange to see her life on screen like that, wasn't it?*

Tiffany: *Have any of you spoken to the police yet? About Erica? About her drinking?*

Bee: *I don't want to get involved. Brad would surely have told them that?*

And then, the last message.

From Jilly, again. *What if it was someone she knew?*

Vanessa's lips curled slightly. Of course, it was. Murders like this were never random, were they?

She didn't reply. Instead, she locked her phone and leaned back against the plush leather couch, watching as Willow Creek unraveled in real time.

~

Jilly sat in the bookstore, staring blankly at the same page of a book she had opened twenty minutes ago, unable to focus on the words.

The shop was empty, despite the news vans outside, despite the growing sense of unease that had settled over the town like a fog. No one was in the mood to browse for new fiction when a real killer might be walking among them.

She pressed a trembling hand to her forehead, trying to force her thoughts into some kind of order.

It had been two days. Two *long* days of trying to process what had happened, of replaying every interaction she'd ever had with Erica, of wondering who could have done something like this.

And now, the police were calling it murder.

The word felt too big, too heavy, like it didn't belong in Jilly's world.

She thought about the book club meeting earlier that week. About how Erica had been her usual loud, reckless self, throwing out cryptic hints, toying with people, drinking too much.

She had said something to Jilly that night.

"I have a secret."

Jilly swallowed hard, gripping the book tighter in her hands. She'd said it would blow the town apart. Had she been joking? Had she known something that big? Or had she just been playing one of her usual games, not realizing she was standing too close to the edge?

The bells above the door chimed.

Jilly looked up, startled, as Dani stepped inside.

She looked pale, her brown hair loose around her shoulders, her eyes darting toward the front window as if she was making sure no one had followed her.

"You see all this?" Charlotte asked, waving her hand at the chaos on Main.

Jilly nodded slowly. "Yeah. It's crazy."

Charlotte hesitated, looking over her shoulder before stepping closer. "We need to talk."

Jilly set the book down, dread curling in her stomach. Because Dani's voice wasn't just worried. It was terrified.

Willow Creek had always prided itself on being a town where nothing bad happened. People living here paid a premium for their peace of mind, for their tree-lined streets and historic homes, for the carefully curated local businesses and the illusion of a world untouched by chaos.

But now, with Erica Miller's death being called a murder, that bubble had well and truly burst.

People gathered outside their homes, in coffee shops, in the aisles of the grocery store, speaking in hushed tones, glancing over their shoulders as if the killer might be lurking behind them.

Even the morning traffic on Main Street felt slower, the usual polite smiles exchanged between neighbors were now edged with uncertainty. No one knew who to trust.

Bee could feel it, even as she walked through the narrow aisles of Margaret's Market, gripping the basket in her hands like it might somehow steady her. She had no real reason to be here, her fridge was fully stocked, but she couldn't go home, not yet.

The store smelled of fresh bread and cinnamon, But, as a place that once felt comforting, now, it felt too quiet, too sterile, too full of people trying to pretend that everything was normal.

Bee caught snippets of conversation as she moved past the shelves.

"I heard she was drinking again the night it happened."

"You don't think Brad had anything to do with it, do you? He always seemed so quiet..."

"God, do you think it was a break-in? No, no, there were no signs of forced entry. That means it was someone she knew."

The last statement made Jilly stop in her tracks.

Someone she knew.

A shiver ran through her. That's what Charlotte had said, too. It's what they'd all thought. God knows, Erica had annoyed enough people in Willow Creek. None more so, perhaps, than the ladies from the book club.

She turned the corner near the produce section and nearly ran straight into Annabelle Harper, a PTA mother who had always been a little too invested in everyone's business. She had a permanent tan, over-bleached hair, and a talent for making even the most mundane conversation feel like a calculated interrogation.

Annabelle's perfectly arched brow lifted as she looked at Bee.

"Ah Belinda," she said, almost rubbing her hands with glee. "I was just saying to Olivia here" she continued, gesturing to Olivia Kemp, another town fixture who had been in Willow Creek long before any of them. "That whoever did this is probably walking around right now, just waiting for the police to knock on their door."

Bee's fingers tensed around the handle of her basket.

Annabelle turned her sharp gaze toward her. "You were in Erica's book club, weren't you?"

Bee nodded slowly. "Yes."

Annabelle's lips pursed like she was *considering* something. "Did she seem... off to you lately?"

Bee didn't want to answer, didn't want to be pulled into the town's growing storm of speculation, but Annabelle was looking at her like she expected something.

"She was always just Erica," Bee said carefully. "But I guess she was drinking more than usual."

Olivia sucked in a breath. "You think she was—?"

"No," Bee interrupted, shaking her head quickly. "I don't know. I mean, I," She hesitated, then sighed. "I just think she had a lot on her mind."

Annabelle tilted her head slightly. "Like what?"

Bee hesitated again. She thought of Erica at book club, swirling her wine, laughing too loudly, dropping cryptic little hints like bait on a hook.

"I have a secret."

Bee exhaled, forcing a small smile. "I really don't know."

Annabelle studied her for a moment before humming, unsatisfied, then turning back to Olivia. "It'll all come out soon enough. People like Erica always get themselves in trouble."

Bee clenched her jaw but didn't say anything. Because wasn't that exactly what Vanessa had said too?

Main Street was still crawling with news vans. Tripods blocked the sidewalk. Reporters did their hair with practiced fingers while producers shouted into earpieces. A small crowd had formed, murmuring like a hive, drawn to the scent of scandal.

Tiffany arrived in a crisp white blazer, heels clacking like punctuation marks on the pavement. She had her phone held aloft, already streaming to her modest but loyal following.

"Omg, you guys," she whispered theatrically, eyes darting to the Channel 5 van behind her. "They've just confirmed Erica's drowning wasn't an accident. There were... *bruises.* Injuries. I'm here to try and find out more for you guys."

She widened her eyes for effect. A couple of bystanders turned.

"This is literally *unreal,*" she continued, pivoting so that a camera crew framed her in soft focus. "She was found in her *pool,* and everyone just assumed she slipped because she drank too much. But now they're saying it looks... *deliberate.*"

A reporter cleared her throat loudly, trying to reclaim her shot. Tiffany offered an apologetic smile and retreated a few steps – still in view, still broadcasting her own piece.

"I mean, Erica wasn't just some random woman," she said. "She was a friend of mine. We went to the same book club. And now? She's dead. Possibly murdered. In *our* town. I'll bring you more updates as I get them. You can count on me for the truth, guys."

She gave the camera a solemn nod and ended the stream.

Across the street, the bookstore *Chapter & Verse* looked sleepy in the fog of all the excitement, its quaint little windows, hand-drawn chalkboard signs, and a cozy yellow glow calling her over. Tiffany made a beeline for it.

~

At home, Vanessa sat at the breakfast bar in her pristine white kitchen, scrolling idly through her phone. The town's local action online group was buzzing.

Mrs. Miller's death ruled a homicide.

Police investigating all possible leads.

A town meeting has been scheduled.

Vanessa smirked as she scrolled past the messages, sipping her imported French coffee. Everyone was in a panic, which made her amused more than anything.

"Mother?"

She turned to see Ellie, her thirteen-year-old daughter, standing in the doorway, her arms crossed over her chest. She had Simon's sharp features, Vanessa's icy blue eyes, and an intelligence that Vanessa knew better than to underestimate.

"Yes?" Vanessa set down her phone, giving Ellie a slow, practiced smile.

Ellie hesitated. "People are saying she was killed?"

Vanessa arched a brow. "That's what the news is saying."

Ellie nodded slowly, looking thoughtful. "Do you think they'll find out who did it?"

Vanessa's smile didn't falter. "Oh, sweetheart." She reached forward, tucking a strand of Ellie's hair behind her ear. "They always *find out* in the end."

Ellie's gaze lingered on her mother for a moment before she nodded, her expression unreadable, and turned back toward the staircase.

Vanessa watched her go, then exhaled, her smirk fading.

She had always taught her daughter to be smart. She just hoped she was smart enough to stay out of any of this.

~

Meanwhile, Pam curled up on the couch that evening, a blanket pulled over her legs, her phone pressed to her ear as Miriam sighed heavily on the other end.

"The whole town is losing it," Miriam muttered. "People are whispering about suspects like they're casting a damn movie."

Pam bit her lip. She hesitated before saying, "Miriam, do you think Vanessa had anything to do with this?"

Silence.

Then, Miriam let out a slow, measured breath. "I don't know. But I do know one thing."

Pam swallowed. "What?"

Miriam's voice was quiet. "She's not acting like someone who lost a friend."

Pam nodded to herself, clutching the blanket tighter around her. She didn't say it out loud, but she knew it too.

Vanessa Caldwell was many things, manipulative, cruel, calculating, but she was also dangerous. And Jilly had a terrible feeling they were only just beginning to understand how dangerous.

~

Vanessa Caldwell knew exactly who she was and exactly what she was worth. It wasn't just money. It was power.

Power over women like Jilly, who had once sat in her kitchen near tears, begging for a loan. Or washed-up has-beens like Pam and Miriam, with all their so-called wisdom. They didn't know the half of it.

But she also had power over men like Simon, who probably still couldn't quite figure out if he loved her or feared her more. But what she loved most was her power over people like Charlotte. People who spent years trying to match her, trying to outshine her, only to fail.

But even queens had to watch their backs. Lately, Vanessa had the uneasy sense that some of her hold over Charlotte was slipping.

It was just a whisper of a thought, a fleeting sensation that crept in when she wasn't paying attention. But it was there. And she hated it.

Vanessa sat at the head of the long marble dining table. Her posture was effortlessly elegant as she sliced into her grilled salmon. The table was set for two, the dining room too large, too formal for a casual weeknight dinner.

Simon sat across from her, barely touching his food.

"You're not eating," Vanessa observed, dabbing at her mouth with a linen napkin.

Simon didn't look up. "Not hungry."

Vanessa sighed, setting down her fork. "Is this about Erica?"

His jaw tightened. "The police questioned me again."

She smiled, unbothered. "And?"

"They asked if she seemed troubled. If she'd told me anything."

Vanessa raised an eyebrow. "And what did you say?"

Simon finally looked at her, his expression unreadable. "The truth. That I hadn't spoken to her in days."

Vanessa tilted her head, studying him like a specimen under glass. "Well, I hope you left out the part where you were sleeping with her."

Simon exhaled sharply, running a hand over his face. "Jesus, Vanessa."

"What?" she asked sweetly, reaching for her wine glass. "Don't act like it's some shocking revelation."

Simon stared at her, something flickering behind his eyes. Guilt? Frustration? Fear?

Vanessa leaned forward slightly. "You were careless."

He tensed. "I…"

"You should have been more discreet," she interrupted, swirling the wine in her glass. "Now look where we are. With you playing the grieving friend and me covering for your mistakes."

Simon paled slightly.

Vanessa took a slow sip of her wine, watching him over the rim of her glass. She loved this part. Watching people squirm.

"You don't actually think I had anything to do with it, do you?" Simon asked finally, his voice quieter now.

Vanessa set down her glass, smiling. "No, darling. You don't have the spine for something like that. But I'll have to think very carefully about what I tell the police if they ask me anything about it, which they're sure to do."

Simon's throat bobbed in a swallow, and Vanessa savored the tension in the air.

Yes. She still had control over him. For now.

Later that evening, Vanessa stood in her walk-in closet, scrolling through her texts.

Nothing from Charlotte. Typical.

Vanessa had let her stew in silence for days, waiting for her to crack. Because Charlotte had been cracking for a while. It was in her eyes. The way she avoided Vanessa's gaze at book club, the way she'd flinched whenever Vanessa made an offhand comment.

Vanessa smirked to herself and typed out a message.

Vanessa: *You've been awfully quiet. Everything alright?*

She watched the screen for several seconds. No response.

Vanessa sighed dramatically. Fine. If Charlotte wouldn't come out to play, then maybe it was time for a little reminder.

She walked over to her desk, pulled open the drawer, and retrieved the folder.

It was neatly organized, filled with documents, screenshots, and carefully collected evidence. Her insurance policy.

She flipped through the contents, pausing at the photos she had printed weeks ago.

Charlotte.

Simon.

A hotel parking lot.

A timestamp that could destroy a marriage.

Vanessa traced her manicured finger over the edge of the photo, her smirk widening.

She was untouchable.

Charlotte could pretend she wasn't afraid. She could try to hide. But Vanessa always won. Always.

The next morning, Vanessa went to the country club.

She had coffee with her usual circle of women, reveling in their adoration, enjoying the way they hung onto every word she said. She had first-hand knowledge of the victim, after all. They were rapt.

But even among her most devoted ladies, she couldn't help feeling something was different. Something was off.

When she made a joke about Erica's drinking, no one laughed. When she walked past a table of younger women, they stopped talking.

She felt the shift before she even understood it. People were looking at her differently now. Not with admiration. Not with envy. But with something else.

Suspicion.

Vanessa took a slow sip of her coffee, scanning the room.

Finally, she found Charlotte sitting alone near the window, staring out at the golf course, tense and silent.

For a moment, Vanessa considered going over. Taunting her about ignoring her message last night. Seeing just how close she could push her to the edge. But then Charlotte's gaze flicked up directly at her.

And for the first time in years, Vanessa felt a strange, unfamiliar sensation curl around her spine.

Was it possible? Was Charlotte finally ready to fight back?

Vanessa smiled. Good. She loved a challenge.

That night, as Vanessa slipped into her silk robe and stepped into her dimly lit bedroom, the feeling from the club hadn't left her. The feeling of being watched. Of being suspected. But now it had been joined by a different, more unsettling feeling. Of being hunted.

She turned off the light and slid into bed alone. Simon was still out. Maybe at the club. Maybe with Charlotte. Vanessa didn't really care where he was. She'd come to bed, but she doubted she would sleep.

Because for the first time, she wasn't sure if she was the one holding the power anymore. And she hated it.

10

THE NOTE

Jilly found it by accident.

She hadn't been looking for anything, just tidying up around the bookstore, trying to distract herself from the way the town felt right now, from the way everyone was talking but no one was saying anything real.

She had been moving books around behind the register, organizing receipts, trying to restore some sense of normalcy. But when she pulled open the drawer where she kept old invoices and book fair sign-ups, there it was.

A note. Folded. Slightly crumpled. Her name scrawled across the front in a way that was unmistakable.

Jilly's breath caught in her throat. She knew that handwriting.

Erica.

Her hands trembled as she unfolded the paper. The ink was slightly smudged, like it had been written quickly, with frantic pressure.

Only one sentence.

I know what she's up to. And I can prove it.

Jilly's mouth went dry. She read it again. And again.

The note wasn't dated, but she knew. She could feel it in her bones. Erica had written this the day before she died. That was the last time she'd been in the store. And Jilly had left her out front here, while she got some stock from the back.

And suddenly, Jilly couldn't breathe.

She sat down hard in the chair behind the counter, her fingers tightening around the paper.

Why so vague? Dammit Erica!

Who was she talking about?

Was it Vanessa?

Was it someone else?

Or...

Her stomach twisted violently. What if Erica had meant her? What if the note was supposed to threaten Jilly in some way? But why? What had she ever done to Erica?

Jilly shut her eyes, forcing herself to stay calm, but her mind was already unraveling.

Had Erica known? Had she figured out the one thing Jilly had never told anyone?

She pressed her free hand to her forehead, her pulse hammering. It didn't make sense. Erica had never said anything to her directly, never hinted at knowing. But she had been nosy. She had liked to play games, to poke at people, to see how far she could push before something broke.

Jilly forced herself to breathe. Even if Erica had known, what could she have proved? And why would the note say 'she' and not 'you'?

Jilly tried to put the idea out of her head. Of course Erica didn't know. But... what if she did? And what if, Jilly swallowed, what if that's why she was dead?

She sat there for what felt like forever, the note crumpled in her hand. She should take it to the police. She knew that. But something in her gut told her not to. The note didn't say who

Erica was talking about. If she handed it over, the police would start asking questions. About Erica. About the others. About Jilly. About things Jilly had spent too much time burying.

Her fingers clenched. If Erica had known something, she should have come to her. But she hadn't. Instead, she had left this note like a warning. Or a threat. Or a goodbye.

Jilly's throat tightened. She couldn't risk keeping it.

She took a shaky breath and reached for the small silver lighter she kept in the drawer. She wasn't sure what she was doing until she was doing it, her hands moving on autopilot, her brain screaming at her to stop but her body refusing to listen.

She flicked the wheel, and a small flame flickered to life.

For a moment, she hesitated. Then, with a sharp inhale, she held the note to the fire.

The paper curled at the edges, the ink darkening, the words erasing themselves as if they had never existed. She held it until there was nothing left but ash. Then she let the corner fall into the waste bin, watching as the embers smoldered and died.

Jilly sat there in the silence of the bookstore, her heart racing, her stomach churning, her hands still shaking. She had just destroyed the only clue Erica had left behind. And she had no idea if she had just saved herself or made a terrible mistake.

Jilly sat frozen as the faint scent of burning paper still lingered in the air. Her fingers twitched where they rested in her lap, her breathing uneven.

She had never felt afraid of Erica.

Annoyed? Sure. Exhausted by her drama? Absolutely. But fear? That was new. Because this wasn't just Erica being reckless. This wasn't just another night of too much wine and careless confessions. This was something else. That note had been more sinister than she ever remembered Erica being.

Jilly swallowed again, her pulse pounding. Erica hadn't just been messy. She had been dangerous. And she'd stuck her nose in where it wasn't wanted. And now, maybe, someone had killed her for what she knew.

Jilly stood suddenly, needing to move, needing to breathe, needing to pretend for a moment that everything was normal.

She went to the register, pressing her palms against the cool glass countertop, staring blankly at the neat stacks of books around the shop. Normally, being surrounded by stories was comforting, the one place where she didn't have to pretend to be someone else. But today, the bookstore felt too quiet. Too still.

She could still feel the weight of the ashes of Erica's note in the trash can beneath her desk, could still see the words seared into her mind.

I know what she's up to. And I can prove it.

Jilly squeezed her eyes shut. She had never wanted to be part of anything like this.

She had come to Willow Creek for a fresh start. A new life. A quiet existence, away from the past, away from the person she used to be. But now Erica was dead. And the police were looking for answers.

The chime of the front door made her jump. Jilly's eyes flew open just as Detective Sam Whitaker stepped inside. Her heart slammed against her ribs.

He was tall, broad-shouldered, the kind of man who carried an air of calm authority, his police badge clipped to his belt, a small notepad already in his hand.

He wasn't alone. A female officer stood just behind him, younger, her expression more neutral, but her eyes scanning the bookstore with quiet calculation.

"Ms. Lawson?" Whitaker asked, his voice even.

Jilly's mouth went dry.

"Y-Yes," she managed, forcing a small, polite smile. Too polite. Too careful.

Whitaker nodded, glancing briefly at his notepad before

meeting her gaze. "We're speaking with folks around town, trying to get a better sense of Erica Miller's last movements. Mind if we ask you a few questions?"

Jilly stiffened. This was it. This was the moment.

She had nothing to hide.

Except she did.

Because perhaps the only evidence Erica had left behind, the only thing that might have told the police that she knew something which someone else wanted to keep secret, was now burned to ash.

Jilly forced her shoulders to relax, stepping forward with what she hoped looked like ease.

"Of course," she said, carefully keeping her voice steady. "But I don't know how much help I'll be."

Whitaker lifted an eyebrow.

"You were in her book club, weren't you?"

Jilly hesitated, just for a second. A second too long.

"Yes," she admitted. "And I guess we were friends."

That part was true. Or at least, it had been true. Even that had drifted with Erica's drinking.

Until now.

Whitaker nodded slowly. "When was the last time you spoke to her?"

Jilly wet her lips, her mind racing.

She could tell them about book club. About how Erica had been reckless, dropping hints that she knew something she shouldn't have.

She should tell them about the note. But then she'd have to tell them why she burned it. And then she'd end up telling them everything. So instead, she did what she had always done best. She lied.

"The night of book club," she said lightly, shrugging. "She

was drinking a lot, but she always did that. We talked about books, gossiped a little. Nothing unusual."

Whitaker studied her for a long moment.

"You didn't see her after that?"

Jilly shook her head. She could feel the female officer watching her, taking in every twitch of her fingers, every shift in her stance.

"Did Erica seem... concerned about anything?" Whitaker asked. "Worried? Anxious?"

Jilly forced out a small laugh. "Erica was always dramatic. It was hard to take her seriously sometimes, especially when she'd had a drink. I can't say she seemed any more anxious than usual."

Whitaker nodded, but he didn't look entirely convinced.

Jilly's stomach twisted painfully. The air in the bookstore felt too hot, too thick, pressing against her like a physical weight.

"Did she ever mention any altercations with anyone specific?" the female officer asked, speaking for the first time. "Anyone she was arguing with? Someone she was afraid of?"

Jilly's fingers curled into her sleeves. Her mind flashed back to the note.

I know what she's up to. And I can prove it.

Jilly inhaled slowly, forcing herself to hold it together.

"No," she said finally. "Not that I remember."

Another lie.

The officers exchanged a glance, then Whitaker nodded, slipping his notepad back into his jacket.

"All right," he said. "If you think of anything else, let us know."

Jilly nodded quickly. "Of course."

She stepped back as they turned toward the door, as if putting as much distance between herself and the police as possible.

As the bell chimed and the door swung shut behind them, Jilly let out a slow, shaky breath. She could still feel their eyes on her. She had lied. She had destroyed evidence. And now, the only thing left between her and the truth coming out was how well she could keep it buried.

~

Willow Creek had always been the kind of town where people left their doors unlocked, where neighbors greeted each other with warm smiles and borrowed sugar without hesitation. But not anymore.

Since Erica's death, everything had changed. The once-lively streets were quieter. Parents kept a closer eye on their children. The morning coffee crowd at the local café spoke in hushed tones, their usual chatter replaced by a singular topic of conversation.

The murder.

Because that's what people could call it now, now that the police had confirmed it.

Nobody drowned in their own pool, in the middle of the night, without something more behind it. Even if they were drunk. Suddenly, it seemed everyone in town had their own theory.

By the time Friday rolled around, Willow Creek was buzzing with speculation.

People whispered at the bakery. Stared a little too long in the grocery store. Conversations died the moment someone new entered the room.

Locks were changed. Security cameras installed.

And now, in the evenings, when the town quieted, people stayed home with their gates and doors locked. Because for the first time, Willow Creek didn't feel safe. For the first time, people weren't sure they really knew their neighbors. And for the first time they had to wonder if the killer was still walking among them.

~

Three days after Erica's body was found, the book club members were brought in for formal questioning.

Not together. One by one.

Jilly was the first.

She sat stiffly in the station's interview room, a place that smelled of old coffee, stale sweat, and bleach, her fingers twisting in her lap. Across from her, a different detective this time – one with tired eyes and a notepad too full of scribbled notes – leaned forward.

"How well did you know Erica Miller?"

Jilly hesitated. "Well enough, I suppose. We were part of the same book club for years."

"And outside of the club?"

She swallowed. "Not much. I mean, I ran into her sometimes at the store or around town. But we weren't close friends or anything."

The detective tapped his pen against the notepad. "Did she have any enemies?"

Jilly blinked. That was a loaded question.

Erica had spent most of her time pushing people's buttons. Was that the same thing as having enemies?

"I, I don't know," Jilly said carefully. "I think she could be difficult, but I wouldn't say she was hated."

The detective didn't look convinced.

~

Vanessa didn't wait to be questioned. She had invited herself in, arriving at the station in dark sunglasses and a perfectly tailored coat, her heels clicking across the linoleum floor as if she had walked into a business meeting rather than a murder investigation.

"I don't know what help I can be," she said smoothly as she took a seat across from the detective. "But I'll answer whatever you need."

The detective didn't look amused.

"Tell me about the last time you saw Erica Miller."

Vanessa barely blinked. "At book club, of course."

"You didn't see her outside of that?"

"No."

The detective stared at her. "You hesitated."

Vanessa smiled tightly. "No, I didn't."

A long pause stretched between them.

The detective leaned forward slightly. "Did you know about any conflicts Erica had?"

Vanessa exhaled. "Detective, we were a book club. Not a cage match."

The detective gave her a pointed look. "That's not a no."

Vanessa tilted her head, adjusting her sunglasses as though suddenly bored. "Women talk. We gossip. It's harmless."

"But was it?"

Vanessa didn't answer. And the detective didn't push. Because something about the way she carried herself, about the way she had marched into the station on her own terms, made it clear she was choosing her words very carefully.

Charlotte sat perfectly still. Her hands were folded neatly on the table.

The detective studied her for a moment before speaking. "How well did you know Erica?"

Charlotte offered a polite, almost rehearsed smile. "We were friendly enough."

The detective raised an eyebrow. "Friendly?"

Charlotte hesitated. "We had our moments. But that's true of any group of women, isn't it?"

"Were you aware of any trouble Erica was having?"

Charlotte didn't flinch. "Trouble?"

"Yes. Financial, personal, or otherwise."

She shook her head. "No, nothing like that."

The detective paused, letting the silence stretch just long enough to make Charlotte shift slightly in her seat.

"Did she ever tell you she felt threatened by someone?"

Charlotte's throat bobbed in a swallow. It was so small, so subtle, but the detective caught it.

"No," she said, too quickly.

Another pause. The detective leaned back, scribbling something in his notebook while Charlotte stayed very, very still.

~

Dani crossed one leg over the other, arms folded tightly across her tracksuit top. Her face was flushed, as though she'd just jogged there.

The detective glanced up. "You say you were at swim practice the morning they found Erica?"

"Yeah," Dani said quickly. "My boys are both training for regionals."

"You and Erica—close?"

Dani shook her head. "She wasn't exactly the carpool kind. Too... high-strung."

"Any tension between you?"

A beat passed. Dani's jaw flexed. "She didn't like that my kids are better at sport than hers, I guess. She thought I was using some influence to get them on the team, you know. Just jealousy, really. I didn't take it personally."

"Did Erica seem afraid? Nervous about anything?"

Dani's gaze flicked to the corner of the room. "She has been on edge lately. Snapped at Tiffany last week over some stupid social post."

The detective nodded. "But nothing specific?"

"Nope," Dani said. "Just drama. Like always."

Bee sat with her hands curled into her sleeves. Her voice, when she spoke, was barely above a whisper.

"Did you and Erica speak much?" the detective asked.

She shook her head. "Not really. She was quite loud. Outspoken, I mean. I... I listen more than I talk."

The detective studied her. "You were at home when you heard the news. What did you do?"

Bee nodded slowly. "I baked. I always do. I just... wanted to keep busy."

"Did Erica confide in you ever?"

"No," Bee said. "To be honest, I don't think she ever really noticed me."

She looked down at her hands, fidgeting in her sleeves. And then she looked up again, as though remembering something.

"But I did see her arguing with Charlotte a week or so ago. In the car park. I was in my car. I heard them both yelling. But I couldn't hear what they said."

"Did you ask what it was about?"

"No," Bee murmured. "But Charlotte looked... cold. Hard."

The detective scribbled something down. Bee flinched at the sound of the pen. Had she said too much?

~

Pam leaned back in the chair, arms loose, fingers clasping the stem of her sunglasses dangling from her fingers. Her tone was dry as dust.

"Well, let's get on with it," she said. "I assume you're asking everyone the same dead-girl questions?"

The detective looked up. "How would you describe your relationship with Erica?"

"Competitive. She wanted to be queen bee. I was the wasp in her martini."

"Did you have any serious arguments?"

"Serious is relative. She didn't like being disagreed with. I didn't like being bossed around. That's suburbia, isn't it?"

"Did you notice any changes in her behavior recently?"

Pam shrugged. "She was twitchier. Bitchier. Checking her phone more. Watching the door like she was expected someone."

"Did she mention being scared?"

"No. But someone like Erica? She'd never admit it, even if she was."

~

Miriam's expression was calm, reflective. She leaned forward, hands clasped.

"You strike me as someone who pays attention," the detective said.

"I try," she replied. "People reveal more when they think no one's looking."

"Did Erica ever mention feeling unsafe?"

"No. But she had the energy of someone being watched. Skittish. Defensive."

"Any theories?"

Miriam paused. "She was arguing with Vanessa a lot lately. And Tiffany's been fishing for drama since day one. She had a snap at Dani about bribing a ball coach. What do you want me to say?"

"You don't want to answer my questions?"

Miriam tilted her head. "How about you answer one of mine? Have you confirmed whether the injuries happened before or after she drowned?"

The detective didn't reply. Miriam smiled, just faintly. "Didn't think so."

~

Tiffany perched on the edge of the chair like it was a photoshoot prop. Her nails clicked against her phone case.

The detective sighed. "Please put the phone away."

"I'm just checking comments. People are freaking out."

"This is a formal interview."

"Fine." She shoved it into her bag with a huff.

"You were the last to join the group chat the night the news broke."

"I was filming a makeup collab. Late upload. You understand, right?"

The detective said nothing.

Tiffany adjusted her scarf dramatically. "Look, Erica and I had our moments. She was jealous. Said my posts were 'tasteless.'"

"Did you feel threatened by her?"

Tiffany scoffed. "Please. I grew up with worse than passive-aggressive texts. Erica couldn't touch me."

"Did she say she felt threatened?"

Tiffany hesitated. "By me?"

"By anyone?"

"No," Tiffany said, voice softer now. "But then she loved winding people up. I doubt she'd ever feel threatened by anyone."

By the end of the week, the police released a statement.

The official cause of death was drowning. But the injuries on Erica's body, bruising around the wrists and arms, a faint scratch along her neck, suggested something more violent.

There were no signs of forced entry into Erica's home.

No fingerprints that weren't supposed to be there.

No clear suspects.

Just questions. And in a town like Willow Creek, questions turned into rumors faster than wildfire.

11

ANOTHER ONE BITES THE DUST

A few days had passed, and the shock of Erica's death had almost begun to settle into something dull and uneasy in Willow Creek. People still whispered, still watched their neighbors a little too closely, still let their eyes linger on the police cruisers parked near the station, but slowly, the town was adjusting.

Because that's what people did when the drama didn't directly affect them. They adjusted. They moved on.

Until Vanessa Caldwell was found dead in her bedroom.

~

It was her daughter, Ellie, who found her.

She had come home from school early, dropped her backpack by the front door, and called out for her mother. When no one answered, she sighed. Vanessa was probably upstairs taking one of her afternoon naps, the ones she only took when she wanted to avoid dealing with whatever her latest problem was.

Ellie made her way up the grand staircase, trailing her fingers along the polished wooden banister, her mind already preoccupied with the unfinished history paper sitting in her bag.

She knocked once.

"Mom?"

No answer.

Another knock, this time harder.

"Mother, are you—"

The door creaked open. And then, Ellie's world stopped.

Vanessa was on the bed. Her silk robe was askew, her blonde hair spread across the pillow like she had simply laid down for a nap, except her skin was wrong.

Pale. Blue.

And her neck...

Ellie made a sound, something between a gasp and a scream, her breath locking in her throat as she stumbled back into the hallway, her knees nearly giving out beneath her.

Her mother wasn't asleep. She was dead.

The investigation into Erica's death had barely begun and now the town was reeling from another blow – one that no one had seen coming.

Vanessa Caldwell. Cold, sharp, untouchable Vanessa. The one so many had whispered might be in the frame for Erica's murder. Larger than life Vanessa Caldwell was gone. Strangled in her own bed.

The perfect house, the perfect family, the perfect life and all of it shattered with one cruel, suffocating act.

Dani was in the bleachers at her son's ball game she got the call from Miriam.

She answered on the second ring, pressing the phone tightly against her ear.

"Have you heard?" Miriam's voice was thin, shaking.

Dani froze.

"Heard what?"

Miriam exhaled sharply, as if she had been holding her breath. "It's Vanessa. She's... Dani, she's dead."

Dani's entire body went cold. Her fingers loosened. She didn't even see the third strike which knocked her son out of the game.

No. Not Vanessa. Not her.

Her mind scrambled to make sense of it, to put the pieces together, but it was too much, too soon, too fast.

"I—I don't understand," Dani stammered. "How?"

"Strangled," Miriam said, her voice barely above a whisper. "In her own bed."

Dani almost dropped her phone. She was glad she'd been sitting down when she took the call.

Two deaths. Two women from their book club, murdered within days of each other.

Dani could suddenly feel the weight of something dark and inevitable pressing down on all of them.

Erica had been reckless. She had told them all she'd known something dangerous. That she was about to share someone's secret.

But Vanessa? She'd had been untouchable. Or at least, that's what they had all thought.

Dani swallowed hard. "Miriam," she whispered. "What's happening?"

Miriam didn't answer because they both already knew.

Someone was killing them. But what if they weren't done yet?

The Caldwell estate looked wrong.

It wasn't just the flashing blue lights of the police cruisers still parked in the driveway, or the crime scene tape that had been stretched across the entrance to Vanessa's bedroom. It wasn't even the cluster of neighbors hovering near the gates, whispering behind their hands, pretending to be concerned when really, they were hungry for details.

It was the silence.

Vanessa's house had always been a place of controlled perfection, a place where appearances were everything. There had been dinner parties with hand-pressed linen napkins, where Vanessa would stand in the kitchen, a glass of expensive wine in hand, entertaining effortlessly while guests marveled at her ability to make everything look easy.

But now, the house felt empty. Cold. Hollow.

Charlotte took a steadying breath and rang the doorbell.

There was a long pause, and for a moment, she wondered if Simon would ignore it. But then the heavy door creaked open.

Simon Caldwell looked wrecked.

His crisp, tailored life had collapsed overnight, and it showed. His shirt was wrinkled, the top buttons undone, his dark hair uncombed, his jaw rough with days-old stubble. His usually sharp blue eyes were clouded with something Charlotte couldn't quite name.

Grief. Or something worse. Resentment, perhaps. Had she misjudged her visit?

"Charlotte," he said, his voice hoarse but curious, though his face revealed a hint of panic at seeing her there on his doorstep.

"I'm so sorry, Simon," she said softly, holding up the foil-covered dish in her hands. "I brought pie. I didn't know what else to do."

Simon exhaled, glancing over his shoulder. "You'd better come in."

Charlotte hesitated, just for a second. She could see a police officer inside, and feel the tension radiating off Simon and lingering in the air like smoke. This wasn't just a house anymore. It wasn't his home. It was a crime scene.

Still, she stepped inside, clutching the dish like it was an offering, a peace treaty, a bridge across something too dark to name.

The kitchen looked exactly the same as it always had, pristine, gleaming, untouched. The countertops were polished to a shine, the stainless-steel appliances glinting. But there was a wrongness to it now, an emptiness that felt unnatural.

The police officer stood near the kitchen counter, flipping through a small notebook, eyes flicking toward them occasionally.

Charlotte placed the pie on the counter carefully.

"I figured Ellie might need to eat something," she said softly.

Simon nodded absently, rubbing a hand over his face. "She's upstairs. She hasn't come down much since..." He trailed off. He didn't need to finish the sentence.

Charlotte shifted uncomfortably. "Simon, if you or Ellie need anything, anything at all, please, just... call me."

Simon looked at her then, really looked at her, and for a moment, Charlotte felt the weight of everything unsaid between them.

Everything too dangerous to name.

His mouth opened like he was about to say something.

"Mr. Caldwell," the officer interrupted, his voice steady but firm. "I just have a few more questions."

Simon's expression shut down immediately. Charlotte watched as his grief rearranged itself into something else. Something colder. Something he quickly hid again.

She stepped back. "I should go."

Simon nodded once, but he didn't say goodbye. Charlotte

turned and made her way to the door, the weight in her chest heavier than before. She hesitated at the doorway, her fingers tightening around the doorknob. She should leave. The police officer was still standing near the kitchen island, watching the exchange with a neutral expression, waiting for Simon to turn his attention back to the interview.

But something in Simon's posture, the way his jaw locked and unlocked, made Charlotte pause. He wanted to say something. He just wasn't sure if he should.

She turned slightly, lowering her voice. "Simon. What is it?"

Simon's shoulders tensed. He exhaled through his nose, rubbing a hand over his jaw, then flicked his gaze toward the officer. For a moment, Charlotte thought he wouldn't answer.

Then, in a voice too quiet, too low, he said, "There was no sign of forced entry."

Charlotte blinked. "What?"

Simon swallowed hard, his Adam's apple bobbing. "Whoever did it, they didn't break in." He paused, voice dropping even lower. "She let them in."

A cold shiver ran down Charlotte's spine. She turned her head slightly toward the officer, but he didn't seem to be paying attention to them anymore, pretending, maybe, not to hear.

Charlotte's pulse quickened. "Simon, what are you saying?"

Simon's expression darkened, his lips pressing into a thin line. "She wasn't afraid before it happened. There wasn't a sign of struggle, no mess, no overturned furniture. Nothing." He exhaled sharply, gripping the counter. "Someone came into our house, into our bedroom, and wrapped their hands around her throat."

He broke off, his fingers curling into a fist.

"I think..." he started, and then gulped. "She might have been having an affair."

"Simon," Charlotte hesitated. What could she say? "I'm sure that's not true," she said, finally.

Simon didn't move for a long time. Then, finally, he turned toward her, and Charlotte almost stepped back at the look in his eyes. Dark. Unsettled.

"I don't know," he admitted, his voice quieter than before. "Someone she knew did this to her. Just like someone Erica knew did the same to her."

Charlotte felt her stomach twist.

The house was so quiet. Too quiet. The kind of silence that came after something awful had happened.

She swallowed, stepping away, her heels clicking softly against the polished floors. "I should go," she murmured.

Simon didn't stop her.

As she reached the door, she glanced over her shoulder one last time. Simon was still standing there, staring at the counter, as if seeing something Charlotte couldn't. Something he would never be able to unsee.

Charlotte stepped into the cold air, the weight of Vanessa's death pressing against her chest.

Willow Creek would never be the same without her.

12

THE COFFEE HOUSE

The air inside The Roasted Bean was thick with the scent of freshly brewed espresso and cinnamon. Normally, it was a warm, inviting space, a place where Willow Creek's well-to-do women gathered to chat over matcha lattes and hand-crafted pastries, a place where people could pretend that life was perfect. The décor was effortlessly chic, with exposed brick walls, vintage chandeliers, and sleek wooden tables, each topped with a small glass vase of fresh-cut flowers. It was a place of routine and comfort, where people came to escape the real world, if only for an hour.

But today, there was nothing comforting about it.

The women from the book club sat at their usual corner booth table near the large bay window. Jilly, Charlotte, and Miriam were crowded into one of the bench seats, while Dani, Tiffany, and Bee occupied the other. Jilly and Pam now had a little more space on the end seat they usually shared with Erica, and Vanessa's chair at the head of the table had been removed completely.

Now, they sat, half numb and in a daze, their coffee

untouched, their movements stiff and uneasy. The atmosphere in Willow Creek had shifted again, and this time, it wasn't just grief or shock. It was fear. The hum of conversation in the café felt different today, more hushed, more urgent, the occasional burst of laughter sounding wrong, misplaced, as if people weren't sure whether it was still okay to act normal.

Across the café, a group of women huddled together, whispering, throwing not-so-subtle glances toward the book clubbers. They weren't even trying to hide their curiosity anymore. They wore perfectly ironed blouses and diamond-studded earrings, their fingers wrapped delicately around porcelain cups, their voices low but buzzing with something that sounded almost like excitement.

Because now it wasn't just Erica Miller. Vanessa Caldwell was dead too. And everyone knew Vanessa Caldwell.

Miriam exhaled sharply, shifting in her seat, adjusting the sleeves of her soft gray sweater. "I don't even know what to say," she admitted, rubbing her temples. Her voice, usually calm and measured, was unsteady, tinged with something too close to panic. "I mean, this isn't just some awful coincidence, is it?"

Jilly sat stiffly beside her, barely moving. Charlotte shook her head, but said nothing.

Normally so put-together, today Miriam thought Charlotte looked drained, her skin pale, her dark hair falling limply over her shoulders. There were dark circles beneath her eyes, like she hadn't slept in days. Miriam was about to ask if she was okay, but stopped herself. None of them were.

Jilly exhaled shakily and murmured, "What if someone is targeting us?"

The words sat between them like a curse, and for a moment, no one spoke.

Bee shivered. She pulled her cardigan tighter around her, as was her habit, as if the soft knit fabric could shield her from the weight of what they were all now fearing.

Miriam pressed her lips together, glancing around the café, suddenly hyperaware of how public this group meeting was. The truth was that none of them had wanted to meet at someone's house. Not now. Not when two of their own were dead. And now, here was Bee, voicing a fear most of them had already felt. What if the group was a target.

The café was meant to feel safe, but now even the familiar setting felt different. The walls that once gave it a cozy intimacy now felt like they were closing in, and the soft background chatter of other customers was a reminder that everyone was watching.

Being in public felt safer, or at least, that's what they had told themselves. But that was before they'd got here.

A shadow moved beside them, and all three women looked up at once as a waitress, young, bright-eyed, and far too eager to be the one that served the group, stepped up to their table, balancing a tray of fresh coffee cups and a plate of cupcakes dusted with powdered sugar.

She set them down with practiced ease, then smiled a curious smile.

She had honey-blonde hair pulled into a high ponytail, a perfectly pressed apron over her fitted uniform. She looked fresh-faced, like she didn't yet know the exhaustion of real life, of real loss.

"Wow," she murmured, her gaze flicking between them. "I mean, just, wow! Right?"

Miriam frowned, her grip tightening around her cup. "Excuse me?"

The waitress, her name tag read BECCA, leaned in slightly, lowering her voice as if she were about to share a juicy secret. "I just mean, *it's crazy*, right?" she said, shaking her head. "First Erica, now Vanessa. And you all knew them both. I mean, they were always here with you. Right... here." As she said the last, she must have realized that she was standing where Vanessa's chair would usually be, because she shifted sideways quickly.

Pam stiffened. Her fingers curled tightly around the handle of her coffee cup, knuckles white against the porcelain. She had no time for this waitress at the best of times.

Bee's stomach turned uneasily. She had never liked attention, and now it felt like all of Willow Creek's eyes were slowly turning toward them, dissecting them, watching their every move.

Becca didn't seem to notice the sudden tension gripping the table. She just grinned, as if she were thrilled to have a front-row seat to a real-life murder mystery. "The whole town is talking about it," she added, her voice practically buzzing with excitement. "About all of you. Like, wow..."

Miriam's eyes narrowed. Her expression, normally open and patient, had turned to stone. "Are you insinuating something?"

Becca flushed slightly, but her smile didn't waver. "Oh, no, no, I didn't mean anything like that!" she said quickly, holding up her hands. "I just meant it's wild, you know? People are saying that the killer might be someone you all knew. Someone close."

Charlotte rose abruptly to her feet. "I don't need coffee," she muttered, grabbing her purse. "I need air."

Jilly and Miriam exchanged a glance before following suit, leaving the untouched pastries behind.

Tiffany. "Great, Becca. Well done. Way to go."

Becca looked suddenly downcast as the remainder of the group got up and shuffled out. She didn't even stop Pam when she grabbed two of the cakes and shoved one in her mouth on the way out.

As they hurried toward the door, Miriam cast one last glance over her shoulder, feeling the weight of Becca's stare still lingering on them. The young waitress didn't look remorseful. If anything, she looked pleased.

In a town like Willow Creek, everyone loved a scandal. And this was shaping up to be the best one yet.

~

The air outside The Roasted Bean was crisp, but Miriam barely felt it. She could still hear the whispers from inside, still feel the weight of the town's scrutiny pressing in on them all, even as they stood beneath the black-and-gold awning of the café.

Inside, even before the group had walked out, the atmosphere had been thick with something unspoken, something tangibly unpleasant. Suspicion.

The café, usually a haven of warmth and routine, had transformed into a gossip mill, grinding every last detail of Vanessa and Erica's deaths into something sensational.

Through the large bay window, Charlotte saw women pressed together at tables, their eyes darting toward their group every few seconds before flicking away again. Their fingers toyed absently with their silver spoons, stirring coffee that had long gone cold, too distracted by the thrill of speculation to actually drink it.

A few older men sat along the bar, pretending to read the paper but tilting their heads just enough to catch pieces of conversation.

The coffee shop had always been a place for quiet talk, small-town musings, and the occasional PTA scandal.

But now?

It was a courtroom. Worse than that. It was a place where it felt everyone had already made up their minds about who was guilty.

And now they, the remaining book club members were at the center of everyone's suspicion.

Charlotte rubbed her arms, trying to shake the feeling of being watched.

"Whoever did this," Jilly muttered beside her, voice soft, haunted, "it has to be someone who knew them both well."

Pam sneered, still chewing her cake.

"Or someone who they both knew something about," Tiffany said. "I mean, let's face it. The last time we were all together, before Erica... well, the last time we were all together, there was a lot of talk about buried secrets."

Jilly flushed, thinking of the note. Of her lie to the detective.

Charlotte frowned. "We were talking about the book, Tiff," she said.

"Or were we?" said Tiffany. "I'm not so sure."

"Remember what Erica said about a secret that would blow the place wide open?" said Dani. "She told us all that, but she told us all individually."

"But what?" asked Bee, still hugging herself. "And why did she want to blow everything out into the open."

"Because," said Tiffany. "She loved things to be messy. Remember what Vanessa said?"

Miriam looked at her. Had that been a defensive tone in her voice? She couldn't tell. She hated that this whole situation was making her question people she felt were friends. But someone had been close enough to both Vanessa and Erica to step inside their homes unchallenged, to touch their lives, to steal their breath away.

It was personal. And whoever had done it was still out there.

Jilly swallowed, adjusting the sleeves of her cardigan. "You know the police are going to interview all of us now."

Miriam let out a slow breath. "They'll have to," she agreed, wondering why Jilly seemed so worried about that. "It's not like they have a choice."

The words sat heavy between them, like their unspoken truths lingering in the cold autumn air.

Then a sharp voice cut through the silence like a knife.

"Funny," someone said, tone dripping with mock innocence, "that you lot have the nerve to still meet as group."

Charlotte turned, her stomach tightening before she even saw the face.

There, standing on the sidewalk, arms folded, lips pursed in quiet calculation, was Laurie Pierce.

Laurie wasn't the type to openly cause conflict, but she had a way of making her words feel like weapons. She was the kind of woman who always knew more than she let on, the kind who waited for the right moment to drop her opinions into the conversation like stones into a still pond, just to watch the ripples spread.

She wore a navy wool coat, her short dark hair meticulously styled, her sharp blue eyes flicking over them like a predator considering its prey.

Charlotte felt her shoulders tighten.

"We weren't," Jilly began, but Laurie cut her off before she could finish.

"Hiding in plain sight?" Laurie tilted her head, mock curiosity lacing her tone. "Because that's certainly what it looks like."

Charlotte's blood simmered beneath her skin.

Miriam, who was usually the most collected of all of them, let out a slow breath, like she was trying very hard to stay calm. "We met for coffee," she said carefully. "Like we do every Tuesday afternoon."

Laurie didn't look convinced. Her gaze lingered on each of them, slow and deliberate.

"Interesting," she murmured.

Charlotte felt something curl tight in her stomach.

"You know what the whole town is saying?" Laurie continued, idly inspecting her manicured nails as she spoke, her tone too casual, too calculated. "That this isn't random. That maybe someone knows more than they're letting on. Someone close to the victims. Someone they thought was a... *friend*."

Charlotte clenched her teeth. Enough.

"What the hell are you suggesting?" she asked, her voice sharper than intended.

Laurie shrugged, her coat shifting slightly with the movement. She wasn't rattled. She wasn't nervous. She was enjoying this.

"You tell me," Laurie said, voice smooth, her gaze cool and assessing.

Charlotte opened her mouth, ready to snap something back, but then, through the café window, movement caught her eye.

She turned, just in time to see Becca the waitress standing behind the counter, watching them. The young woman wasn't even pretending to hide her interest, or her phone, which she had held up to record the altercation. Her lips were slightly parted, her brown eyes practically glowing with excitement, like she was watching a movie unfold right before her. She stood frozen, a coffee pot in one hand, completely enthralled by the drama playing out on the sidewalk.

Charlotte felt sick. Because this wasn't just gossip anymore. This was a witch hunt. And they were right in the middle of it.

Miriam's voice was the first to break the silence.

"Let's go," she muttered under her breath, placing a hand on Charlotte's arm. "Now."

Charlotte inhaled sharply but nodded, tearing her gaze away from Becca's eager expression.

"Don't worry about her," Tiffany said. "I'll make sure that little clip never sees the light of day."

They all turned away from Laurie without another word, walking briskly down the sidewalk, their shoes tapping against the pavement.

But even as they left, Miriam could still feel the weight of Laurie's stare burning into their backs.

13

THE SUSPECT

The morning fog hung low over Willow Creek, swallowing the streets in a cold, eerie quiet. The sidewalks were slick with last night's rain, the air thick with the lingering scent of damp earth and freshly brewed coffee from the bakery down the road. Normally, Jilly liked mornings like this, slow and peaceful, where she could pretend, for a little while, that life was still normal.

But nothing was normal anymore.

She walked through town with her head down, her pulse thrumming beneath her skin, every step feeling heavier than the last.

She had never been someone who stood out in Willow Creek. She had always been just Jilly, the quiet woman who owned the failing bookstore, the one who never quite fit in with the polished perfection of the other women. She wasn't flashy like Vanessa. She wasn't charming like Erica. Or sporty like Dani, upbeat like Tiffany, kind like Bee or even hilariously cynical like Pam.

She had always been the one left on the outskirts, looking in. Not observing, like Miriam, but just not quite in the gang.

But now? Now, everyone was looking at her.

She could feel their eyes on her as she passed the local market, the way conversations stopped just a second too late, the way people suddenly found something very interesting on their phone screens when she walked by.

It wasn't just paranoia. They were whispering about her. Because now, she was a suspect.

She first heard the rumor at the bakery.

It was the only place she could stomach going into since even the bookstore felt suffocating, and home wasn't much better. She just wanted one cup of coffee, something warm in her hands to keep them from shaking.

The moment she stepped inside, she felt the shift in the room.

The bakery had always been one of the warmest spots in town, the smell of butter and flour rich in the air, the glass displays lined with golden croissants, plump blueberry muffins, and delicate raspberry tarts. It was a place people lingered in, chatted in, gossiped in.

Today, the warmth felt absent. The bakery felt darker.

Two women, Penny Manson and Rosie Clarke, stood near the counter, their voices low and conspiratorial.

Jilly recognized them from the PTA years ago, women who had never paid her much attention, who had always been wrapped up in their own world of well-planned charity events and tennis matches. Women who floated through life without a care in the world. Women who were lucky. Unlike Jilly.

Today, those women were talking about her.

Penny pressed a hand to her mouth in mock surprise before whispering something to Rosie. They hadn't seen her come in.

Jilly could feel it, even before she heard it.

"Well, it's not that much of a leap is it?" Rosie murmured, not even trying to lower her voice. "Vanessa had money. A lot of money. And everyone knows the bookstore is failing. Apparently, Vanessa had money owing from a lot of quarters. I wouldn't be surprised if one of them is that Jilly from the workshop."

Jilly's stomach dropped. Her fingers curled tightly around the strap of her purse.

She wanted to tap them on the shoulder and demand they say it to her face, wanted to tell them they had no idea what they were talking about.

But the worst part was they weren't wrong. Vanessa had had money. And Jilly's financial struggles were an open secret.

Jilly didn't wait for her coffee. She turned and walked out, leaving the warmth of the bakery behind, the cold air slapping her in the face as she stepped back onto the street.

Back at the bookstore, Jilly paced behind the counter, her mind running in circles.

She hadn't told the police about the loan. She hadn't told anyone. And now, it felt like the walls were closing in on her.

She ran a shaky hand through her hair, trying to steady herself. Could they find out? Could the police dig through Vanessa's bank records and see the money trail?

Vanessa had certainly never let her forget about it.

"I was generous, but I'm not a fool, Jilly."

"You're running out of time."

Jilly closed her eyes, her pulse pounding.

What if people found out about the money? Would they think she did it?

The bookstore felt too quiet. The shelves were too full of books that no one was buying.

Jilly had built this place with everything she had, poured her savings into it, believing and hoping that a bookstore in Willow Creek would survive. But it wasn't surviving. And now, with Vanessa gone, her debt was in danger of coming out. The anger was still here. Hanging over her. Waiting to ruin her.

The sudden sound of the bookstore bell jingling made Jilly jump. Her body went rigid, her breath catching in her throat as the door swung open. A police officer stepped inside.

Not Detective Whitaker, someone younger, sharper, with dark eyes that didn't miss a thing. His uniform was neatly pressed, his belt gleaming with the weight of his radio and handcuffs. He had the look of someone who had done this exact thing a thousand times before, walked into a small-town shop, asked polite questions, and watched as people squirmed under the weight of them.

"Ms. Lawson," he greeted, his tone polite, but too careful.

Jilly's throat went dry. "Yes?"

He pulled out a small notepad, flipping it open. "We'd like to ask you a few questions about Vanessa Caldwell."

Jilly felt the blood drain from her face. She nodded slowly, forcing herself to breathe evenly. But her fingers curled into fists at her sides. She knew. She knew exactly why they were here. And she still wasn't sure if she could tell them the truth.

~

The fluorescent lights in the market buzzed faintly overhead, casting a dull glow over the neatly stocked aisles. The store smelled of fresh bread and floor cleaner, the familiar scent of something ordinary, routine, safe—except nothing in Willow Creek felt safe anymore.

The produce section gleamed with perfectly arranged apples, oranges stacked in neat pyramids, bundles of fresh herbs tied together with twine. The shelves were lined with artisan pasta sauces, imported olive oils, and organic snacks that no one really needed but bought anyway because they could afford to.

The town's wealth was everywhere, even here in a convenience store.

Miriam and Dani moved through the store side by side, both clutching small hand baskets, their steps eerily in sync. None of them shopped alone anymore. Not after Erica. Not after Vanessa.

In fact, the silent rule had settled over the whole town like a fog, women pairing off, watching each other's backs, scanning faces in the aisles as if one of them might be the killer, as if one of them might be next.

Miriam studied Dani carefully as they passed the rows of canned goods, her fingers trailing absently along the edge of a shelf, her mind turning over the details that weren't adding up.

Dani had barely spoken since Vanessa's death. And when she did, she never said her name.

It was always:

"When it happened."

"After what happened to her."

"You know, when everything changed."

But never Vanessa. Never her name.

Miriam pretended to inspect a bag of coffee beans, weighing it in her hand, her eyes flicking toward Dani's reflection in the glass of the refrigerator doors.

Unlike her usual vibrant, athletic self, Dani looked exhausted. Her complexion was pale, her hair hanging loose around her shoulders in soft waves, slightly tangled as though she had been running her fingers through it all day. Her clothes, tailored gym gear in a muted shade of blue, were pristine as always, but something about the way she wore them today made her seem smaller, more fragile.

"Did you see that the police were at Jilly's store today?" Miriam asked, voice light.

Dani didn't look up. She reached for a box of tea, chamomile, the expensive kind, the kind someone bought when they were trying to sleep through something they couldn't quite forget.

"I heard," Dani murmured. She placed the tea in her basket, adjusting the strap over her arm, her movements calculated, careful. "People have been talking. Apparently, Vanessa had loaned her money to help with the bookstore. Tiffany said she heard Vanessa had been putting pressure on her to pay up."

Miriam nodded in agreement, setting the coffee back on the shelf.

"You think she did it?" she asked, watching Dani out of the corner of her eye.

Dani tensed, just slightly, barely enough to notice.

"God no," she said quickly. Then, "I don't know." She brushed a strand of hair behind her ear. "She has seemed unusually jumpy lately. And Vanessa could be a real bitch when she had something over you."

Miriam raised an eyebrow, but said nothing. There was something in Dani's tone that said she was speaking from experience.

Dani didn't respond right away. She turned the corner into the produce aisle, inspecting a row of apples, her fingers tracing the smooth red skin before finally choosing one.

"Look. I think Jilly's been struggling," Charlotte said finally. "And now people have heard about the loan, and they're looking for someone to blame."

Miriam let out a slow sigh pretending to inspect a bag of oranges.

"You talk like you think Vanessa had it coming," she said, keeping her tone light, careful.

Dani's jaw tightened.

"I didn't say that."

Miriam tilted her head slightly, watching her.

"Didn't you?"

Dani exhaled in frustration, grabbing another apple, dropping it into her basket with a little too much force.

"I just," she hesitated, rubbing her temple. "I don't know what to think anymore, okay?"

Liar. Miriam knew that tone.

Dani was choosing her words too carefully, as if she had already played out this conversation in her head, as if she had rehearsed exactly what to say.

Miriam rolled an orange between her palms, studying her. "You never say her name."

Dani fingers froze mid-reach. She turned to face Miriam, her expression carefully neutral, blank in a way that only made Miriam more suspicious.

"What?" Dani asked, her voice too even.

"You never say Vanessa's name," Miriam said, holding her gaze. "You always talk around it."

Dani let out a small, tight laugh, one that didn't reach her eyes.

"That's ridiculous," she said.

But she still didn't say her name.

Miriam set the orange back down on the display, dusting her hands off against her jeans.

"I just think it's strange," she said, watching Dani carefully. "That's all."

Dani opened her mouth like she wanted to say something, a denial, an excuse, a reason for her hesitation. But before she could, a sharp voice cut through the air.

"You two look serious."

They both turned, and Miriam felt a small spike of irritation at the interruption.

Standing near the end of the aisle, gripping a basket full of overpriced organic snacks, was Becca. The waitress. The one who had been watching too closely at the café. The one who had been waiting for this town to fall apart just so she could have something interesting to talk about.

Becca tilted her head slightly, giving them both a curious, knowing smile.

She was dressed casually, in dark leggings and an oversized sweatshirt, her brown hair pulled into a loose ponytail. Her makeup, heavy mascara and a matte lipstick that was just a little too dark for her skin tone, looked like it had been applied carelessly, like she had somewhere better to be but showed up here anyway, just in case something interesting happened.

Dani tensed beside Miriam, her fingers tightening around the strap of her basket.

Becca's gaze flickered between them, her lips twitching like she was trying to hold back a smirk.

Miriam didn't trust her either.

But not in the same way she didn't trust Dani right now – where there was something Dani was hiding.

No. Becca was different. Becca was hungry. She wanted this. She wanted the scandal, the drama, the unraveling of a town that had always looked down on her. And now she was thriving. Miriam felt her patience snap.

"Do you need something, Becca?" she asked, voice sharp, edged with irritation.

Becca laughed softly, shifting her weight onto one foot. "No, just, people are asking questions, you know?" she said, in that sickly sweet, amused tone. "Figured you two would know more than the rest of us."

Dani glared at the waitress. Miriam smiled tightly.

"Well, we don't," she said coolly.

Becca's gaze flickered over them one last time, assessing, waiting, before finally shrugging.

"Well," she said, grinning as she turned away, "I guess we'll all find out soon enough."

The moment she was gone, Dani let out a breath, her shoulders sinking slightly.

Miriam watched her for a long moment. She had seen the way Dani had reacted to the question about Vanessa's name. And she had seen the way Becca had smiled like she already knew how this was going to end.

14

UNDER SCRUTINY

The knock at the door was sharp and deliberate, the kind that made Miriam's stomach tighten instinctively.

She had been expecting this. It was only a matter of time.

Taking a slow breath, she smoothed down the front of her blouse, silky, olive green, chosen carefully to give off the impression of composed cooperation, and walked to the door.

When she pulled it open, Detective Whitaker stood on the porch, his expression polite, unreadable, the late afternoon sun casting a long shadow over the front steps.

"Mrs. Reed," he greeted, his voice steady, his eyes assessing.

She hated that. The way he was already taking her in, categorizing her reaction, reading into the way she was standing, the way her fingers curled slightly against the edge of the door.

"Detective," she said smoothly, offering a tight smile, carefully measured. "I assume this isn't a social call?"

Whitaker barely blinked. "Mind if we come in?"

We?

Miriam's gaze flicked past him to see another officer, a younger woman with sharp cheekbones and dark hair tied into a low ponytail, standing just behind him, her notepad already in hand.

Miriam hesitated, just for a fraction of a second.

Then she stepped back. "Of course."

Her house was pristine, as always, a reflection of her own meticulous nature, her need for control.

Whitaker and the young officer, Detective Riley according to her badge, took seats in the living room. The room was warm and elegant, decorated in earthy tones, a lit candle flickering softly on the coffee table. It smelled like orange zest and vanilla, the faint trace of something freshly baked still lingering in the air.

It was the kind of house that didn't belong to a murderer.

But Miriam knew better than anyone that appearances could be deceiving.

She settled into the chair opposite them, tucking one leg over the other, careful to keep her body language open, neutral, unaffected.

Whitaker flipped open his notepad.

"I appreciate you taking the time to speak with us, Mrs. Reed," he said, glancing up. "I'm sure you understand that we're trying to piece together what happened to Vanessa Caldwell and of course to Erica Miller, and since you were part of a book club with both of them, we'd like to ask you a few questions."

Miriam nodded, keeping her expression even.

"I'll help however I can," she said.

Whitaker tilted his head slightly. "You and Vanessa were friends?"

Were they? It was a loaded question.

Vanessa had been many things. A book club member. A socialite. A woman who thrived on control and manipulation. But a friend?

Miriam folded her hands neatly in her lap. "We were little

more than acquaintances," she said carefully. "We spent time together through the book club, but I wouldn't say we were particularly close."

Whitaker watched her closely, his pen hovering over his notepad.

"But you were at her house for book club fairly regularly," Riley pointed out, flipping through her notes. "And you and the other women met again for coffee after she was killed. Is that correct?"

Miriam felt her pulse kick up, but she kept her face calm, unreadable.

"We wanted to check in on each other," she said smoothly. "Losing Erica was shocking enough, and then Vanessa, well, it shook all of us."

Whitaker nodded, but Miriam noticed a subtle shift in his posture, a slight narrowing of his gaze, the way his pen tapped once against the edge of the notepad.

"Do you know anyone who would have wanted to hurt Vanessa?" he asked.

Miriam paused. She could answer this question in so many ways.

Did Vanessa have enemies? Absolutely. But giving names, offering ideas, that was dangerous. So instead, she gave the safest answer possible.

"Vanessa had, let's say... strong opinions," she said, tilting her head. "She wasn't exactly known for her kindness. But murder? That's something else entirely."

Whitaker nodded, scribbling something down.

Miriam's hands curled slightly into the fabric of her pants. She needed to know what they knew. So, she leaned forward slightly, feigning curiosity.

"Detective," she said lightly, "I don't mean to overstep, but do you have any leads? I assume you wouldn't be here unless you were looking for something specific."

Whitaker's mouth twitched slightly, not quite a smirk, but close.

"You'd be surprised," he said. "People have a habit of revealing things without realizing it."

Miriam felt the weight of his gaze, her stomach twisting. She smiled, but it felt tight, wrong. "I suppose they do."

There was a beat of silence, thick with unspoken words. Then Riley closed her notepad, glancing at Whitaker. "That's all for now."

Whitaker nodded, standing. "We appreciate your cooperation, Mrs. Reed."

Miriam stood as well, walking them to the door, keeping her movements smooth, controlled. But just as Whitaker stepped onto the porch, he turned back, his eyes sharp.

"Oh, one more thing," he said, casually. "Where were you the night Vanessa was murdered?"

Miriam's breath hitched. But only for a second. Then she smiled.

"At home," she said simply. "Alone."

“Where is Mr Reed, if I may.” Whitaker inquired.

“He died last spring. Cancer.” Miriam said flatly.

Whitaker held her gaze for a beat longer than necessary. Then he nodded.

"Good night, Mrs. Reed."

Miriam showed them out, and then returned to her lounge, via the kitchen where she poured herself a decent glass of wine.

She had always been the quiet observer, comfortable on the outskirts, watching, absorbing. But there had been a time when she'd been at the center of her own story, a chapter she kept carefully guarded, like an old photograph tucked away between pages of a seldom-read book.

She had met Arthur in graduate school. Miriam, studious and reserved, spent most evenings lost in stacks of history books in the university library, sipping lukewarm coffee and scribbling meticulous notes. Arthur, charming and impossible to ignore, was studying literature but seemed to spend most of his time roaming campus corridors, sparking conversations with anyone willing to engage.

Their paths collided in the most clichéd of circumstances, Miriam accidentally knocking over a pile of books onto Arthur's table, his notes scattering across the floor. Instead of annoyance, he had laughed, eyes bright with amusement, and as she helped him pick up every page of his notes, he insisted she owed him dinner as an apology.

It was the first time Miriam could recall genuinely smiling without restraint. Arthur had a way of disarming people, peeling back layers they didn't even realize they wore. With him, Miriam found herself talking more openly, laughing more freely, living more vividly than she ever thought possible. They married two years later, a quiet ceremony attended by a handful of close friends and family. Miriam wore her mother's pearls, and Arthur had tucked a handwritten poem into her bouquet.

Life with Arthur was an endless conversation, punctuated by his humor, his curiosity, and his boundless optimism. Even their arguments, rare as they were, ended with laughter or gentle teasing. He adored her for her mind, her steadiness, and her unwavering dedication to truth, even when it was uncomfortable. Miriam adored him for everything she wasn't, outspoken, warm, endlessly adventurous.

But fate, ever indifferent, intervened.

Cancer arrived without ceremony, a cruel intrusion into their carefully constructed world. Arthur faced it the same way he faced everything, with humor, defiance, and quiet bravery that shattered Miriam's heart. She became his caretaker, balancing hospital appointments with her teaching schedule, holding herself together by sheer force of will.

Arthur fought for two years, smiling through treatments, joking with nurses, holding Miriam's hand tightly when the pain became too much to mask. He was strong for her until the very end, even when his body betrayed him, even when hope slipped away quietly, unnoticed until it was too late.

His death had carved a hole in Miriam, a void she filled with routine, discipline, and the comforting familiarity of her history lectures and her carefully maintained home. Her grief became quiet, contained, a private pain she shared with no one. She was alone now, the gentle echo of Arthur's laughter forever fading, the shadow of his presence a constant but silent companion.

And that had only gotten worse since she retired. Now, it was only really the book club that kept her going. But something about these murders was pricking a new sense of engagement in her.

She was still the quiet observer, now with secrets buried deeper, her loss of Arthur a silent chapter in a story she never wanted to share.

She sat on her sofa, sipping her wine, and running back over her conversation with the detectives.

The visit had gone exactly how she expected, the questions, the careful prodding, the way Whitaker had watched her just a little too long.

She had answered everything correctly. She had kept her story clean, vague, untouchable. But she knew, without a doubt, Whitaker didn't trust her. And now? She had no choice but to be very, very careful.

She turned away from the door, rolling her shoulders, her pulse still not quite steady. She had always been good at keeping her composure, but tonight, it had felt like walking a knife's edge.

She headed back to the kitchen, and was just reaching for the bottle of wine, when she heard a frantic knock at the back door. Miriam froze.

For a long second, she didn't move, didn't breathe. The knock came again, louder this time, more urgent.

She set down the glass carefully and made her way to the back of the house, her shoes treading softly on the hardwood floors. She pulled the curtain aside just enough to see Jilly.

Standing on the small back porch, her face pale, her eyes wide and wild, her coat pulled tightly around her like she had run here in a panic.

Miriam hesitated for a second before finally unlocking the door.

Jilly pushed inside the moment the door cracked open, shoving past her, her breath coming in quick, shallow bursts.

Miriam frowned, shutting the door behind her. "Jilly?"

"I didn't do it!" Jilly blurted out, her voice sharp, breaking, like the words had been ripped from her throat.

Miriam stared at her.

Jilly ran a hand through her tangled hair, pacing the kitchen in jerky movements, her whole body too tense, too tightly wound, like a violin string pulled too tight, just waiting to snap.

"I swear to God," she choked out, "I, I would never..."

Miriam watched her carefully, her expression unreadable. "I never said you did."

Jilly froze, spinning toward her, her eyes searching Miriam's face for something, reassurance, absolution, anything.

"But they think I did," she whispered. "The whole town does. And the police, Miriam, they came to my store today. They think I had a reason. They think because of the money..."

She stopped herself, her eyes going wide like she had just realized she said too much.

Miriam tilted her head slightly, her lips curving into something small, knowing.

So. The rumor that vanessa had lent her some money was true. That explained a lot.

"I didn't kill her," Jilly insisted, shaking her head, her voice cracking. "You believe me, right?"

Miriam watched her for a long time, too long. Jilly's hands were trembling, her face washed out, her eyes glossy with unshed tears. She was scared. Genuinely scared. And yet.

Miriam had spent enough time around people, watching, learning, dissecting, to know something wasn't adding up. Maybe Jilly was innocent. Or maybe, maybe she was just a very good liar.

Miriam took a slow step forward, reaching for the half-empty wine bottle she had set down earlier. She poured them both a glass, calm, controlled, utterly unaffected by the unraveling woman in front of her.

"You need to breathe," she said finally, her voice smooth, quiet. She slid one glass toward Jilly, who hesitated before grabbing it with shaking fingers.

Jilly downed half of it in one go.

Miriam leaned against the counter, crossing her arms. "The police," she said carefully, watching Jilly's reaction. "Do they actually think you did it, or are they just looking for answers?"

Jilly swallowed hard, setting the glass down.

"I don't know," she admitted. "They kept asking me about Vanessa. If we were close. If I knew anything about her personal life. If I knew anyone who wanted to hurt her."

Miriam arched a brow. "And what did you say?"

Jilly exhaled, running a shaky hand down her face.

"The truth," she muttered. "That I didn't know anything."

Another lie? Miriam took a slow sip of her own wine.

"You're not telling them about the money."

Jilly flinched.

"She had lent you money, hadn't she?"

Jilly looked away, biting her lip hard, her hands gripping the edge of the counter like she needed something solid to hold on to.

Miriam felt something cold settle in her stomach.

"Jilly," she said, her voice soft, but weighted with seriousness. "Why are you here?"

Jilly's breath caught and for a moment, the room was quiet.

Jilly looked at her, really looked at her, and Miriam saw something flash in her eyes, uncertainty, fear, hesitation. And suddenly, Miriam wondered if Jilly afraid of being framed? Or was she afraid of being found out?

Miriam set her glass down, stepping closer, watching as Jilly's breath shuddered slightly at the movement.

"Wait. You don't think I did it, do you?" Miriam asked. "Is that why you've come? You want to clear your name by blaming me."

Jilly didn't answer immediately. And that? That was very interesting.

Miriam let the silence stretch, watching her, letting the tension settle like a noose tightening around both their throats.

Then Jilly shook her head. "No," she whispered. "No, I don't."

But Miriam wasn't convinced. Not at all.

She took a slow step back, lifting her wine glass once more, her eyes never leaving Jilly's face.

"I think you should go home," she said smoothly.

Jilly hesitated, like she wanted to say something more, something else, but in the end, she just nodded tightly.

She grabbed her coat, her movements too jerky, too rushed, and Miriam knew that she was scared. She knew that she was hiding something.

"I'm sorry," Jilly muttered as she left.

And as the door clicked shut, leaving Miriam alone in the kitchen once more, she let out a slow sigh.

She had spent the past few days wondering about Jilly, about her lies, about what she wasn't saying.

But now? Now, she had a different question.

Did Jilly really think she was the one who had done it? Miriam smiled slightly to herself, turning her wine glass in slow circles against the counter. Maybe she should let her think so. Just for a little while. The investigation hadn't just changed the town, it had changed the women in the book club.

Sleep came in fits and starts, whispers followed them through grocery store aisles, and even within their own homes, there was a creeping sense of paranoia.

The police hadn't made an arrest. They hadn't even named a suspect. But the book club knew that one of them was hiding something.

~

Dani had always been a morning person. She woke early, went for a run, and made breakfast for her family before her husband, Clint, shuffled down the stairs in his usual half-asleep state.

Now, she spent her mornings staring at the ceiling, waiting for the sun to rise.

The dark circles under her eyes were new, hidden beneath layers of expensive foundation. Her runs had become aimless walks, her usual high energy replaced with a heavy, sinking feeling in her chest.

At breakfast, Clint watched her with a new kind of scrutiny.

"You're not eating," he said one morning, studying the untouched toast on her plate.

Dani forced a smile, lifting her coffee to her lips. "I'm fine."

Clint didn't look convinced. "You've not been yourself since..." He stopped short, shaking his head. "Since everything happened."

Dani's grip on her mug tightened.

"I think I'm entitled to be acting a little strange, don't you?" she said lightly, though her voice wasn't as even as she wanted it to be.

Clint exhaled, rubbing his face. "The boys have noticed too."

Dani froze.

"They said you're quieter than usual. Distracted." Clint's voice softened. "Are you okay?"

She wanted to snap at him. Wanted to accuse him of not knowing her at all. But instead, she smiled, perfectly composed, the way she always did.

"I'm fine," she repeated.

But as she took another sip of coffee, the bitter taste did nothing to calm her nerves.

~

Jilly had always found comfort in her bookstore. The smell of old paper. The soft creak of floorboards. The weight of books in her hands.

Now, it felt different.

The front doorbell jingled too loudly, making her flinch. Customers lingered too long near the counter, and when they asked about Erica's death, she struggled to keep her voice steady.

The worst part was closing at night. She double-checked the locks. Then checked them again.

One night, she was halfway home when a cold fear gripped her chest, she hadn't locked the back door.

She turned around and the whole drive back, her hands trembled against the wheel.

When she arrived, the door was locked. It had been locked the whole time. But Jilly still stood there, heart pounding, staring at the bookstore in the dim glow of the streetlights.

Her sanctuary wasn't safe anymore. Nothing was.

Meanwhile, her conversation with Miriam played in her head. She didn't think Miriam was the killer. Why would she think that? But then, why would Miriam jump to that conclusion?

Did she have something to hide? And how had she known about Vanessa's loan? Had Vanessa told her? Or was it just because Miriam saw everything. Knew everything.

So many questions circled her head. She was exhausted. Her nerves frayed to tatters. She just wanted all this to be over.

~

By the time the weekend arrived, the town had changed beyond recognition.

The coffee shop wasn't as crowded. The country club was unusually quiet. And when a car backfired on Main Street, someone actually screamed.

People were on edge.

And the book club had come apart at the seams. Because it wasn't just grief anymore. It was paranoia. And no one knew who to trust.

15

THE CIRCLE

The air in Miriam's living room was thick with something unspoken, something that clung to the walls, pressing in around them like an invisible hand at their throats.

They sat in a loose circle, the remaining women of the book club, Charlotte, Jilly, and Miriam, Dani, Tiffany and Pam. Bee had cried off at the last minute, saying she wasn't feeling well enough to be out.

None of them were relaxed. The seating arrangement alone spoke volumes.

Charlotte perched on the edge of an armchair, her posture stiff, her arms crossed tightly over her chest. Jilly sat on the couch, her fingers wrapped around a steaming cup of tea, her knuckles white against the ceramic.

Miriam, the hostess, was poised in her usual way, wine glass in hand, legs crossed neatly, expression unreadable.

Tiffany sat back, stretching out her legs, a forced boredom in her posture, but her eyes were sharp, scanning, absorbing. She had been reluctant to come after he and Dani fell out about a post Tiffany had uploaded from outside Vanessa's house.

Pam had squeezed on the sofa next to Dani, and offered her

a cookie from a Tupperware box. Outside, a storm gathered, the wind pressing against the windows, making the room feel like it was under siege.

The mood was tense. Nobody trusted each other anymore. They had all shown up out of obligation, but no one actually wanted to be here.

Not now. Not with Erica drowned. Not with Vanessa murdered in her own bed. Not when they were all waiting to see who would be next.

Charlotte was the first to break the silence, clearing her throat and shifting uncomfortably.

"We should stop meeting," she said bluntly.

Jilly's head snapped up. "What?"

Charlotte exhaled, rubbing her temples. She looked exhausted. "Well, it's ridiculous, isn't it? This isn't a book club anymore," she said, shaking her head. "It's a..." She stopped, struggling for the right word.

"We can't stop," Jilly scoffed, setting her cup down with a little too much force. "That's exactly what the killer would want."

Charlotte's eyes narrowed slightly. "What are you saying?"

"I'm saying," Jilly said, leaning forward. "That we're all safer if we stick together."

Dani let out a dry laugh, flipping her hair over her shoulder. "Are we?"

Pam's gaze snapped to her. "What's that supposed to mean?"

Dani smirked. "Oh, come on. We're all thinking it. What if one of us did it?"

Pam laughed out loud. "Do you really think one of us is responsible?"

The room went still. The wind rattled the windows, the faintest creak of the old house settling filling the silence as Tiffany shifted uncomfortably.

Miriam tilted her head slightly, watching the exchange with interest.

Jilly's jaw tensed. "You think one of us did it?"

Dani shrugged, her casual indifference grating. "Well, it wasn't me," she said. "And let's be real, whoever killed Vanessa was someone she let into her house. Someone she clearly trusted. It could be any of you."

Jilly looked down at her hands, fidgeting nervously in her lap.

Dani continued her rant. "And it's not like any of us didn't have a reason to want Vanessa quiet. Or Erica, for that matter."

Pam half-nodded. "She has a point," she said. "But wanting them to dead is a bit of a leap. I mean, it is for me. Far too much effort!"

Miriam took a slow sip of wine, her gaze flicking between them all. "Dani," she said smoothly. "If you really think someone in this room is a murderer, why did you come here?"

Dani smirked. "A bit like Tiffany, really. I'm just here for the show."

Tiffany was about to protest, when Jilly shot up from her chair, her fists clenched at her sides. "You think this is entertaining?"

Dani sighed dramatically. "Relax, Jilly. I'm just saying, if you all want to keep meeting, go ahead. Just don't be surprised if there are fewer of us next time. In fact, after this, I'll sure be watching my back."

Charlotte exhaled sharply, shaking her head. "This is insane."

"No," Jilly said, her voice fierce, certain. "What's insane is pretending we can just go back to normal. That we can stop meeting and hope this awful reality goes away."

Charlotte looked deeply uncomfortable, shifting in her seat. Miriam just watched, saying nothing. Tiffany typed something on her phone. And Pam sat with her mouth open in surprise at Jilly's sudden outburst. Miriam thought she looked like a fish out of water.

Dani, amused, sipped from her water like this was a reality show she was enjoying far too much.

"Maybe we should stop," Charlotte insisted again. "Just for a little while."

Jilly shook her head and sat down.

The storm outside grew stronger, the branches of the trees casting long, eerie shadows against the walls.

No one spoke.

For the first time, it was impossible to tell whether they were all in this together or if one of them was waiting to strike next.

Thunder rumbled in the distance, an ominous low, rolling sound. The wind outside had picked up, rattling the windows, making the old house creak as if it were listening.

Inside, the tension had thickened to something almost suffocating. No one was speaking, but Dani's accusation was rolling around all of their minds.

Miriam tapped a single nail against the stem of her wine glass, her gaze flicking over the women in the room. Jilly, too tense, too defensive. Charlotte, exhausted, unwilling to look any of them in the eye. Dani, smirking, watching like she was just waiting for someone to crack. Tiffany, purposely disengaged and fiddling with her phone. Pam, doing everything she could to look relaxed.

Now that Dani had voiced their fear, that one of them might be a killer and a liar, Miriam wondered for the first time if it wasn't just about who killed the two women, but more about who had benefited from their deaths. Miriam broke the silence first.

"What if," she said carefully, "It wasn't one of us. But someone else that knew them both."

Charlotte rubbed at her temple. "Like who."

"Like one of their husbands?"

Jilly shot her a look. "But Brad doted on Erica. He was always picking up the pieces after her drunken rants. Besides, did he even know Vanessa?"

Dani arched a brow. "How do we know? They could have been having a fling that none of us knew about."

Charlotte cleared her throat but said nothing.

Pam nodded again. "That might make sense of the bickering between Vanessa and Erica at that last book club."

Tiffany looked up from her phone, head tilted. "Well, out of the two husbands, Simon is definitely the more likely to be having an affair."

Charlotte stood up. Sat back down again. "It wasn't Simon, I'm sure of it. He would never hurt Vanessa. Although, God knows she hurt him enough."

Miriam narrowed her eyes. Charlotte's comment seemed strangely defensive of Vanessa's husband. She filed the thought away. She leaned forward, placing her wine glass down with careful precision. "We need to ask ourselves who benefits?" she asked.

The question hung in the air.

Charlotte shook her head. "You think that's what this is about? Gaining something?"

"Murder often is, isn't it?" Miriam said evenly. "Money, love, or silence. Those are your three big motivators."

Jilly exhaled sharply. "Erica didn't have money."

Tiffany smirked. "No, but Vanessa did. And I've heard rumors that she had been running a few loans in town. Maybe she was getting a bit heavy calling them in."

Miriam noted the flicker of panic in Jilly's eyes, but Jilly recovered quickly, wrapping her arms around herself.

"So what? You think someone killed Vanessa for money?"

"You tell me," Tiffany said, pointedly.

"People have killed for less," Miriam murmured.

Dani grinned. "Okay, forget Vanessa's money for a moment. Let's play. Who benefit from Erica's death?"

Pam looked away, staring at the rain streaming down the windowpane. "It has to be someone who benefits from both of them being dead," she muttered.

Miriam nodded. "What if Simon didn't know Vanessa had been loaning money. What if they're secretly in difficulty, and he found out. Sure, he'd be angry, but if she was dead, he'd get the life insurance, wouldn't he?"

"And Erica?" Tiffany asked.

"She knew things," Miriam replied. "She enjoyed knowing things. And she told all of us, one way or another, that she had a big secret she was about to blow."

Dani tapped a manicured nail against her knee. "So, if Erica knew something about Vanessa and Simon, and she used that knowledge against them..."

Charlotte shuddered. "Blackmail."

Jilly swallowed. "Maybe."

Silence.

Miriam turned back to Charlotte, watching her carefully. "You knew Vanessa best. Are you surer she didn't say anything to you?"

Charlotte let out a bitter laugh. "I obviously didn't know her as well as you think. I had no idea about any loans. Or any affairs."

"Still," Miriam pressed, "you were close enough to know if she had secrets."

Charlotte sighed, rubbing her hands over her jeans. "She was controlling. She liked things a certain way. But secrets?" She hesitated. "She would have destroyed anyone who tried to blackmail her. She wouldn't just let someone control her like that."

Dani tilted her head. "Unless the secret was that bad. I mean, we all have something we'd rather keep hidden."

Jilly shifted in her seat. Miriam caught it immediately.

"Jilly," she said smoothly. "Is there something you want to say?"

Jilly's head snapped up. Her eyes were wide and defensive. "No!"

Dani grinned. "Touched a nerve there, did we?"

Miriam just watched her. Jilly was crumbling. She was hiding something.

Miriam leaned back, sipping from her wine glass. "So, here's where we're at," she said, voice light, but firm. "Vanessa had money. Erica had secrets. Someone benefited from both of their deaths. And whoever that person is," she set her glass down carefully. "They probably aren't done yet."

The storm outside raged on, drowning out the silence. No one argued. Because they all knew she was right.

16

THE GOSSIP FACTORY

Charlotte sat at her desk, staring at the glowing screen of her laptop, the cursor blinking like a taunt. Erase. Delete. Wipe it all clean.

Her fingers hovered over the keyboard, trembling slightly, not from fear, not exactly, but from something colder and more calculated. Self-preservation.

She could do it. She could erase every old email, every text, every stupid, impulsive message that now felt like a ticking bomb waiting to explode. And yet, her hands stayed frozen.

Her reflection stared back at her from the darkened window, the faint glow of the screen casting her features in sharp relief. Her hair, normally sleek and styled, hung loose and unruly around her shoulders, and there were faint shadows beneath her eyes that hadn't been there before.

She was unraveling. Charlotte wasn't a woman who unraveled. Not ever.

She had built herself too carefully, had spent years becoming exactly the kind of woman people respected, admired, maybe even feared just a little. Not the way they feared Vanessa, but still. And now?

Now she was sitting in her dimly lit home office, debating whether to erase the parts of her life that might come back to haunt her, to ruin her.

Charlotte had spent her entire life clawing her way up from nothing.

People saw her now, the polished exterior, the refined taste, the carefully cultivated life in Willow Creek, but they didn't know where she had come from.

They didn't know about the apartment with peeling wallpaper and thin walls, where she could hear her mother crying at night, where she had come to dread the sound of eviction notices slipping under their door.

They didn't know what it was like to wake up cold in winter because the heating bill hadn't been paid, or to pretend she wasn't hungry at school because there wasn't enough food at home.

Her mother had done the best she could, Charlotte knew that. But being raised by a woman who had lost everything, a woman who had married young, loved too much, and been abandoned when her husband found someone shinier, wealthier, easier to control, had made Charlotte realize something very early on.

Love was a weakness. Money was power.

She had made a vow to herself before she was even old enough to fully understand it. She would never be her mother. She would never depend on anyone else for stability.

She would be the woman with the perfect life, the perfect house, the perfect family, the kind of woman no one pitied, the kind of woman no one abandoned.

And so, she worked harder than anyone.

She was the best in every class, the one who won the scholarships, the one who had three jobs in college and still managed to graduate at the top of her class.

She had reinvented herself, piece by piece, learning how to speak, how to dress, how to move through a world that had never been meant for girls like her. She learned how to control every aspect of her life, because control meant security. It meant never being vulnerable. And it had worked. For a while.

She had married well. Bobby had seemed like the right choice. Successful. Respected. He had the kind of wealth she had spent her life chasing, the kind that meant never worrying about whether the bills would be paid, never having to hold her breath when she swiped her credit card. But Bobby had never really seen her.

He had liked the version of Charlotte that was easy, the version that smiled at dinner parties, the version that fit neatly into his well-planned, slightly boring life.

The moment she had wanted more, the moment she had started to outgrow him, their marriage had turned into something that felt like a performance neither of them wanted to be in anymore. But they stayed, because neither of them was will to divorce. Neither of them willing to admit.

And now, here she was.

Still fighting to hold onto everything she had built, still trying to control a life that felt like it was slipping through her fingers.

Charlotte moved slowly, pushing back from her desk, dragging her hands down her face.

She needed to pull herself together. She had felt off all day, that prickle at the back of her neck, the phantom weight of a gaze she couldn't see.

At the store, she had noticed a car lingering too long at the far end of the parking lot.

When she walked home, she had sworn she heard footsteps behind her. And now, as she sat in her dimly lit home office, she glanced toward the window, and she heard movement.

Charlotte's heart slammed against her ribs. She turned sharply, eyes locking onto the darkened street outside. The storm had settled into a slow drizzle, the streetlights casting long, distorted shadows against the pavement.

The world outside her window was still. Too still. But something had been out there. She was sure of it.

Her breath came fast, her fingers digging into the desk.

No. No, she was not losing control. She was not unraveling.

Charlotte pushed back from her desk and stood, forcing herself to move, to act, to take control again.

She wasn't deleting anything. Not yet. Because before she erased her past, she needed to know who was watching her. And when she found out she would deal with it. Swiftly. Completely. Without hesitation.

Because Charlotte wasn't the kind of woman who unraveled. And she sure as hell wasn't the kind of woman who got caught.

~

The next morning, Charlotte forced herself into routine.

She rose at dawn, just like always, her alarm a sharp, punctual chime that she silenced with a practiced swipe. She took a long shower, steam curling around her as she stood beneath the water, willing the previous night's paranoia to wash away with the shampoo.

She dressed in muted power, slipping into an elegant black sheath dress, a fitted blazer, heels that gave her an extra two inches of confidence. No hesitation, no cracks in the armor. She swiped on a layer of mascara, brushed her hair into a sleek wave, checked her reflection one last time.

She looked the part. She always did. But beneath it all, something felt different. She could still feel the weight of unseen eyes, the quiet hum of paranoia at the base of her skull. She was being watched. She was sure of it. And now, she had to pretend she wasn't.

Charlotte arrived at the prestigious real estate firm where she had worked for the past eight years at exactly 8:30 a.m., same as always.

The building was sleek and modern, floor-to-ceiling windows offering panoramic views of Willow Creek's wealthiest neighborhoods. The office smelled of fresh coffee, expensive perfume, and the faint tang of high-stakes ambition.

She walked in like nothing was wrong. Like she hadn't spent the night convinced someone was watching her from the dark. Like she hadn't hesitated over her laptop, wondering if deleting old messages, photographs, and receipts would protect her or damn her.

She strode past the receptionist, offered a perfectly neutral smile, and settled into her glass-walled office, placing her designer handbag carefully beside her chair.

Everything in her space was immaculate, just as she always left it, stacked folders, a neat row of pens, a framed photo of her, Bobby, and the kids from a vacation they took three years ago, before everything soured.

Everything looked normal. But somehow nothing felt normal.

She flipped open her planner, forcing herself to focus. Her schedule was full, as always, back-to-back meetings, two property showings, a high-profile listing appointment that could mean a seven-figure sale if she played it right. This was what she excelled at. Control. Presentation. Perfection. She could do this. She would be fine.

But People Were Watching.

Just like it had for poor Jilly, the paranoia started with the whispers.

Soft, quiet exchanges behind polished desks, the barely

disguised flickers of side glances as she walked by. Charlotte ignored it at first.

She was used to office gossip, the petty competition that came with being a top agent in a firm full of people who wanted her job. But today felt different.

She caught snippets of conversation as she passed the breakroom, two colleagues, low voices, huddled near the coffee machine.

"She's acting weird."

"You think it's because of... you know?"

"Well, yeah. First Erica. Then Vanessa. And now she's..."

Charlotte's heels scuffed against the tile as she abruptly turned toward them. The two women, Beth and Kate, both junior agents, froze like startled deer. Their eyes went wide, mouths slightly parted.

Beth recovered first, flashing a tight, fake smile. "Oh, Charlotte! We were just..."

Charlotte tilted her head slightly, her own expression perfectly neutral. She didn't need to raise her voice. Her silence was enough to make them squirm.

Kate cleared her throat, adjusting her blazer. "We were just talking about the market."

Charlotte lifted a single perfectly arched brow. They both shut up.

She held their gaze for a beat longer than necessary, then simply said, "Try focusing on your numbers instead of your theories." She turned and walked away, leaving them shifting uncomfortably in her wake.

But her heart was pounding. Because she knew they weren't the only ones talking. And the worst part? She *was* acting strange. She *was* acting guilty. She *did* have a secret that she couldn't tell.

She could feel her behavior growing more erratic as the day

went on. The tiny lapses in her perfect composure, the way her nerves had started betraying her in the smallest, most unforgivable ways. The way she had snapped at Bobby this morning when he asked if she was okay. The way she had lingered too long at her office window, staring out at the street below, half-expecting to see someone staring back up at her. The way she had flinched when her phone buzzed, like she was afraid of what it might say.

She could hear Vanessa's voice in her head, mocking, amused, cold as ever.

"What's wrong, Charlotte? Losing your mind?"

Charlotte swallowed, sitting at her desk, staring down at her perfectly manicured hands.

She couldn't afford to unravel. Not now. Not when everyone was watching. And definitely not when she was so damn sure that someone, somewhere, was waiting for her to slip up.

Her phone buzzed again. She reached for it but paused before flipping it over. Because for once, she wasn't sure if she wanted to know who was on the other end.

17

THE HOUSE OF GRIEF

A week had passed.

The shock of Vanessa's murder had settled into the veins of the town like an illness, infecting everything, twisting even the most mundane conversations into something coated with suspicion.

The book club no longer felt like a book club. They weren't just a group of random women who ahd once gathered to discuss thrillers anymore, they were the center of the town's most gruesome mystery.

And Erica Miller was already the half-forgotten tragedy. Miriam knew how these things worked.

People were morbidly fascinated by the spectacle of Vanessa's murder, a beautiful, rich woman, strangled in her own bed.

Erica's death, on the other hand, was less glamorous, more tragic. Alcoholic drowned in her own pool. Drunk, reckless, careless, that's what they were saying.

Maybe it was murder. But the general view was that somehow, Erica had it coming. And that was what bothered Miriam the most. Because for all of Erica's flaws, her sharp tongue, her cruel amusement at stirring up drama, she had been a real person. And now she was just a headline people barely cared about. Because someone more popular, prettier, richer, had been killed in an even more brutal way.

That's why Miriam had suggested the visit.

Officially, she, Pam, Bee, and Jilly were here to pay their respects, and to see how Brad and the kids were coping. To offer support in their hour of need, while the rest of the town pointed fingers. In reality, Miriam wanted to see for herself what had been left behind. And she wanted to know what Erica had known, what she was threatening to share before she died.

The Miller house had once been beautiful.

Nestled at the end of a tree-lined street, the two-story colonial had perfect bones, wide bay windows, and a wraparound porch that, once upon a time, had probably been covered in pots of fresh flowers. Now, it was a ghost of what it had been.

The lawn was overgrown, weeds creeping through cracks in the brick pathway leading up to the front door. The paint on the shutters had begun to peel, revealing the raw wood beneath. A week's worth of newspapers sat untouched on the front step, soggy from the rain, curling at the edges.

Jilly shifted beside Miriam, tucking her hands into the sleeves of her oversized cardigan. She looked uneasy, hesitant, like she was already regretting coming. Bee didn't look much better. She hesitated on the path, as though even reaching the front door would taint her somehow.

"Maybe this was a bad idea," Bee murmured.

Miriam sighed, adjusting her coat. It was cold today, a sharp wind cutting through the street, the sky heavy with the threat of rain. Clouds hung low, pressing against the tops of the houses, making the air feel thick, stifling.

"They deserve to know people still care," Miriam said, and then, before Jilly could protest, she knocked.

The sound echoed through the house, swallowed by the silence inside.

A few seconds later, the door swung open far too quickly, and a boy stood in the doorway, his face pale, his eyes hollow.

Erica's son, James. Miriam's chest tightened. She had forgotten how young he was. Just eleven, he looked even younger today. Smaller somehow, wrapped in a hoodie that seemed too big for his thin frame, his shoulders hunched forward, like he was trying to make himself disappear.

Jilly shifted beside her, clearing her throat awkwardly.

"Um, hi," she said, offering a small, hesitant smile. "Is your dad home?"

The boy, James, just nodded and disappeared inside without another word.

A moment later, Brad Miller appeared in the doorway.

Miriam felt her stomach drop. He looked terrible. His shirt was wrinkled, the collar stretched, as if he had yanked it over his head too many times without bothering to button it properly. His stubble had grown too long, shadowing his jawline in uneven patches. His eyes, bloodshot, sunken, held the same hollow vacancy as his son's.

Miriam had never particularly liked Brad. She thought he was a bit wet. He was the kind of man who faded into the background, overshadowed by Erica's sharpness, her confidence, her presence.

Now he just looked lost.

"Brad," Miriam said gently. "I hope we're not intruding, but we wanted to stop by and see how you were all doing."

"See if there was anything you needed," Pam added leaning in around Miriam.

"Or the kids," Bee said quickly.

Brad blinked at them like he had forgotten how to process kindness. Then, after a moment, he stepped aside. "Come in."

As they stepped inside, Jilly sucked in a quiet breath. The house was in disarray. It was not just untidy, it was collapsing. Dishes sat piled in the sink, crusted with food. The air smelled stale, thick with the remnants of forgotten meals, unopened windows, and raw grief. A half-empty bottle of whiskey sat on the coffee table, next to a crumpled tissue and an overturned picture frame.

Miriam's eyes caught the broken glass on the floor, shards scattered beneath the table like something had been thrown.

This family wasn't just grieving. They were drowning.

James slouched back on the couch, eyes glued to a muted television screen that he wasn't watching. His fingers twitched, drumming continuously against his knee, restless, anxious.

Brad rubbed a hand over his face. "Sorry about the mess," he muttered. "I keep meaning to..." He cut himself off with a hollow laugh, shaking his head.

Jilly fidgeted, clearly uncomfortable. "You don't have to apologize," she said quickly.

Miriam's eyes flicked toward the staircase.

A pile of Erica's things sat at the base of the steps, a designer handbag, a half-folded sweater, a pair of shoes she would never wear again.

Miriam felt something sharp twist in her gut. This wasn't just a house in mourning. This was a house that didn't know how to move forward.

Brad exhaled heavily, sinking into an armchair, his gaze unfocused.

"She would have hated this," he muttered.

Miriam and Jilly both turned toward him.

Brad let out a quiet, bitter laugh. "The house, I mean. She was always so... put together. Everything had to be *just right*."

Jilly pressed her lips together, exchanging a glance with Miriam.

Erica had been meticulous. Controlled. Calculated. And she had died in complete chaos.

Brad shook his head. "I keep thinking, what if I had been home? What if I had heard something?"

Miriam hesitated. "You weren't home that night?"

Brad blinked. "No, I..." He scrubbed a hand down his face. "I was staying at my brother's place for a few days. Erica and I... we weren't in a great place."

Jilly frowned. "I thought you two were fine?"

Brad let out a bitter, humorless laugh. "Is that what she told you?"

Miriam leaned forward slightly. "Were you arguing about something?"

Brad hesitated. His hands curled into fists at his sides.

"It was the drink. It was making her angry. Paranoid. Spiteful." He shook his head. "Kept saying *she knew things,* that she had proof of something."

Miriam and Jilly exchanged a glance.

"Proof of what? Have you mentioned this to the police?" Jilly asked quietly.

Brad shook his head. "I don't know what she meant. She wouldn't tell me. She said I'd see, like the rest of you. Of course I told the police. It doesn't make any sense."

Miriam's skin prickled. Erica's death wasn't just tragic. It was intentional. And whoever had killed her had made sure she never had the chance to share what she knew.

A gust of wind rattled the windows, making the curtains shiver as if the house itself was listening. Outside, the clouds had thickened, gray and swollen, threatening rain, the kind of weather that made everything feel heavier.

Brad leaned forward, rubbing at the dark circles beneath his

,es, his whole body sagging with the weight of grief, exhaustion, or maybe something worse. Maybe guilt. His fingers drummed against his knee, restless, distracted.

Miriam waited. She had always known that silence made people uncomfortable. And Brad was no exception.

Jilly stood rigid, hands clasped tightly in front of her, as if she were trying to physically hold herself together. Miriam noticed the way her shoulders tensed with every breath, her gaze flicking toward James, who hadn't moved from the couch, staring blankly at the TV, volume low.

Brad let out a sigh, shaking his head. "She was acting different. Before she died, I mean."

Miriam exchanged a glance with Jilly. "Different how?"

Brad frowned, his jaw tightening, his fingers twitching against his jeans. "More paranoid. More secretive. And obviously, the drinking had gotten worse." He let out a bitter laugh. "But, hell, no one even questioned that, right? Everyone just assumed Erica was always like that. But she wasn't."

Miriam raised a brow, keeping her voice neutral. "What do you think changed?"

Brad hesitated. And then, almost reluctantly, he said, "She kept getting these calls. Late at night. She'd step out onto the back porch to take them."

Jilly stiffened beside Miriam.

Miriam tilted her head, interest piqued. "Who was calling her?"

Brad hesitated, then shook his head. "I don't know. But sometimes I'd wake up in the middle of the night and hear her whispering. Hushed, urgent. Like she didn't want anyone to hear."

Jilly shifted uncomfortably. "Did you ask her about it?"

"Of course," Brad scoffed, rubbing a hand over his face. "She just brushed me off, said I was imagining things. But I wasn't."

He let out a slow, measured breath before adding, "One time, I actually heard a name."

Miriam leaned forward slightly, fingers tightening around the armrest of her chair. "Who?"

Brad's eyes flicked between them before he said it.

"Charlotte."

The name landed between them like a match dropped onto gasoline.

Jilly's breath caught in her throat. She turned to Miriam sharply, her expression shifting—suspicion flickering across her face like a shadow.

Miriam's stomach coiled. *Charlotte.*

Charlotte and Erica. Charlotte and hushed, late-night phone calls. Jilly swallowed hard, her mind racing.

She hadn't thought much of it at the time, but now it felt like something. A memory surfaced, sudden and sharp. That last book club meeting.

Charlotte had been her usual self, controlled, poised and unreadable. But when she had reached for her glass of wine, Jilly had noticed something, something small, something fleeting.

Her hand had trembled. Only slightly. Only for a second. But it had been there.

At the time, Jilly had chalked it up to stress, the tension of the evening, the passive-aggressive snipes, the underlying hostility that always simmered beneath the surface of their meetings.

But now she wasn't so sure. Had Charlotte been afraid? Or was she guilty?

Miriam spoke first. Her voice was steady. "Did Erica ever say why she was talking to Charlotte?"

Brad shook his head. "No. And I didn't push. I should have, but," he shrugged, "Erica didn't like to be questioned. Besides, that's just a name I heard her say. I don't know if she was talking to her, or about her."

Miriam nodded, her mind still spinning, piecing things together.

Pam, ever composed, took a slow sip of her tea, gaze unfocused, lost in thought.

Charlotte.

Jilly thought of the way she had looked the last time they'd all gathered. Not just tense, but something more. Something off. And suddenly, for the first time, Jilly saw her in a different light. Because Charlotte had always been in control. But now she too had started looking a little frayed around the edges. Jilly was beginning to wonder, had Charlotte been hiding something all along?

Brad leaned back into the armchair, his expression shifting, the hard lines around his mouth softening just slightly. He rubbed a hand over his face, as if trying to shake off the weight of the conversation, the accusations, the memories.

"You know," he said suddenly, voice quieter, raw in a way that caught them all off guard. "For everything people said about Erica, for all the gossip, all the speculation about her drinking, her affairs, whatever it was people wanted to whisper about, she was a good person. And a great Mom."

Bee blinked, surprised by the tenderness in his voice.

"She used to leave notes in James's lunchbox," Brad continued, a small, tired smile tugging at the corner of his mouth. "Every morning. Silly ones. Jokes, reminders to be brave, sometimes just a heart. He'd pretend it embarrassed him, but he saved them. I found him sitting reading them all the other day."

Miriam and Jilly both turned toward James, who sat curled into himself on the couch, his face blank but his fingers clenching against his knee.

Brad let out a breath, shaking his head. "She loved fiercely.

Even when things were hard. Even when we were fighting, she'd still make sure my favorite coffee was stocked in the pantry. Still booked those stupid couple's massages, even when we both knew neither of us wanted to go."

His voice cracked, just slightly. Then he cleared his throat, his grief twisting back into something harder.

"But, of course, that's not what people are going to remember, is it?" His gaze flicked to Jilly, something sharp behind his tired eyes. "People are going to remember the drinking. The shouting. I've heard them talking. Whispering. Saying that I was struggling, that I wanted out."

Jilly stiffened.

Brad let out a humorless laugh. "And maybe I did, sometimes. But I never wanted this."

Jilly hesitated, then forced a small nod. Because she had thought it, hadn't she? Hadn't they all? That Brad had struggled with Erica's drinking? That it had been too much for him? That maybe, on some level, he had wanted it to be over.

She looked at him now, slouched in his chair, his hands gripping the armrests like they were the only thing tethering him to this world. And she wondered if she had been wrong about him.

Miriam sat back, watching him, silent. Calculating. Perhaps the murders weren't connected. But Miriam strongly suspected they were. Somehow, she had to find out what Erica had been about to reveal.

Outside, the wind howled, shaking the trees. And Jilly had never felt more unsure of anything.

18

THE THIN LINE

The knock at the door was sharp and deliberate, the kind that made Charlotte's stomach tighten instinctively.

She had been expecting this. It was only a matter of time.

She glanced toward Bobby, who was already halfway out of his chair, frowning toward the door. He looked confused but not surprised, like he had been waiting the sharp knock, too.

"I'll get it," she snapped.

The late afternoon light streamed through the expansive windows, turning the pristine white walls of her foyer into a soft gold. Outside, the wind whispered through the neatly trimmed hedges lining the driveway, carrying the distant scent of cut grass and approaching rain.

Charlotte adjusted her blouse, silk, ivory, perfectly fitted, and forced a slow, measured breath before walking to the door.

She opened it to find Detective Whitaker and his ever-present shadow, Detective Riley, standing on her porch.

Whitaker, tall and broad-shouldered, with the look of a man who had seen too much and trusted too little, tilted his head slightly, his polite expression laced with something else—

curiosity, suspicion, calculation. Riley, younger but just as sharp, stood beside him, dark eyes scanning Charlotte in that quiet way that made her skin prickle.

"Mrs. Davenport," Whitaker greeted, his voice smooth. "I hope we're not interrupting."

Charlotte gave them her well-practiced, neutral smile, stepping back. "Not at all. Please, come in." She didn't have a choice, anyway.

The detectives settled into the living room, their presence imposing against the clean, controlled perfection of Charlotte's home.

The room was immaculate, as always, cream-colored walls, tasteful furniture, carefully curated decor that exuded quiet wealth without looking ostentatious. A candle burned on the coffee table, the air tinged with the faint scent of bergamot and vanilla.

It was a room that didn't belong to a murderer.

Bobby sat beside her on the couch, arms crossed, expression tense. She could feel the way his knee bounced slightly, a nervous tick he had never been able to hide.

Whitaker leaned forward slightly, flipping open his notepad. "We appreciate your time, Mrs. Davenport. We just have a few follow-up questions."

Charlotte folded her hands neatly in her lap. "Of course."

Whitaker tapped his pen against the page. "Can you describe your relationship with Erica Miller?"

Charlotte barely blinked. "Again?"

Whitaker nodded.

"I didn't really know her that well. Like I told you. It's not like we were friends."

Whitaker raised an eyebrow. "Friends?"

Charlotte kept her expression carefully neutral. "We were in the same book club. We saw each other regularly. I don't know what else to say."

Riley jotted something down, not looking up.

Whitaker tilted his head slightly. "Did you two ever argue?"

Charlotte inhaled slowly. "Not any more than anyone else. Erica had a way of stirring things up sometimes. But that was just who she was."

"And Vanessa Caldwell?"

Charlotte felt something cold curl in her stomach. She forced a slow, even breath, keeping her hands still, her voice calm.

"Vanessa and I were... complicated."

Whitaker's gaze sharpened. "Complicated how?"

Charlotte smiled tightly. "She liked to be in control. She wasn't exactly the warmest person, but we tolerated each other."

"Because of book club?"

Charlotte hesitated just for a fraction of a second before nodding. "Yes."

Whitaker watched her closely. "Were you in contact with Erica before her death?"

Charlotte's breath caught, but she recovered quickly.

"As I said, we saw each other at book club," she said smoothly. "Beyond that? No. Not really."

Whitaker didn't look convinced.

There was a moment of silence, thick and heavy.

"So you didn't see her? The night she died? Didn't speak to her?"

"No, I told you. I was home all night."

Then Bobby shifted beside her, rubbing a hand against his jaw. "Well, I mean, Charlotte. You were out for part of it. Right? You ran down to the store."

Charlotte's blood ran cold. She felt the shift in the room, the weight of the detectives' attention snapping to her all at once.

Whitaker's pen stilled. Riley finally looked up from her notepad.

"The store?"

Charlotte's pulse hammered in her ears. But she didn't let it show.

Instead, she turned to Bobby smoothly, her smile still in place, her hand settling lightly on his knee, a silent command for him to shut the hell up.

"Actually," she said, voice even, calm, steady, "You're wrong, Bobby. I went to the store the night before. We had steak, remember?"

Bobby hesitated and for one horrible second, Charlotte thought he was going to correct her.

But then he cleared his throat, nodding. "Yeah. Right. My mistake."

Whitaker's eyes lingered on them, dark and knowing. But he didn't push. Instead, he simply flipped his notepad shut.

"Thank you for your time, Mrs. Davenport," he said. "We'll be in touch if we have any further questions."

Charlotte smiled, standing. "Of course. Happy to help."

She walked them to the door, keeping her movements smooth, controlled but the moment the door clicked shut behind them, she whipped around.

"What the hell is wrong with you?"

Bobby flinched, running a hand through his hair. "I, I don't know! It just slipped out!"

Charlotte let out a sharp, disbelieving laugh, pressing a hand against her temple.

"Slipped out?" she hissed. "Bobby, I swear to God—"

"It's not like I was lying!" he shot back. "You did go out that night, didn't you? You took a call and shot off like you were on a mission."

She turned away, pacing the length of the living room, fingers twitching at her sides.

"I don't see how that's relevant," she said finally.

Bobby let out a harsh, humorless laugh. "Oh, sure. Not relevant. Not like your friend drowned in her own damn pool that night or anything."

Charlotte whipped around, her eyes burning. "Don't."

Bobby held up his hands. "I'm just saying..."

"I know exactly what you're saying," she snapped.

Bobby let out a long breath, shaking his head. "Jesus, Charlotte. What is going on with you?"

Charlotte inhaled sharply, steadying herself.

"You just need to be careful," she said quietly. "You can't just run your mouth to the police."

Bobby frowned, studying her. "You're acting like you have something to hide."

Charlotte's pulse thumped against her ribs. She took a deep breath to calm herself, stepped forward, and placed a hand on his chest, tilting her head slightly.

"You trust me, don't you?" she murmured.

Bobby hesitated. And for the first time in their marriage, Charlotte saw it. Doubt. It flickered across his face, just for a second, but it was there.

Charlotte swallowed, stepping back, composing herself.

"Just be careful what you say to the police," she said, voice softer now. "Please. I don't want them getting the wrong idea."

Bobby exhaled, rubbing a hand over his face. "Fine. Whatever."

He turned and walked out of the room, leaving Charlotte standing alone in the too-quiet house.

Her fingers clenched at her sides. She had managed to hold everything together. For now. But Bobby was a problem. And if he kept slipping up she wasn't sure what she would do.

Later that day, Miriam was in her kitchen, the soft hum of jazz floating through the air, the evening light filtering through the wide bay windows. She had just poured herself a second cup of coffee when her phone buzzed sharply on the counter.

She glanced down at Tiffany's name. A slight frown creased her brow. Tiffany wasn't the kind of person who called just to chat.

Miriam swiped to answer. "Tiff?"

A sharp intake of breath. A pause.

"I don't feel safe anymore."

Miriam froze. Tiffany's voice was tight, shaken, edged with something raw.

She turned toward the window, looking out into the evening shadows.

"Tiffany," she said carefully. "Calm down. What's going on?"

"I just..." Tiffany stopped herself, her breathing unsteady. "I keep thinking... someone's watching me."

Miriam set her coffee down, a ripple of unease curling in her stomach. This wasn't like Tiffany. She was always on display, always projecting an image of complete togetherness. She was never this paranoid.

"Has something happened?" Miriam asked.

Tiffany hesitated. Then, in a small, tight voice. "I had a message from a follower. A fan. They said they know something about one of our group. But they want to meet up with me to tell me face-to-face."

Miriam let out a slow breath. "You know who they are?"

Tiffany let out a soft, bitter laugh. "No. But they seem to know a lot about us. They said something about Erica and Vanessa having more in common than we think."

Miriam frowned deeper.

"What is that supposed to mean?"

"I don't know. What should I do?"

"Call the police. Tell them. And let them work it out. Whatever you do. Don't meet up with anyone without telling me first."

19

BEHIND CLOSED DOORS

The house was quiet, almost eerily so, the faint sound of the refrigerator filling the silence. The dim lighting of the kitchen made the room feel smaller than it was, the shadows from the overhead light cutting sharp angles into the walls.

Charlotte stood by the sink, scrubbing at an already-clean glass with mechanical precision. She focused on the rhythm, the scrape of the sponge, the cool water running over her hands, trying to quiet the storm of thoughts swirling in her mind.

The day's events looped on a constant reel: the police visit, Bobby's slip up to the cops, the relentless weight of suspicion pressing down on her.

Bobby sat at the kitchen table now, his posture slumped, his hands clasped loosely in front of him. He was a tall man, though his years of quiet disappointment and uncertainty seemed to have shrunk him somehow. His once-athletic frame now carried a slight softness, barely a hint left of the man he had been when they first met. His face, now lined with subtle creases, bore the wear of time and unspoken frustrations.

His brown hair had started to gray at the temples, something Charlotte might once have found distinguished, but now it only seemed to remind her of how much had changed between them. And yet, despite his weary exterior, there was something solid about Bobby, a kind of quiet resilience that she had once loved about him.

Now, he was looking at her with a gaze that felt sharp, his brown eyes narrowed with suspicion, his lips pressed into a tight line.

Charlotte could feel his judgment like a weight on her chest, and it was beginning to suffocate her.

When Charlotte had first met Bobby, he had been everything she thought she wanted.

He was steady, reliable, someone who had grown up in a stable home with parents who were still happily married, a stark contrast to Charlotte's own fractured childhood. His upbringing had given him a kind of grounded optimism, a belief that hard work and honesty could solve most problems.

Bobby had been the kind of man who held doors open, who brought flowers just because, who always called when he said he would. He was wealthy. Old money. But he wasn't flashy or ambitious. He was just, well, dependable. And in the beginning, that had been enough.

He had been working as an accountant when they met, solid, secure, respectable. Charlotte had been drawn to his quiet confidence, the way he seemed to anchor her in a world that often felt chaotic.

But as the years passed, that same stability had begun to feel more like stagnation, and that had in turn started to feel like imprisonment

Bobby had never wanted more than what he had. He was content with his modest successes, his steady paycheck, his predictable routines. And Charlotte? Charlotte had wanted the world.

She had wanted the big house, the picture-perfect family,

the kind of life people envied. She had worked tirelessly to create that life, to sculpt their marriage into something that looked flawless from the outside.

But Bobby had never been able to keep up.

He wasn't the kind of man who cared about appearances. He didn't understand why Charlotte insisted on hosting elaborate dinner parties, or why she obsessed over the perfect shade of paint for the living room walls.

They had started to drift apart, their conversations becoming shorter, their silences longer. And now, as Bobby sat across from her, his brow furrowed in suspicion, Charlotte could feel the distance between them like a chasm she couldn't cross.

"Charlotte," Bobby said, his voice breaking the heavy silence.

She didn't turn around.

"What is it?" she asked, her tone sharper than she intended.

Behind her, she could hear the scrape of his chair against the floor as he shifted uncomfortably.

"Are you hiding something from me?"

The words hit her like a slap. She froze, the glass slipping slightly in her hands, the sponge falling into the sink with a soft plop. For a long moment, she didn't move.

Then she turned, setting the glass down with deliberate precision, her movements controlled, measured.

"What did you just say?" she asked, her voice low and dangerous.

Bobby's shoulders were hunched, his hands clasped together on the table. The overhead light cast harsh shadows across his face, highlighting the worry lines etched into his forehead.

"You heard me," he said, his gaze meeting hers. "Are you hiding something?"

Charlotte let out a short, incredulous laugh, crossing her arms over her chest.

"Huh," she said sharply. "Is that what you think? Is that why you nearly handed me over to the police this afternoon with your little slip-up."

Bobby flinched, his mouth tightening, but he didn't back down.

"Don't turn this around on me," he said, his tone firmer now. "I just," he exhaled heavily, running a hand through his hair. "You've been acting different. Ever since Erica died. And now Vanessa. It's like you're..."

"Like I'm what?" Charlotte snapped, her voice rising.

"Like you're scared of something," Bobby said, his voice quieter but no less piercing. "Or guilty."

Charlotte's stomach churned, but she refused to let it show. Instead, she took a step closer to him, her eyes narrowing. "Guilty of what, Bobby? Enlighten me."

Bobby hesitated, his hands tightening into fists on the table.

"I don't know," he admitted. "But you're not acting like yourself. And the way you lied to the police today..." He shook his head. "It's like you're trying too hard to stay calm. Too hard to seem innocent."

Charlotte felt her pulse quicken, her chest tightening with a mix of anger and fear.

"You have no idea what you're talking about," she said coldly.

Bobby leaned forward, his gaze unrelenting. "Don't I?"

Charlotte felt something snap inside her.

"How dare you," she hissed, her voice trembling with rage. "How dare you sit there and accuse me after everything I've done for this family. After everything I've sacrificed."

Bobby stood abruptly, the chair scraping loudly against the floor.

"Then tell me, Charlotte," he said, his voice rising to match hers. "Tell me what's going on. Because I can't keep pretending that everything's fine when it's not. I'm your husband, for God's sake!"

Charlotte laughed bitterly, shaking her head. "My husband? You haven't acted like my husband in years, Bobby. You've been checked out for so long, you wouldn't notice if I wasn't even here at all."

The words came out sharper than she intended, and she saw the way they landed like a physical blow. Bobby's face fell, his shoulders sagging.

"That's not fair," he said quietly.

Charlotte pressed her lips together, turning away, her arms still crossed tightly over her chest.

The kitchen felt too small, the walls closing in around her.

"I just want to know the truth," Bobby said finally, his voice softer now, almost pleading.

Charlotte gripped the edge of the counter, her knuckles white.

"You don't want the truth," she said, her voice barely above a whisper.

Bobby stepped closer, his presence behind her heavy and uncertain.

"Try me," he said.

Charlotte turned to face him, her eyes hard, her jaw tight.

"The truth," she said slowly. "Is that I am doing everything I can to keep this family together while you sit there and question me like I'm some kind of criminal."

Bobby stared at her. His expression was unreadable.

"And if you can't see that," Charlotte continued, her voice rising again. "Then maybe you don't deserve to know anything at all."

"I just wanted to give you the chance to tell me where you'd really gone. To tell me who you'd really gone to see. To tell me about... about him.

The words hung between them, heavy and final. Bobby

blinked, his mouth opening like he wanted to say something more, but no words came.

Charlotte froze. She'd underestimated him. But how long had he known? She wanted to ask him, but to do so would be to admit he was right.

"You know?"

"I've known for months. You're not as smart as you think you are. And he certainly isn't. He couldn't help but gloat every time he saw me. Thought he was being clever with it. But I knew straight away."

Maybe she had under-estimated him. Maybe he did see more than she gave him credit for. She thought she'd played her affair brilliantly. But as even that had begun unravelling, she'd grown more careless. She'd been desperate to cling on to the thrill of it. Of being desired.

"Why did you do it?" Bobby asked. A seemed broken, now that the affair was out in the open. "Why all the lies?"

"Bobby, I..." she started. But she had no words. It was better that she stayed silent.

Finally, he shook his head, turning away.

"Goodnight, Charlotte," he said quietly, walking out of the kitchen.

Charlotte stood there, her heart pounding, her chest tight. He was right about one thing. She'd been hiding something. But the affair was only the half of it. If he kept pushing, she wasn't sure how much longer she could keep the whole truth hidden.

20

A MEDIA STORM

The camera panned across a packed room in the Willow Creek town hall. Reporters jostled for position, their faces lit with a mix of urgency and morbid fascination, their notepads ready, microphones extended toward the podium. The room hummed with tension, the kind of charged energy that accompanies both tragedy and spectacle.

Detective Whitaker stood tall at the podium, his tailored navy suit crisp but slightly creased, as though he had been wearing it for far too many hours. His face was hard, lined with exhaustion and resolve, and his graying temples gave him an air of authority that commanded the room.

Beside him stood Detective Riley, her sharp, hawk-like gaze scanning the crowd, her posture rigid, as if daring anyone to interrupt.

The press conference had drawn reporters not only from Willow Creek's small local outlets but from national networks. Bright lights from camera crews turned the usually subdued town hall into a glaring stage, highlighting every crevice of the wood-paneled walls and the worn carpeting that bore the marks of decades of use.

Whitaker adjusted the microphone, his deep voice cutting through the low murmur of the room.

"Thank you all for being here," he began, his tone steady and laced with gravity. "We are here to provide an update on the ongoing investigations into the deaths of Erica Miller and Vanessa Caldwell. While we cannot share certain details at this time, we want to emphasize that these murders are believed to be connected."

The room stilled. The rustling of paper stopped.

"We have every reason to believe that the perpetrator was known to both victims," Whitaker continued, his gaze sweeping the crowd like a spotlight. "These crimes were personal. And we are confident that someone in this community has information that could help us solve these cases."

Cameras clicked furiously.

"We are urging anyone who may have seen or heard something, no matter how insignificant it might seem, to come forward. Your information could be the key to bringing justice for Erica and Vanessa's families."

Whitaker paused, letting the weight of his words settle over the room.

He leaned slightly closer to the microphone, his voice dropping just enough to add an edge of warning.

"We have our suspicions," he said, his sharp gaze unwavering. "And we are following a number of leads. So, I can assure you, this investigation is far from stalled. We are watching. We are listening. And we will not stop until we find the truth."

Behind him, Riley's expression was cold, unyielding.

"Thank you," Whitaker concluded, stepping back. The room erupted into a flurry of shouted questions, but Whitaker ignored them all, stepping aside and whispering something to Riley as they left the stage.

Tiffany's living room was bathed in the cozy glow of the fire, but tonight, the room felt cold, almost sterile. The light from the television flickered, its bluish glow casting long shadows across the glossy tiled floor.

Tiffany sat, legs stretched out on the couch, a glass of wine balanced precariously on the arm. Her face was pale, her lips pressed into a tight line as she stared at Whitaker's face on the screen.

"Personal," Whitaker's voice echoed. "The perpetrator knew both victims."

Her eyes darted toward the large bay window across the room. The curtains were drawn, but she imagined shadows shifting outside, imagined eyes peering in.

Tiffany lifted the glass of wine to her lips, taking a slow, deliberate sip. But the wine did nothing to steady her nerves. She had told the detective about the message from her follower, and he'd eyed her suspiciously, but said he'd follow it up.

"We have our suspicions," he'd just said. She wondered if her follower was among the suspects. She aimed the remote at the television and shut it off, forcing herself to exhale slowly.

Her phone buzzed on the coffee table. She glanced at the screen. It was a text from Bee:

Did you see that? It sounds like they're onto someone, doesn't it?

Tiffany stared at the message for a long moment.

Do you want to come over? She sent the reply quickly. She could do with some company, and of all the women in the book club, she trusted Bee the most not to hurt her. Bee couldn't kill a soul. She even rescued spiders.

I'll bring wine came the reply.

Miriam's kitchen was warm, lit by the soft glow of under-cabinet lighting. The faint aroma of chamomile tea filled the air, but the cup in her hands had gone cold, untouched.

The small TV mounted under the cabinets flickered with end of the broadcast, Whitaker's face sharp and serious as he addressed the reporters.

"Personal."

Miriam tilted her head slightly, her brow furrowed. She leaned forward, her elbow resting on the counter as she studied the screen, her fingers lightly tapping against her chin.

Her home was quieter than usual tonight, the usual hum of the radio in the kitchen replaced by the steady ticking of the wall clock. The stillness felt heavier now, the kind that made you hyper-aware of every creak, every shadow.

On the counter beside her sat a notepad filled with her own scrawled notes, observations, timelines, fragments of conversations from the book club that now seemed more important than ever.

Miriam wasn't afraid, not exactly. But she was unnerved. Because Whitaker was right and this wasn't random.

She couldn't ignore her own growing suspicions. She knew she'd need to start tackling some of her questions soon. She would need to talk to Charlotte about what Brad had overheard. Why would Erica have been talking about her. And who to?

Miriam flinched as her phone buzzed. She glanced at the screen.

Dani: *Can you believe that press conference? Think they're really onto something?*

Miriam's lips pressed into a thin line. Something, she thought. Or someone.

~

Meanwhile, Jilly's small living room was a mix of chaos and coziness. A stack of books leaned precariously on the side table, and a half-folded blanket was draped over the arm of the couch. The TV sat in the corner, its volume turned up louder than usual, Whitaker's voice filling the room.

Jilly sat curled up on the couch, a throw blanket wrapped tightly around her shoulders. She clutched a mug of hot chocolate in her hands, her fingers trembling slightly, the drink sloshing dangerously close to the rim.

"Personal," Whitaker said, and Jilly flinched.

Her stomach churned, her thoughts racing. She couldn't stop thinking about Erica's note, the one she had destroyed, the one that might have changed everything.

And then she thought about what Brad had said. About the secret phone calls. Could Erica have been gathering evidence on someone. Who was the mystery caller, and why had she threatened to expose their secrets?

The sound of a car passing outside made her jump, her head snapping toward the window. The curtains were drawn, but she could feel the darkness outside pressing against the glass, heavy and watchful.

Her phone buzzed in her lap, and she nearly dropped it. She glanced at the screen. The message was from Miriam:

We need to talk.

She set the mug down carefully, her hands shaking too much to hold it. Her gaze flicked back to the television, where Whitaker's face remained calm but firm.

The words he had spoken echoed in her mind. *Personal. Suspicions. Leads.*

As the press conference drew to a close, the televisions in Willow Creek flickered off one by one, leaving behind a lingering sense of unease.

In their separate homes, the ladies of the book club digested what had been said, their thoughts tangled with fear, suspicion, and the creeping sense that the walls were beginning to close in. Each of them with something that they wanted to keep secret. Something they needed to stay buried. But one of them, perhaps, with more to hide than the rest.

The truth was coming. And none of them were ready for it.

21

BOOKS AND SECRETS

The curtains were open, but the mood was claustrophobic. Sunlight filtered through the tall windows of Miriam's crisp white lounge, but it couldn't cut the tension. The seven women from the book club sat in a loose circle, the air between them thick with unspoken questions. Mugs of untouched coffee steamed quietly on coasters.

Pam was the first to break the silence.

"So," she said, tapping a chipped nail against her mug. "We all saw the press conference, right? We've all been interviewed by the police at least once. And now they're saying they have leads. Does that mean one of you has told them something you're not sharing with the group?"

"They seemed pretty sure the killer knew both of them," Bee said, her voice tremulous. "I think they're looking at one of us."

Tiffany glanced up from her phone. "People in the comments on the stream think it's a man. A stalker maybe."

Miriam raised a brow. "Except neither of them mentioned anything about feeling watched or followed."

"I've been feeling like I'm being watched lately," said Jilly.

All eyes shifted to Jilly.

"We all are," said Charlotte bluntly. "The cops have got us all under surveillance, I bet."

Miriam looked at Charlotte.

She sat upright, composed, dressed immaculately even for a mid-morning emergency. But Miriam could see the twitch around her eyes. The harsh line of her lips. She made a decision. It was time to tackle the elephant in the room.

"We went to see Brad. Me, Pam, Jilly and Bee. He's in a bad way."

The others all nodded sadly.

"Anyway, he told us she'd been getting late-night calls," Miriam said evenly. He thought she might be having an affair. She was being very secretive. Sneaking out all the time."

Pam nodded, arms folded. "And he said once, in the middle of one of those calls, he heard her say a name."

Jilly shifted uncomfortably. "Your name, Charlotte."

A beat. The room stilled.

Charlotte blinked, lips parting slightly. "My name?" She seemed genuinely surprised.

Miriam nodded slowly. Charlotte laughed nervously.

"I... I don't know anything about late-night calls," Charlotte said. "But... Erica and I were on the fundraising committee for the new park renovations. She called me a few times, late. Usually to vent. She said she had something on someone on the planning committee. That's she'd use it if she had to."

Dani looked skeptical. "That's the best you've got?"

Charlotte met her gaze. "If you don't believe me, fine. But Erica had plenty of secrets, didn't she?"

She let that hang.

Then: "Anyway. She was having an affair. And Vanessa knew about it," Charlotte said.

Everyone stared, mouths gaping.

"She told me a few weeks ago. Said she thought Erica was

screwing her husband. She was livid. Asked if I'd ever noticed anything between them." She gave Jilly a pointed look. "And we all know Vanessa wasn't exactly shy about getting even with people who crossed her."

Jilly's mouth twitched. "You're saying Vanessa killed Erica?"

"I'm saying," Charlotte replied smoothly. "That Vanessa had motive. Maybe she confronted Erica. Maybe it went wrong. And *someone* killed Vanessa to keep her from talking."

"But if that's true," Bee whispered. "What was the secret Erica said would 'blow the town's mind'?"

Silence again.

Tiffany's eyes lit up. "What if it wasn't just an affair?"

"What then?" Pam asked. "Erica was secretly a Russian spy?"

"No," Tiffany said, leaning forward. "What if it wasn't just one affair? What if the dirt she had on the guy on the planning committee was on someone big? The mayor? The principal? Hell, isn't Vanessa's husband on that committee?"

Miriam's voice was calm, but cold. "She was going to tell me. Said she was tired of being scared. But she didn't get the chance."

Charlotte's smile was tight, calculated. "Or maybe she was bluffing. Maybe she thought the threat would keep someone in line. Only she misjudged how far they'd go."

Another silence.

Tiffany's phone vibrated against the table. She didn't pick it up.

Charlotte stood. "Believe what you like. I spoke to her a few times about the fundraiser, but that was it. I've told you the truth. But if you want to waste your time pointing fingers, maybe start with the ones who actually had *real* reasons to want her gone."

She swept out, leaving the women in stunned silence.

22

UNRAVELING A MYSTERY

Miriam sat at the small desk in her home office, the soft light of a desk lamp illuminating the scattered notes and open books before her. The room smelled faintly of chamomile and old paper, a comforting contrast to the turmoil of her thoughts. Rain tapped lightly against the window, a soothing backdrop to the storm of possibilities swirling in her mind.

She flipped through the notepad she had started keeping after Erica's death, her pen tapping absently against the edge of the desk. The pages were filled with scribbled thoughts, timelines, and connections, fragments of a puzzle she couldn't quite piece together.

The news from the book club's latest gathering replayed in her mind. Erica's affair. The cryptic way she had confided in Miriam months ago, her voice slurred from too much wine but tinged with something deeper, guilt, maybe. Or fear.

Miriam had brushed it off at the time, chalking it up to Erica's flair for drama. But now, knowing what she knew, it felt significant. The kind of secret someone might kill to protect.

She leaned back in her chair, staring out the window at the darkened street. Willow Creek was a quiet town, but tonight, it felt unnervingly still, the rain blurring the glow of streetlights. It was hard to believe such violence had seeped into their carefully curated suburban lives.

"Who were you about to expose, Erica?" Miriam murmured aloud, her voice barely a whisper.

It had to have been someone close. Someone with something to lose.

And then there was Vanessa.

Miriam couldn't ignore the growing sense that Vanessa's death wasn't just a coincidence. Vanessa wasn't the type to overlook something as juicy as an affair. She thrived on control, on knowing things others didn't.

Miriam let out a slow breath, her gaze drifting to the neatly stacked books on the corner of her desk. One of them caught her eye, a thriller they had read in the club months ago, where the murderer had silenced witnesses to cover their tracks. A chill crept up her spine.

What if Vanessa had challenged Erica about the affair? What if that had gone wrong, and ended up with Erica face down in her pool? What if Vanessa's husband, Simon, had found out what she'd done. Was he so overcome with grief for Erica that he lashed out at his own wife for killing her?

The idea felt disturbingly plausible. Perhaps she should call Detective Whitaker right now, and tell him everything she knew. But something was stopping her. Something wasn't quite adding up.

Simon was notorious for his affairs. And Vanessa for her ability to turn a blind eye. It seemed unlikely that she'd get upset enough with Erica to kill her. There had to be something more. Something she was missing.

She thought back to the last time she had seen Vanessa alive, sitting smugly in her perfectly styled living room, sipping wine like she didn't have a care in the world. Miriam had always admired her confidence, but now, she wondered if that confidence had been her downfall. Whoever she'd let into her house had come bent on murder.

Miriam stood, stretching her stiff legs, and wandered into the kitchen. The rain had picked up again, its steady rhythm filling the silence of the house. She poured herself a glass of water, her thoughts still racing.

She couldn't shake the feeling that they were all missing something obvious, something right in front of them.

Her phone buzzed on the counter, startling her. She glanced at the screen: a message from Jilly.

Do you really think the affair has something to do with it?

Miriam hesitated before replying:

It feels connected. But there's more to this. We're not seeing the whole picture yet.

Jilly's response came almost instantly:

I'm scared, Miriam. What if we're next?

Miriam frowned, her grip tightening on the phone. She didn't know how to answer that. Because deep down, she couldn't shake the feeling that Jilly might be right. And the more she delved into it, the more at risk she was.

As Miriam returned to her desk, her tea now lukewarm, she flipped back through her notes. She was convinced the affair was at the center of it all. She sat back in her chair, her pen tapping against the edge of the desk as she stared at her notes. The timeline of Vanessa's last days felt muddled, but certain moments stood out, glinting like shards of broken glass, sharp, dangerous, and begging to be pieced together.

She thought back to their last book club meeting, replaying the snippets of conversation she could remember. Vanessa had been her usual self that evening, charming, smug, subtly goading everyone just enough to keep them uncomfortable but not enough to outright offend.

And then there was that comment.

"I had a very interesting conversation last night," Vanessa had said, a sly smile tugging at the corners of her lips. "People really do surprise you, don't they?"

At the time, Miriam had dismissed it as one of Vanessa's many vague attempts to stir the pot. Vanessa thrived on knowing things others didn't, on dropping hints without ever revealing the full picture. But now, the memory struck Miriam differently.

Who had Vanessa spoken to? And what had surprised her?

Miriam frowned, her pen pausing mid-tap.

Charlotte had been adamant that she hadn't spoken to Vanessa before her death. She had said so during the book club meeting, her tone clipped, almost dismissive. And she'd had a reasonable enough excuse for why her name may have been on Erica's lips in a late night call.

But Vanessa's comment from that night suggested otherwise.

Was it possible that Charlotte was lying?

Miriam's mind raced as she considered the possibilities. Charlotte had always been careful, controlled, her emotions measured to perfection. But at the last meeting, Miriam had noticed something, a flicker of unease in Charlotte's expression when Vanessa made that comment.

It was subtle, the kind of thing most people wouldn't have caught. But Miriam wasn't most people.

She thought about Charlotte's behavior when they'd all met after Erica's death. She'd seemed shocked, but also distant. Withdrawn.

Was it guilt? Or fear?

Miriam's fingers tightened around her pen.

She flipped to a blank page in her notepad and began sketching out everything she knew, or thought she knew, her handwriting neat and methodical. With her thoughts all on paper, her gaze drifted toward the window, where the rain had slowed to a light drizzle, the droplets streaking down the glass like tears.

Vanessa had always been careful about who she let into her life. But if she had discovered something about Erica's affair, maybe she had let the wrong person get too close.

And maybe that person had decided to silence her before she could say more.

Miriam exhaled slowly, her thoughts churning.

Instead of the police, she thought, she could bring this up to some of the others in the book club. Maybe mention Vanessa's cryptic comment, point out the potential contradiction in Charlotte's story. But still, something held her back.

There was an unspoken rule in Willow Creek, a line you didn't cross unless you were willing to deal with the consequences. Secrets were currency here and revealing them often cost more than they were worth.

And then there was the nagging feeling Miriam couldn't shake.

If she shared this information, she would be putting a target on her own back. Because whoever had killed Erica and Vanessa wanted their secret to stay very much buried. That was clear.

No, she decided. For now, she would keep this to herself.

She closed her notebook and leaned back in her chair, her gaze drifting to the window once again. The faint glow of a streetlight illuminated the rain-slicked pavement outside, casting long shadows that swayed with the wind.

She felt a chill creep up her spine, her skin prickling as if she were being watched. She shook off the feeling, but it lingered, settling uneasily in her chest.

Miriam had always prided herself on being an observer, on staying one step ahead. But tonight, she felt uncertain. Because there was something about all of this, about Vanessa, about Erica, about Charlotte, that didn't add up.

And for the briefest moment, as she sat alone in the quiet of her home, she wondered: What if she wasn't as far removed from this as she thought? The thought sent a shiver through her, and she reached for her tea, her fingers trembling slightly.

Outside, the rain continued to fall, each drop a reminder that in Willow Creek, nothing stayed hidden forever.

23

A REAL-LIFE MURDER MYSTERY

The bell above the door jingled softly as Miriam stepped into Jilly's bookstore, the familiar scent of old paper and polished wood enveloping her. Dust motes floated lazily in the pale afternoon sunlight streaming through the front windows, casting a golden glow over the worn wooden floors.

The usually cozy felt awkward today. The air was heavy, tinged with unease, and Miriam could feel it as soon as she stepped inside.

Jilly stood behind the counter. Her head was bent low as she stacked books into a neat pile. Her sweater, a pale lavender that once might have been cheerful, hung loosely on her thin frame, and her dark hair was pulled back in a messy bun, strands escaping to frame her face. Her hands trembled slightly as she worked, the stack of books wobbling with each movement.

"Hi, Jilly," Miriam said, her voice soft but purposeful as she approached the counter.

Jilly startled, looking up sharply. Her wide hazel eyes, ringed with dark circles, were filled with the kind of nervous energy that made Miriam's stomach tighten.

"Miriam," Jilly said quickly, forcing a smile that didn't quite reach her eyes. She tucked a strand of hair behind her ear, a nervous habit Miriam had noticed before. "I didn't hear you come in."

Miriam studied her carefully, taking in the faint sheen of sweat on her brow, the way her fingers clutched the edge of the counter. Jilly looked like she hadn't slept in days, her usually warm demeanor replaced by jittery unease.

"Busy day?" Miriam asked lightly, nodding toward the books on the counter.

Jilly let out a laugh, but it was high-pitched and strained. "You could say that. Everyone's suddenly very interested in murder mysteries. I can't keep Agatha Christie on the shelves."

Miriam raised an eyebrow. "I imagine people are curious. Small towns love their gossip."

Jilly's forced smile faltered, and she looked away, her fingers tightening around the edge of the counter.

Miriam stepped closer, lowering her voice. "But it seems to me like you're worried about more than just gossip."

Jilly's face paled visibly, and she glanced down at the books in front of her, avoiding Miriam's gaze. The warm afternoon light illuminated her face, emphasizing the tension in her furrowed brow and the slight tremor in her lips.

For a moment, the only sounds in the room were the faint hum of the heater and the soft footsteps of a customer browsing in the back.

Finally, Jilly let out a shaky breath and looked up, her eyes brimming with anxiety.

"Miriam," she began hesitantly, her voice barely above a whisper. "Do you think Charlotte is hiding something?"

Miriam blinked, startled by the directness of the question. She opened her mouth to respond but stopped herself, choosing her words carefully.

"What makes you ask that?" Miriam said instead, her tone calm but probing.

Jilly hesitated, her gaze darting toward the lone customer in the back, a middle-aged woman leafing through a memoir. She leaned in closer to Miriam, lowering her voice.

"It's just, she hasn't been acting like herself," Jilly said, her voice trembling. "At the book club meetings, at her house, even in her texts. She's so *careful.* Like she's afraid to say the wrong thing."

Miriam nodded slowly but her face was unreadable. "That doesn't mean she's hiding anything."

Jilly swallowed hard, her eyes dropping to her hands. "I know. But..."

"But what?" Miriam pressed gently. Her tone was soft but insistent.

Jilly looked up, with eyes wide with fear. Her lips parted slightly, as if she were about to say something, but she hesitated, glancing toward the back of the store again.

"I think she's afraid of something," Jilly finally said, her voice trembling.

Miriam leaned back slightly, crossing her arms as she studied Jilly. "Afraid of what?"

"I don't know," Jilly admitted, shaking her head. "But it's like she's always looking over her shoulder. Like she's waiting for something bad to happen."

Miriam's mind raced as she pieced together fragments of memories. She thought about Charlotte's tightly controlled composure at the last book club meeting, the way her hand had trembled slightly as she poured herself a glass of wine. Charlotte was too poised, too measured, and it was beginning to feel like a performance.

"What are you saying, Jilly?" Miriam asked, her voice quiet but firm.

Jilly's gaze dropped to the counter, her fingers twisting nervously in the hem of her sweater. "I'm saying, I don't know. I don't think she'd hurt anyone. But there's something she's not telling us. I can feel it."

Miriam tilted her head slightly, her piercing gaze fixed on Jilly. "Have you noticed anything else? Anything she's said or done that seemed off?"

Jilly hesitated, chewing on her bottom lip. "No, not really. Just, I don't know. It's a feeling. Like she's always watching everyone. Like she's waiting for the other shoe to drop."

The soft chime of the bell over the door signaled the departure of the lone customer. Now, it was just Miriam and Jilly in the small shop, the silence pressing in around them. The warm light filtering through the windows seemed dimmer now, the shadows stretching longer across the floor.

Miriam glanced around the store, her eyes lingering on the darkened corners and the bookshelves that seemed to tower over them. The cozy space suddenly felt claustrophobic.

Jilly shifted nervously, breaking the silence. "Do you think she could have done it?"

Miriam hesitated, her mind racing through everything she knew about Charlotte. The perfect house. The perfect family. The perfect image she presented to the world.

"No," Miriam said finally, but her voice lacked conviction. "I don't think Charlotte is the type. But there is definitely something she's hiding."

Jilly nodded, but she didn't look convinced.

Miriam placed a hand on Jilly's trembling arm, her touch firm and reassuring. "Listen to me," she said quietly. "Let's not jump to conclusions. The police will figure this out. In the meantime, just keep your head down and your eyes open. You've done nothing to hurt anyone, so there's no reason they'll hurt you. But whoever has done this will slip up at some point, and we should be ready to see it."

Jilly nodded again, pressed her lips into a thin line, and looked down at her hands, her fingers fidgeting with the hem of her sweater. "I don't know. It feels wrong, Miriam. Like we're prying."

"We should be prying," Miriam said firmly. "Two of our friends are dead, Jilly. Do you really think this is going to stop? Because I don't."

Jilly hesitated, her face pale, her lips pressing into a thin line. "But what if it makes things worse?"

Miriam exhaled sharply, her patience thinning. "Worse how? Jilly, we're already in the middle of this whether we like it or not. You said it yourself, Charlotte's hiding something. Pam's not herself. Tiffany is loving the sudden limelight in an unhealthy way. Even Bee is more skittish than usual. Any one of them could hold the key to it all. Don't you want to know what it is?"

Jilly glanced toward the window, the faint drizzle outside casting shadows across the glass. "Of course I do," she admitted quietly. "But what if we dig too deep and we find something we can't handle?"

Miriam straightened, crossing her arms over her chest. "What's the alternative? Sitting around, hoping the killer doesn't come for one of us next?"

Jilly flinched at Miriam's bluntness, but she didn't argue. She wrapped her arms around herself, her voice barely above a whisper. "I just don't want anyone else to get hurt."

Miriam softened slightly, stepping closer to the counter. "Neither do I, Jilly. But if we don't get ahead of this, we're just sitting ducks. The longer we stay silent, the more power we give to whoever is behind this."

Jilly swallowed hard, her fingers clutching the edge of the counter. "So, what are you suggesting?"

Miriam's tone shifted, becoming more deliberate, more controlled. "We meet. Somewhere neutral. Somewhere public. The coffee shop, maybe. We get everyone together and we talk. No pretense of discussing a book. Just honesty. Transparency. We lay it all out."

"And what if no one says anything?" Jilly asked, her voice trembling.

"They will," Miriam said confidently. "People slip up when they're cornered. Someone knows more than they're letting on, and we need to find out who."

Jilly's unease deepened, her shoulders hunching as if the weight of the conversation were pressing down on her. "And what if we're wrong? What if it's none of them?"

Miriam hesitated, her mind racing through the possibilities. "Then at least we'll know we tried. At least we'll know we didn't just sit back and let this happen."

Jilly sighed, her hands falling to her sides. "Fine. But you're the one arranging it. I don't want to be the one to call them all together."

Miriam gave a small, satisfied nod. "I'll handle it. Don't worry."

As Miriam turned to leave, the bell above the door jingling softly, she cast one last glance over her shoulder. Jilly was still standing behind the counter, her expression troubled, her shoulders slumped.

Miriam stepped out into the rain, pulling her coat tighter against the cold drizzle. Her mind was made up. She would gather the group, whether they wanted to meet or not.

Because someone knew the truth. And Miriam was determined to find out who.

As she walked down the quiet street, her heels clicking against the damp pavement, she couldn't help but feel the weight of unseen eyes on her back. But she didn't look back.

She had already made up her mind. No more waiting. No more wondering. It was time to act.

She pulled her coat tighter around her, her mind churning with possibilities. Whatever the group truth was, Miriam knew it wouldn't stay hidden for long. And when it finally came out, Miriam had a sinking feeling it would shatter everything.

24

THE BOOK SHOP

The coffee shop was packed for a weekday afternoon, though most of the patrons weren't there for coffee.

The usual cozy atmosphere, warm lighting, the scent of freshly ground beans, the gentle hum of conversation, felt wrong today. The tension in the air was too thick, the chatter too forced, the usual clatter of cups and cutlery too loud.

Miriam sat at the center of the long wooden table, her hands folded neatly in front of her, a cup of untouched coffee cooling beside her. She had spent the last two days piecing together fragments of conversations, scanning old texts, and making quiet inquiries that no one had noticed. She had her suspicions now and she was ready to see if anyone else did, too.

Around her, the remaining book club members had gathered. Charlotte, Jilly, Bee, Pam, Tiffany, and Dani.

Charlotte sat stiffly, her navy-blue blouse pristine, her hair perfectly arranged, her face a carefully controlled mask of polite disinterest. She had barely touched the tea in front of her, her hands folded in her lap, her fingers twisting slightly against each other.

Jilly looked a mess of nerves, her cardigan hanging loosely

over her thin frame, her lips pressed into a tight line as she clutched her coffee cup with both hands. She kept glancing toward the window, as if expecting someone, or something, to appear.

Tiffany and Dani sat across from each other, their usual camaraderie absent today, their postures tense. Pam, usually the first to throw out a smart comment, was uncharacteristically quiet, stirring her cappuccino with slow, methodical movements.

No one had spoken much beyond pleasantries, and the silence had stretched long enough for it to become noticeable. Miriam looked like a hawk waiting to pounce, and Bee appeared as sheepish as usual.

Finally, Miriam cleared her throat.

"I thought it was time we all sat down," she said smoothly, her voice calm, controlled. "A lot has happened. And I think we need to talk openly and honestly."

Charlotte exhaled softly, shaking her head. "Miriam, this isn't some kind of game. We can't just sit here and play detective. There are real police officers investigating this. They'll figure it out."

Miriam didn't so much as blink. "Will they? They don't seem to be getting very far."

Charlotte's eyes flickered with something too quick to name, fear, maybe, or frustration.

Tiffany let out a breath, rubbing her temple. "I don't think any of us feel particularly comfortable playing 'who's the murderer' over lattes."

Pam let out a short, humorless laugh. "Speak for yourself."

Jilly shifted in her seat. "I don't think this is a good idea," she mumbled. "Being here together, I mean. I don't think we should be sitting here, talking about this like it's... normal."

"Nothing about this is normal," Miriam said, her voice

smooth but unwavering. "But sitting around pretending like we don't all have questions? That's not helping, either."

Jilly's eyes darted around the café. She felt watched. Every time the door swung open, she stiffened slightly, expecting something. Someone to burst in and accuse her or the police to drag someone away in cuffs. Or worse still, for whoever had killed Erica and Vanessa to be sitting right there with them.

She pulled her cardigan tighter around herself, her pulse hammering.

"I just don't want to make things worse," she murmured.

Miriam studied her. "Worse than what, Jilly?"

Jilly's breath caught, and for a fraction of a second, something passed across her face. Panic. She shook her head quickly. "Nothing. I just—" She trailed off, looking at her lap.

Charlotte's voice cut through the tension. "This is ridiculous," she said crisply. "We shouldn't even be discussing this. We're not detectives."

"Maybe not," Miriam agreed, tilting her head slightly, "But that doesn't mean we don't know things."

Charlotte went very still. For the first time, she reached for her tea, lifting the cup but not drinking from it, her fingers gripping the porcelain tightly.

The café had grown too quiet. Even the background murmur of other patrons felt strained, as if the whole room was teetering on the edge of something.

None of the women noticed the way certain customers lingered a little too long at the counter, how the barista exchanged quick, knowing glances with a man sitting alone near the window.

None of them noticed how a woman flipping through a magazine wasn't really reading at all. Plainclothes officers moved through the space, careful, inconspicuous. Watching. Listening.

Miriam had known they would. She had set this meeting up in the coffee shop for a reason.

Jilly finally broke the silence, her voice barely above a whisper. "Do you think whoever did this is sitting right here?"

The table fell into stillness. No one breathed.

Then Charlotte let out a soft scoff, shaking her head. "This is insane," she muttered. "We're all just scared."

Miriam watched her closely. "Are you?"

Charlotte's eyes snapped up. "Excuse me?"

"Scared," Miriam said lightly. "Are you scared, Charlotte?"

Charlotte stared at her, her mouth parting slightly, as if searching for the right response.

Then, too carefully, she said, "Of course I am. We all are."

But Miriam wasn't convinced. Because fear and guilt can look awfully similar if you don't know what to watch for. She leaned back, taking a slow sip of her coffee, her eyes never leaving Charlotte's.

She was waiting for someone to slip. And she had a feeling it would happen very, very soon.

The coffee shop felt smaller now, the walls pressing inward with each passing second. The tension at the table had thickened, stretching tight between the women, fraying at the edges. Outside, the rain drizzled against the windows, soft and steady, a contrast to the electric current running beneath the surface of the conversation.

Miriam let the silence linger just a moment longer, savoring the discomfort in the air. Then, with a slow, measured breath, she spoke.

"You know," she said casually, swirling the coffee in her cup, "I've been thinking about something Vanessa said at our last book club meeting."

Jilly's fingers tightened around her mug. Charlotte, who had been idly smoothing the cuff of her blouse, froze for just a fraction of a second before recovering, taking a small, measured sip of her tea.

Miriam didn't miss it.

"She mentioned," Miriam continued, watching them carefully. "That she had a very interesting conversation the night before. She didn't say with whom, but she certainly seemed amused by it."

Jilly let out a short, nervous laugh, shifting uncomfortably in her seat. "Vanessa said a lot of things," she muttered. "She loved stirring the pot."

"She did," Miriam agreed, tilting her head. "But this wasn't just gossip. She was smug about it. Like she had something over someone."

Charlotte exhaled, setting her cup down a little too carefully. "And?" she asked, her voice level, but there was a tightness in her tone, a thin thread of strain. "What's your point?"

Miriam leaned forward slightly, her gaze flicking between Jilly and Charlotte. "I find it interesting that neither of you asked who she was talking about."

Jilly's breath hitched. She quickly masked it by shifting in her seat, pretending to glance at the café entrance.

Charlotte, however, held Miriam's gaze steadily. Her nails tapped once against the ceramic of her cup, then stopped. A pause. A calculation.

"She was probably just being dramatic," Charlotte said smoothly. "Vanessa loved making people squirm. That doesn't mean she actually knew anything."

Miriam smiled. Too sharp. Too knowing.

"Maybe," she murmured. "Or maybe she knew something she wasn't supposed to."

Jilly's hands trembled slightly as she reached for her napkin, dabbing at her lip even though there was nothing there. Her eyes flicked toward Charlotte, a glimmer of something unreadable passing between them.

Miriam did not miss it.

Charlotte exhaled through her nose, shaking her head slightly. "You're reaching, Miriam. Just because Vanessa liked to stir up drama doesn't mean it got her killed."

Miriam tapped a finger against her cup, her expression thoughtful. "Maybe not. But what if it did?"

A sharp inhale from Jilly. A tiny flicker of something in Charlotte's otherwise perfectly composed face.

Miriam could feel it now. The shift. The pressure. She was getting somewhere. She let the silence stretch again, letting them sit in their own unease.

Jilly was afraid. And Charlotte? Charlotte was keeping something buried.

Outside, the rain picked up, tapping harder against the windows. The coffee shop had grown strangely quiet, save for the faint murmur of voices at the counter.

Miriam's gaze flicked subtly around the room. The plainclothes officers were still there. Sitting inconspicuously, flipping through newspapers, drinking their coffee, waiting. Watching.

Jilly licked her lips, then spoke hesitantly. "So, what are you saying, Miriam? That Vanessa *did* know something? And that's why she was—" She trailed off, as if saying the word murdered would make it more real.

Miriam didn't answer right away. Instead, she glanced at Charlotte. Charlotte sat very still. Then she yawned slowly, shaking her head as though she were tired of all of this.

"Look," Charlotte said, "whatever Vanessa was talking about, it's irrelevant now. She's gone. Speculating about things we can't prove doesn't help anyone."

Miriam's lips curved into a small smile.

"It helps me," she said simply.

Charlotte's eyes flickered just slightly, the briefest loss of control before she regained her carefully built composure.

Miriam knew then. Charlotte was afraid of something getting out and Miriam was going to find out exactly what it was. The room buzzed with unspoken tension. The game had changed but Miriam was going to keep playing.

25

SKELETONS IN THE CLOSET

The tension in the café felt thicker now, as though the air itself was pressing in around them. The rain continued to tap softly against the windows, the sound rhythmic, almost hypnotic, a quiet metronome to the growing unease at the table.

Miriam tilted her head, watching, calculating.

The cracks were forming. Now she just had to press a little harder.

She let the silence linger just a moment longer before shifting slightly in her seat. She reached for her coffee, taking a slow sip, then placed it carefully back on the table. Her fingers traced the rim of the cup absentmindedly as she spoke.

"There's something else that's been on my mind," she said casually, her tone light, conversational. "Vanessa's finances."

Jilly flinched this time. Not much. Just a little. But it was enough.

Charlotte, however, barely hesitated. She let out a short, sharp breath, too controlled, too dismissive. "Vanessa always had money, and she was always flashing it about. What about it?"

Miriam studied her carefully. Charlotte was usually a master of composure, of turning conversations exactly where she wanted them to go. But not today. Not with Miriam watching.

"She had money," Miriam agreed, nodding slightly. "But she also had power. And people like Vanessa? They don't just hand either of those commodities out for free."

Jilly's fingers twisted into the fabric of her cardigan. She was staring at the tabletop now, her breath coming in short, uneven bursts.

Miriam sensed the shift immediately.

Charlotte, however, just scoffed, shaking her head. "Vanessa was always controlling everything. She wanted to own people."

The words left her lips too fast. Too sharp. The moment they were out in the open, the energy in the room changed. A heavy silence followed.

Charlotte realized her mistake too late. Her spine straightened, her jaw tightening, but the damage was done. The words had landed. And they had been felt.

Miriam placed her hands flat against the table, leaning forward slightly. "Own people?" she echoed, her voice dangerously soft.

Charlotte hesitated for half a second. Then she rolled her shoulders back, feigning nonchalance. "You know what I mean. Vanessa loved being in control. Of her house. Of Simon. Of her reputation. Of everything."

Miriam said nothing. She just let the words settle between them. Jilly couldn't take it anymore.

"I borrowed money from her."

The confession tumbled out, breathless, shaky. Like it had been dying to be spoken. All eyes snapped to Jilly. She was trembling now, her hands gripping the edge of the table as if it were the only thing keeping her upright.

Charlotte's face went blank. Not shocked, not surprised, just unreadable.

Miriam smiled to herself.

Jilly let out a shaky breath, blinking rapidly. "It wasn't a lot. I mean, it was a lot to me, but not to her. She barely even hesitated when I asked."

"When was this?" Miriam asked, keeping her voice carefully neutral.

Jilly swallowed hard. "Last year. When the store was struggling. I tried to go to a bank first, but my credit..." She shook her head. "Vanessa found out and offered to help."

Pam, silent until now, let out a low whistle. "That doesn't sound like an offer. That sounds like a deal with the devil."

Jilly flinched. "It wasn't like that. At first. She said she wanted to help me, that she believed in local businesses. That she believed in me. But after a while, she started..." Jilly's voice faltered, her fingers gripping the edge of the table even tighter.

"She started what?" Tiffany asked, her voice unusually sharp.

Jilly hesitated, then whispered, "She wanted favors." The words hung in the air, suffocating.

When Charlotte finally spoke, her voice was too smooth. "That sounds like Vanessa."

Miriam turned her gaze to Charlotte again, watching her reaction. "What kind of favors, Jilly?"

Jilly bit her lip. "Just little things. Hosting events here in the shop. Inviting certain people. Dropping her name when I spoke to suppliers."

"That doesn't sound so bad," Dani muttered, but even she sounded uncertain.

Jilly's hands tightened into fists. "She also wanted updates on what people were saying about her. She made it clear that I owed her. And that I'd better remember it."

Miriam sat back in her chair, tapping her finger against her cup.

It made perfect sense. Vanessa loved control. And she would have loved having someone like Jilly, a nervous, soft-spoken bookseller, wrapped around her finger.

But the real question was: Had Vanessa pushed too far? Had she threatened someone she shouldn't have?

Jilly let out a slow, uneven breath. "I was going to pay her back. I tried to. But then..." Her voice broke off, and she gave a watery laugh. "Well. Then she died."

Another silence fell over the table. And then, ever so softly, Charlotte exhaled through her nose. The sound was barely noticeable. But to Miriam, it was everything.

Miriam folded her hands together, her gaze flicking from Jilly to Charlotte. The pieces were moving into place now.

Vanessa had money. Power. Influence. And she had used it to keep people indebted to her. The real question was: Who had finally decided they'd had enough?

Miriam glanced around the café. The plainclothes officers were still there, lingering, observing. They wouldn't intervene. Not yet. But they were listening.

Miriam leaned forward slightly, her voice gentle, almost kind. "Jilly, did Vanessa ever threaten you?"

Jilly's breath hitched. She opened her mouth, then hesitated.

Charlotte cut in smoothly. "Vanessa implied things. She never outright said them."

Miriam turned her gaze to Charlotte. "But she had information that could ruin people, didn't she? She said so herself."

Charlotte's shoulders stiffened. "She liked people thinking that."

Miriam smiled slightly. "But could she?"

Charlotte's jaw tightened and that was all the answer Miriam needed.

The table fell into a thick, unbearable silence.

Jilly stared down at her lap, blinking rapidly. Pam and Dani exchanged wary glances. Tiffany sat back, rubbing her temple.

Charlotte sat perfectly still. Composed. Silent. Watching.

Miriam took a sip of her coffee and let her words settle, let them seep into the spaces between the women at the table. She could feel them absorbing what she'd just asked, bracing themselves, waiting.

She traced the rim of her coffee cup with one steady finger, her posture relaxed, composed, but her eyes sharp, watchful.

Finally, she spoke again, her voice measured, almost gentle.

"Vanessa wasn't just rich. She had leverage over people. We know she had something over Jilly with the loan. Did she have leverage over you, Charlotte?"

The question hung in the air like an axe poised to drop. Charlotte didn't answer.

She didn't flinch. She didn't shake her head in denial. She just sat there, her expression unreadable, her fingers curled loosely around her teacup as though the warmth was the only thing grounding her.

The silence stretched too long. Too heavy. Too revealing.

The other women exchanged glances, Jilly, Pam, Tiffany, Dani, and Bee, a flicker of realization passing between them that Miriam was on to something, a slow-building awareness that something wasn't adding up.

Miriam waited, watching Charlotte's stiff posture, the way her chest rose and fell just a little too quickly.

Bee swallowed hard and set her coffee down with a shaky clink. "Charlotte?" she asked, hesitant, uncertain.

Still, Charlotte didn't speak.

Miriam's lips curled into something that wasn't quite a smile.

There it is. That carefully curated poise, that pristine control, beginning to unravel at the seams. The truth was close now. So close. And then Miriam leaned back, crossed one leg over the other, and dropped the bomb.

"We know Erica was sleeping with Simon. But was she the only one? Because Vanessa seemed to infer there was another secret she knew. And she seemed pretty bitter about it."

The reaction was instantaneous.

Jilly gasped loudly, her hand flying to her mouth. Pam let out a sharp breath, as if someone had just struck her in the chest. Dani and Tiffany stiffened, exchanging looks of shock. Bee went white.

Charlotte stayed completely still. Not a blink. Not a flicker of emotion. Just pure, practiced stillness.

The coffee shop felt smaller now, the walls pressing in, the noise around them dampened by the weight of what had just been asked.

From across the room, at a quiet table near the back, two plainclothes officers sat motionless, coffee cups untouched. They weren't reading the newspapers in front of them. They weren't scrolling through their phones. They were listening. Watching. Taking in every reaction.

One of them, a younger woman with keen, calculating eyes, had been pretending to flip through a book for the last half hour, but now she had it resting open in her lap, barely disguising the way she was hanging on every word.

The older officer, a man with a face lined with quiet skepticism, reached for his coffee without drinking it. He exchanged a single glance with his colleague. Because even they felt something brewing.

Charlotte's hand trembled as she finally lifted her tea to her lips. Not much. But enough. Jilly saw it. Tiffany saw it. Miriam saw it. The cracks in Charlotte's pristine composure were spreading.

Jilly shook her head, her voice tight. "If Vanessa knew, she wouldn't have kept quiet about it. She wouldn't have let that go."

"She didn't," Miriam said, still watching Charlotte. "And I think that's why she's dead."

Jilly let out a shaky breath, realization dawning across her features. "Oh my God."

Pam leaned forward, her voice a whisper. "Do you think she was... blackmailing them?"

Miriam tilted her head slightly. "Or worse. Maybe she was planning to tell everyone in the town. Maybe she'd had enough of Simon's cheating and thought it was time the town knew everything about who he was cheating with."

Jilly shuddered. "Vanessa wasn't the type to forgive betrayal."

"No," Miriam agreed, her voice low. "She wasn't."

Another silence. Then, slowly, so carefully, Charlotte placed her cup down on the table.

When she spoke, her voice was flat. Controlled. Devoid of emotion.

"None of this proves anything," she said, her tone perfectly even.

But it was too late. The damage had been done. The shift had happened. And everyone at the table knew she had spoken too carefully, too deliberately.

Miriam smiled. Because she wasn't done yet. She leaned forward, her voice dropping just slightly. Just enough to make Charlotte sweat.

"You're right," she said sweetly. "It doesn't prove anything." Then, she let the words sink in before delivering the final blow. "But it does make you wonder, doesn't it? Who that other woman was, and what they stood to lose if their secret came out."

Charlotte's lips parted slightly, just the tiniest fraction, as if she had no response.

Miriam smiled again. Because the truth was clawing its way out. And soon there would be no stopping it.

26

THE FINAL ACT

For a moment, there was nothing. No one spoke. No one breathed.

The coffee shop, the muted conversations around them, the low hum of the espresso machine, all of it faded into a distant blur. And then Charlotte laughed. A short, sharp, bitter sound that sliced through the thick tension like a blade.

Jilly flinched. Pam blinked, stunned. Tiffany and Dani exchanged looks of disbelief, and Bee looked like she might be sick.

But Miriam leaned back, watching. Waiting.

Charlotte's laughter was hollow, a humorless thing that echoed in the stunned silence of the group.

She shook her head, lifting a hand to her temple as if steadying herself, as if even she couldn't believe what she was about to say. And then, finally, she snapped.

"You want the truth?" she asked, her voice razor-sharp, her carefully composed exterior fracturing right in front of them. "Fine. You want to know what Vanessa was holding over me? What her precious leverage was?"

She let out a shaky breath, her gaze flickering around the table before she dropped the bomb.

"I was sleeping with Simon too."

The weight of her confession slammed into the table like a thunderclap.

Jilly gasped audibly, her eyes wide with shock, her fingers frozen around her coffee cup.

Dani's mouth fell open. "Oh. No."

Tiffany pressed a hand to her chest, whispering, "Jesus Christ."

Even Pam, who had remained carefully detached until now, looked visibly rattled.

Miriam stayed quiet, her heartbeat steady, her expression unreadable. She had suspected as much, but hearing Charlotte say it out loud was something else entirely.

Jilly blinked, shaking her head rapidly, as if she could somehow process the impossible weight of what she had just heard. "You were having an affair with Simon too?"

Charlotte let out another bitter laugh, but this time, it sounded like defeat.

"Oh, don't look so surprised," she muttered, running a hand through her perfectly styled hair, unraveling it slightly. "Isn't that what men like him do? Take and take and take? And we let them. I let him."

Silence. A long, heavy, unbearable silence. Then Bee, still reeling, shook her head in disbelief. "But, how?"

Charlotte exhaled, finally collapsing under the weight of it all. "It was a mistake," she muttered. "A long, stupid mistake. It started before Erica started sleeping with him. I don't even know why I let it happen. But Vanessa," her breath caught, "Vanessa found out."

Jilly swallowed hard, her hands trembling against her lap. "How?"

Charlotte's lips parted, but no sound came out at first.

Then she let out a slow, shuddering breath. "She found proof. Because Simon is careless."

Miriam's grip on her cup tightened. There it was. Vanessa had caught her. And Vanessa, being Vanessa, had known exactly what to do with that information.

Charlotte shook her head, letting out a shaky, breathless laugh. "She had text messages. Photos. Videos."

Jilly covered her mouth, her face paling.

"Oh my God," Maddie whispered.

Charlotte exhaled shakily, her hands gripping the edge of the table as if it were the only thing keeping her from falling apart.

"She told me she was going to destroy me," Charlotte murmured, staring at the table but not really seeing it. "Expose me to Bobby, to my kids, to everyone. She said she would make sure I lost everything."

The confession settled over them, heavy and suffocating.

Jilly spoke first, her voice trembling. "So, she was blackmailing you."

Charlotte let out another humorless laugh. "She never outright said the word, but of course she was. That was Vanessa's game. She wanted to own people. Wanted to watch people squirm. She lived for it. She said she would ruin everything I had."

"And she died for it." Miriam's jaw clenched. Just like Jilly said before. Just like they all knew, deep down, about Vanessa – she didn't just hold power she wielded it like a weapon. And it got her killed.

From across the room, at the table near the back, the plainclothes officers exchanged glances. The younger officer, her posture rigid, lowered her coffee cup slowly, her expression sharp, calculating. The older officer, pretending to scan his phone, kept his attention firmly on Charlotte.

The confession had changed everything. Charlotte had a motive now, and she had lied to them in questioning. That was all they needed.

Miriam placed her coffee cup down carefully. Her gaze drifted over the table, studying the fallout. Charlotte, pale and shaken. Jilly, fearful and reeling.

Pam, Tiffany, Dani and Bee, all grappling with this new, impossible truth. Miriam spoke softly, but the words cut deep.

"So let me get this straight," she murmured, her voice deceptively even. "Vanessa caught you cheating with Simon. She had proof. She was going to ruin you."

Charlotte didn't speak. She didn't deny it. She just sat there, her fingers twitching against the ceramic of her cup, her silence stretching too long, too thin.

Miriam leaned forward slightly, her voice lowering. "And then," she said quietly, "Vanessa turned up dead."

The words landed like a slap. Charlotte's entire body tensed. Jilly let out a shaky breath. The others watched in stunned silence, waiting. Tiffany's hand clasped around her phone, as though sensing something needed to be recorded here.

Charlotte's throat bobbed as she swallowed. Her eyes flicked up to Miriam's, and for the first time that day, Miriam saw it. The hint of true, unfiltered fear. Charlotte opened her mouth. And then the café door swung open, the bells jingling violently.

Everyone jumped at the sound.

The room turned to see who had arrived. And there, standing just inside the entrance, was Simon Caldwell. Dripping wet from the rain. His face a mask of unreadable tension. And his eyes were fixed directly on Charlotte's face. For a moment, the entire café held its breath.

Simon stood in the doorway, rain dripping from his dark

coat onto the tiled floor, his chest rising and falling just a little too fast. His deep eyes, usually so carefully blank, were locked onto Charlotte.

The warmth of the café had vanished. Conversations stalled. The barista froze mid-pour, her hand hovering over a cappuccino.

At the back of the café, the plainclothes officers stiffened. They hadn't expected him.

One of them, the younger woman with the bright eyes, exchanged a loaded glance with her partner. This was no coincidence. Someone had orchestrated this. And that someone was sitting calmly at the table, stirring her coffee.

Miriam.

She didn't move, didn't flinch, didn't so much as blink as Simon stepped forward. She had planned this. Every moment, every calculated sentence, every layer of tension that had built and built and built, all of it had led to this.

Simon had no idea he had just walked into a trap.

Charlotte, on the other hand, looked like she was going to be sick. Her grip on her cup had turned knuckle-white, her breath uneven. She hadn't even turned fully toward Simon. She couldn't.

Jilly, beside her, was trembling visibly. Pam, Dani and Bee sat frozen, trapped in the reality of what was unfolding. Tiffany held her phone almost hidden in her lap, now definitely filming what was happening.

Miriam simply sat back and watched the final act begin.

"Charlotte." Simon's voice was quiet, measured, dangerous.

She flinched. Just barely. But enough for everyone to see it. A second stretched between them, too long, too fragile.

Then, suddenly, Charlotte laughed again. That same short, sharp, bitter sound that wasn't humor at all. Her head tilted back slightly, her nails digging into the smooth ceramic of her teacup. The sound made Jilly flinch, and even Simon seemed unsettled.

Pam's voice was barely a whisper. "Charlotte, what the hell is wrong with you?"

Charlotte wiped at her eyes, but it wasn't remorse that twisted her face. It was relief.

"You want the truth?" she asked, her voice razor-sharp, brittle with exhaustion, yet laced with something dangerously close to satisfaction. She exhaled, a slow, eerie sigh. And then, finally, she broke.

"She told me she was going to destroy me," Charlotte murmured again, staring at the table but not really seeing it. "She said she'd tell Bobby. She'd tell the kids. She'd tell the whole town. And I'd lose everything. My family. My home. My kids. My.... My reputation."

And then she looked up. And for the first time, they saw it. She wasn't sorry. Her lips curled slightly, her eyes glinting with something almost smug.

"So, I killed her," she said, shrugging.

Jilly gasped. Pam shook her head violently.

Charlotte leaned back, smirking.

"I begged her," she said, voice like silk. "I told her to let it go. But she wouldn't." Her fingers drummed lightly against the table. "She laughed in my face. Called me pathetic. Said I was weak."

Then, her voice dropped lower, colder.

"She shouldn't have done that. I grabbed her," Charlotte continued, her tone disturbingly casual now. "She fought, but not much. Not at first. I think she was enjoying it." She let out a soft, dark chuckle. "Until she realized I meant it."

Jilly covered her mouth, tears spilling down her face.

"She clawed at me," Charlotte went on, tilting her head slightly. "Begged me to stop. But she never gave me the same mercy, did she? She would've ruined me, just like she was going to ruin you, Jilly."

Jilly flinched as though struck. Charlotte's gaze flicked to her, mocking, amused.

"She blackmailed you too," Charlotte reminded her. "We all know it. She wasn't a saint."

Miriam had orchestrated this moment perfectly. She had spent days watching, waiting, pushing, until finally, Charlotte cracked.

Now, the women of the book club sat frozen, eyes wide, hearts pounding, the scent of old books and tea turning sour in the heavy silence.

Charlotte sat at the center of it all, shoulders squared, chin lifted, like a queen who had just lost her crown but refused to kneel. She had laughed when she confessed. A short, bitter sound that sent a chill skittering down Jilly's spine.

"I killed Vanessa," she said, her voice eerily calm. "There. You happy now?"

And then, as the gasps rose around her, she smirked.

"And you know what? Honestly?" Charlotte continued, her voice almost conversational. "It was way easier than I imagined."

The bookstore's cozy, familiar air had turned stifling, thick with something uglier than fear. It was truth.

Jilly clutched the edge of the table, her nails digging into the wood. "Oh my God."

Pam covered her mouth, eyes glistening. Dani muttered a whispered, "Jesus."

Even Vanessa, for all her cruelty, hadn't deserved this. Miriam sat still, unblinking, watching Charlotte unravel in real time.

"You don't even sound sorry," Tiffany whispered, her phone still filming Charlotte's confession.

Charlotte turned to her, that same, strange smile still painted across her lips. "Would it make you feel better if I did?"

A sharp breath. A choking sound. Then silence.

Charlotte let it hang there for a long moment before she sighed, leaning back in her chair. "You all act so surprised. But let's be honest. Who here hasn't thought about killing Vanessa at least once?"

More silence. Because none of them could argue. Charlotte tilted her head, studying them like a puzzle she had already solved.

"No one?" she pressed. "Not even you, Jilly?"

Jilly flinched, her face going pale.

Charlotte smiled, slow and knowing. "Or what about you, Miriam? You're the one who set this little trap, aren't you?"

Miriam didn't flinch. Didn't blink. "I didn't need to. You've been wearing your guilt like a badge."

Charlotte let out a breath, shaking her head. "I was never the villain in Vanessa's story, you know. I was just another one of her pawns. She thought she could frighten me. That I'd fall in line, like everyone else."

Jilly's voice was shaky. "So, you... what? You just snapped?"

Charlotte's laugh was soft, hollow. "You make it sound so dramatic."

For a second, Charlotte's face shifted, just for a second, something raw and jagged and bleeding flickered in her expression.

Then she smoothed it away.

"I didn't plan it," she admitted. "I just wanted her to stop."

She exhaled, shaking her head. "I went to her house that night. I begged her. I told her I would do anything."

The memory of it flooded back, sharp and bright as a camera flash:

Vanessa in her silk robe, leaning against the doorway, smirking. Enjoying the power she had.

'Oh, Charlotte,' she had purred. 'You don't get to make demands. That's not how this works.'

Charlotte's hands clenched into fists. "She laughed at me. She said it was all a game. That she was bored with me. That she'd already won." Her eyes darkened. "So, I wrapped my hands around her throat."

A strangled gasp rippled through the room. Charlotte's voice didn't waver. "And I squeezed. And squeezed. And do you know what the last thing she did was?"

She leaned forward, her eyes sharp, burning.

"She smiled."

Jilly's stomach turned violently. Dani covered her face, her shoulders shaking.

Bee was crying now, soft and broken. "You, you're a monster."

Charlotte let out a soft, breathy laugh. "You think I don't know that?"

She leaned back, eyes flitting across their faces. Simon, shaking and pale, stepped forward now.

"But you still haven't asked her the real question." He said, his voice cracking.

Jilly swallowed hard. "What question?"

Simon swallowed hard. "What about Erica?"

The room turned ice cold. No one spoke. No one breathed.

Miriam, still eerily calm, tilted her head. "Did you?"

Charlotte lifted a single shoulder. "That's for me to know."

Jilly shook her head, her hands shaking. "Oh my God. You did."

"Guess we'll find out in time, won't we?"

Jilly shook her head violently, her body trembling. Charlotte smirked.

"She deserved it, too" she said simply. "You should never have dumped me for her, Simon."

Miriam finally exhaled, slowly placing her cup down. She had won.

Now, the plainclothes officers moved. Fast. Charlotte barely registered them before they were on her.

A sharp voice. "Charlotte Davenport, you're under arrest for the murder of Vanessa Caldwell, and the murder of Erica Miller..."

A stunned gasp from the crowd. A rush of movement. Jilly clamped her hands over her ears. Simon stared at Charlotte like she was a stranger.

Charlotte didn't fight it. Didn't argue. Didn't resist as they pulled her from her chair, as they yanked her arms behind her back, as the cold snap of handcuffs echoed through the café. She just smiled.

Miriam reached for her coffee, took one last sip.

The handcuffs clicked into place, the cold metal biting against Charlotte's wrists, but she didn't flinch. She stood tall, her chin lifted, her lips curved in a slight, knowing smirk.

Dani had her hands pressed to her temples, shaking her head. Tiffany was still filming, but staring, wide-eyed, frozen in horror. Bee had gone completely pale.

Jilly, however, was shaking. Her breath was shallow, her body trembling as the reality of it all came crashing down. Charlotte had killed Vanessa. And Erica. And she didn't even care.

And as Charlotte was led out into the rain, into the flashing lights, into the open arms of justice, her smile never wavered.

The door swung shut behind her. And in the coffee shop, where the weight of her words still hung heavy in the air, no one knew what to say.

27

THE AFTERMATH

Willow Creek had never felt quieter.

Even in the busiest places, the grocery stores, school drop-offs, church services, there was a lingering hush, an unnatural weight pressing over the town like a storm cloud that refused to break. Conversations were subdued, eyes wary, whispers hushed, but ever-present.

Charlotte's arrest had finally shattered the carefully maintained illusion of their picture-perfect suburban life. And no one knew what to do with the fragments left behind.

The coffee shop where Charlotte had confessed was still the epicenter of gossip. People gathered there not just for coffee, but for information.

The small café, usually filled with soft music and idle chatter, now felt heavy, like a courtroom after a guilty verdict. The baristas worked in near silence, handing out cappuccinos to customers who were too busy whispering to properly thank them.

"She just admitted it?" a woman at a corner table whispered, her voice tinged with disbelief.

"In front of everyone," another murmured, shaking her

head, her fingers curled around her cup like she was trying to hold onto something less tangible.

"She didn't even look sorry," a third voice said, quieter, as if saying it any louder would summon Charlotte back.

Across town, the local news cycled through the story on repeat.

"Willow Creek resident Charlotte Davenport, once a respected member of the community, was arrested earlier this week after a shocking public confession."

The words echoed through homes, through car radios, through the stiff corridors of the country club where Charlotte had once reigned supreme.

The women who had admired her, envied her, feared her, they all now spoke of her in hushed, scandalized tones. But the worst of it was that Simon Caldwell had become a pariah. He walked through town like a ghost, hollowed out, unreadable.

At the grocery store, women pulled their carts away from him as if murder were contagious. At the gas station, a group of men fell into an awkward silence as he walked past, muttering to each other as soon as he was out of earshot.

He was the man both his wife and mistress had died for. And no one knew whether to pity him or despise him.

Miriam watched it all unfold quietly. From the coffee shop, from the bookstore, from the aisles of the grocery store where mothers clutched their children's hands just a little tighter. She saw the way people avoided eye contact, how they talked in corners, how they searched for someone to blame. She saw the way Jilly had stopped looking people in the eye altogether. She saw the way Simon moved through town with his head bowed, as if waiting for the next blow to come. And she saw the way the remaining book club members could barely stand to look at one another.

None of them trusted each other anymore. Even though

Charlotte had been arrested, something didn't feel over. Something was still missing.

Three days after Charlotte's arrest, Miriam found Jilly at the bookstore.

It had once been a comforting place, warm and lived-in, with stacks of well-loved books and the faint smell of chamomile tea. Now? It felt abandoned.

Jilly was sitting behind the counter, a cup of tea in front of her, untouched and long gone cold. Her eyes were puffy, her hair unbrushed. She looked like she hadn't slept in days.

The bell above the door jingled as Miriam stepped inside. Jilly barely looked up. Miriam approached carefully, resting her hands on the counter.

"You haven't called," she said softly.

Jilly flinched slightly, then forced a small, tight smile. "Been busy."

Miriam raised an eyebrow. "Lying to me?"

Jilly let out a breath, shaky and uneven. Miriam waited. Then, finally, "She wasn't sorry," Jilly whispered, voice hoarse. "Not even a little."

Miriam said nothing.

"She..." Jilly swallowed hard. "She enjoyed it, Miriam. You heard her. She wanted Vanessa to suffer."

Miriam nodded, because she had heard it too.

"She smirked when I asked about Erica," Jilly continued, voice breaking now. "She didn't even deny it. She just smiled. But why did she do it? I just don't understand."

Miriam's chest tightened. Because that moment hadn't left her, either.

Jilly sat hunched behind the counter, her hands wrapped tightly around a cup of long-cold tea, her knuckles white. The shadows beneath her eyes looked even deeper in the soft glow of the shop's warm lighting.

Miriam watched her carefully, sensing the fragile edge of her unraveling composure.

Outside, Willow Creek moved on or at least it pretended to. Cars rolled down the wet streets. Children laughed on their way home from school. People picked up dry cleaning, made dinner reservations, acted like life wasn't permanently stained.

But Miriam knew better. This wasn't over. Not yet.

Then, Miriam's phone rang. A shrill sound that cut through the silence.

Jilly flinched, and Miriam reached for her device.

"This is Miriam."

A deep, clipped voice came through the line.

"Mam, we have Charlotte Davenport in custody, as you know." His tone was neutral but loaded. "She's requested to speak with you."

Miriam's grip on the phone tightened.

Jilly's head snapped up. "Who is it?" she mouthed.

Miriam ignored her, her pulse quickening. "She asked for me?"

"She did," the officer confirmed. "Said she has something she needs to tell you."

Miriam felt a chill creep down her spine. Charlotte didn't want the police or a solicitor. She wanted her.

Jilly was staring now, her face pale. "Who is it?" she whispered again, more urgently.

Miriam covered the receiver. "The police," she murmured. "Charlotte wants to see me."

Jilly blanched. "Miriam, no."

Miriam turned back toward the phone. "Did she say why?"

"No," Holt admitted. "Only that she'll talk to you. No one else."

Miriam exhaled slowly, staring out the front window of the

bookstore. Rain dripped from the awning, pooling in the cracks of the sidewalk.

Jilly's chair scraped loudly against the floor as she stood. "Miriam, this is a bad idea."

Miriam knew it was. She knew she should say no, let Charlotte rot in her cell with her secrets. But curiosity was a dangerous thing. And it had Miriam wrapped around its finger. She brought the phone back to her ear.

"Fine," she said, her voice steady. "When?"

The officer didn't hesitate. "Tomorrow. Two p.m." Another pause. Then he added, "Please be punctual." The line clicked dead. Miriam lowered the phone slowly, her mind racing.

Jilly's voice was tight with panic. "You can't seriously be considering this."

Miriam looked at her, forcing a small smirk. "We both know I am."

Jilly ran a hand over her face, exhaling sharply. "Miriam, she's a psychopath. She doesn't feel anything. She's playing you."

Miriam's fingers drummed against the counter. Maybe she was. But Charlotte had smirked when Jilly asked about Erica. And that meant something.

Maybe Charlotte wasn't done confessing. Maybe, there was still one more secret left to tell. Miriam exhaled, her breath fogging up the glass of the window. Tomorrow, she'd find out. One way or another.

28

PRISON BAIT

The Willow Creek Holding Facility wasn't much to look at, a squat, gray building on the outskirts of town, surrounded by a high, chain-link fence. The parking lot was cracked and uneven, small puddles collecting in dips along the concrete from last night's rain.

It didn't belong here, not in a town like this.

But neither did a murderer.

Miriam stepped through the front entrance, greeted immediately by the sterile scent of bleach and something metallic. The waiting area was a pale shade of green, the chairs bolted to the floor, the ceiling buzzing with fluorescent lights.

Everything about the place was ugly and functional.

She checked in at the front desk, where a tired-looking officer gave her a quick once-over before leading her down a long, dimly lit hallway. Her footsteps echoed. The air was thick with something unspoken.

Miriam had visited plenty of uncomfortable places in her life, but this was different. This wasn't a visit. This was an interrogation.

She passed several holding cells on the way, the occasional

glimpse of a figure behind steel bars, slouched or pacing, staring vacantly at nothing. A guard stood at the end of the hall, arms crossed, eyes flicking up at her briefly before he opened a heavy, reinforced metal door.

"She's waiting for you," he said.

His voice was gruff, uninterested, but there was something else beneath it. A wariness. Miriam wasn't sure if it was for her sake, or his own.

The room was small, cold, windowless. Just a metal table, two chairs, a single overhead light casting sharp shadows against the walls.

Charlotte was already waiting for her. Her wrists were cuffed to the table, her ankles chained to the floor. But despite her restraints, despite everything, she still managed to look composed. Poised. Dangerous, even.

Her once carefully styled blonde hair was now a wild, tangled mess, falling in uneven waves around her face. Dark circles bruised the skin beneath her eyes, but her expression remained serene.

She had swapped her designer dresses for an orange prison jumpsuit, baggy and ill-fitting, yet somehow, she still managed to wear it with an air of quiet defiance. Like the walls around her, the shackles on her wrists, none of it could touch her.

Miriam had expected some kind of deterioration. Some sign that Charlotte was breaking. But instead, she was smirking.

"You came."

Miriam pulled out the chair opposite her and sat down. Charlotte's eyes flickered over her, assessing, calculating. Something about her demeanor was almost relaxed. And that, more than anything, unnerved Miriam the most.

"You said you had something to tell me." Miriam kept her voice neutral, calm.

Charlotte exhaled slowly, leaning back in her chair as much as her chains allowed. "You want the truth?"

Miriam didn't blink. "That would be a start."

Charlotte's smirk widened just slightly. Then she leaned forward, lowering her voice as she said, "You already know I killed Erica, too."

Miriam had prepared for this moment. She had expected it and yet, hearing it out loud again still felt like a punch to the stomach. She forced herself to remain still, to not react. But Charlotte noticed anyway. Her lips curled.

Miriam exhaled slowly. "Why?"

Charlotte's smile dimmed. For the first time since she had walked into the room, something shifted. Something darker.

"She knew about me and Simon." Charlotte's voice was quiet now, controlled. "She found out. And she was going to tell Vanessa."

Miriam's stomach twisted.

Charlotte's eyes darkened. "What I didn't know at first, what I only later figured out," a slow, bitter laugh escaped her lips. "Was that she was sleeping with him too. And it seems that that's why he had gone cold on me."

Miriam held her breath. Charlotte's lips pressed together, a small twitch in her jaw.

"I didn't understand why she was so angry about him sleeping with me," she admitted. "She was furious, almost betrayed." Charlotte shook her head. "I thought she was trying to take the moral high ground. But no. She was jealous."

A pause. A long, terrible pause. Then Charlotte let out a breath.

"She was drunk when I got there," she said flatly. "Slurring. Dramatic. She said she was going to ruin me, that Vanessa deserved to know the truth. That I deserved to have my life ripped apart."

Charlotte exhaled slowly.

"She was in the pool, floating like she didn't have a care in the world. I asked her to stop, to just let it go. But she just..." her fingers flattened against the table. "She just laughed at me."

Miriam's chest tightened. Charlotte lifted her gaze, her voice softer now.

"I walked over to her. Told her to get out. She ignored me. So, I leaned down, grabbed her wrist. She yanked away, told me to get off her."

Charlotte tilted her head slightly.

"So, I pushed her under."

Miriam stiffened.

"She fought," Charlotte continued, her tone chillingly detached now. "Not at first. At first, she thought I was just messing with her. But then..." her eyes flickered. "She started panicking."

Silence.

"She clawed at my arms. Kicked. But I was stronger. And she was drunk. She got too tired to fight..."

Charlotte gave a slow, deliberate shrug. Miriam swallowed the nausea rising in her throat.

Charlotte smiled. "And you know what's funny?"

Miriam didn't want to know. But Charlotte told her anyway.

"I didn't have to." She exhaled a soft, bitter laugh. "I thought I was silencing her. That if I just stopped her from talking, I'd be fine."

She leaned forward, her cuffs rattling slightly against the table.

"But Vanessa already knew." A cruel smirk played on her lips.

"All that effort," she murmured. "All that panic. And it was pointless."

Miriam stared at her, horrified.

Charlotte let out a breath. "I suppose that's the real tragedy, isn't it?"

Miriam stood up abruptly, her chair scraping against the floor, the sound slicing through the cold silence.

Charlotte's smirk didn't falter. If anything, it grew. But Miriam wasn't finished. She took a step closer to the table, leaning in just slightly, lowering her voice to something only Charlotte could hear.

"You think you're clever," she said, her tone calm, even. Too even.

Charlotte's smile twitched, just slightly.

Miriam held her gaze. "But you're not as smart as you think you are."

Charlotte blinked, the smallest flicker of irritation flashing across her face.

Miriam tilted her head. "You thought you could control everything. That no one would ever be able to touch you." She exhaled, slow and deliberate. "But you made one mistake."

Charlotte's fingers tightened into fists against the metal table. "Oh?"

Miriam smiled. "You got caught."

Charlotte's jaw clenched.

Miriam straightened. "And now? You get to spend the rest of your life right here, in places like this, wearing that jumpsuit, waiting for guards to tell you when you can eat, when you can sleep, when you can breathe."

She leaned in just a little closer, voice a whisper now.

"You don't own anything anymore, Charlotte. No power, no influence. Just time to think. And that's the cruelest punishment of all, isn't it?"

Charlotte didn't move. Didn't smirk. Didn't blink.

For the first time since Miriam had stepped into the room, Charlotte had nothing to say.

Miriam gave her one last look, then turned on her heel.

The guards moved in, unlocking Charlotte's cuffs from the table, ready to lead her back to her cell.

As Miriam stepped toward the door, she glanced back, just once. Charlotte was staring after her. Not smug. Not amused. Just silent.

As Miriam stepped out into the fluorescent-lit hallway, the door slamming shut behind her, she knew Charlotte would finally have to face something she had spent her entire life avoiding. The consequences.

29

A NEW CHAPTER

It had been several weeks since Charlotte Davenport's shocking arrest, but the ripple effects still lingered in Willow Creek. The town, once proud of its postcard-perfect streets and tight-knit community, had become a shadow of its former self.

Residents locked their doors now, double-checking the bolts before they went to bed. Windows that once stood open to let in the crisp autumn breeze were shut tight, blinds drawn, curtains pulled.

The sidewalks, once bustling with friendly chatter and carefree strollers, were eerily quiet. People walked quickly, heads down, glancing over their shoulders as if danger might be lurking in every shadow.

Children no longer played freely in the parks without an adult hovering close by. Even the usual cheer of the Saturday farmers' market had dimmed; vendors stood stiffly behind their stalls, their smiles strained, their eyes darting nervously.

Willow Creek, with its white picket fences and manicured lawns, had always prided itself on being safe. Untouchable. But now it felt like a place where anything could happen.

The absence of Charlotte's family in Willow Creek was palpable, like a hole torn in the town's fabric. Bobby and the kids had vanished almost as quickly as the moving van had arrived, their departure as sudden and quiet as the collapse of a house of cards.

There had been no goodbyes, no tearful farewells, no acknowledgment of the life they'd left behind.

The house, once a symbol of the Davenport's status and success, now sat empty and lifeless, its windows dark, the front yard untended.

"Did you hear?" whispered a woman at the grocery store. "He didn't even tell the school they were leaving. Just pulled the kids out."

"Can you blame him?" another replied. "Imagine growing up knowing your mother was a murderer."

Jilly had overheard a dozen conversations like this in the past week, each one tinged with a mix of pity, judgment, and morbid curiosity.

She couldn't help but feel a pang of sadness for Charlotte's children. They were just kids, after all, innocent bystanders in the fallout of their mother's crimes.

She wondered what their lives looked like now. Were they huddled in some distant town, trying to start over? Did they even understand what their mother had done?

And Bobby? Jilly felt a complicated swirl of emotions when she thought about him.

Part of her despised him for being weak, for looking the other way when Charlotte's life began to unravel. But another part of her felt a twinge of pity. He had been caught in the storm, too. Not innocent, perhaps, but certainly not deserving of all this.

The memorial for Erica and Vanessa was held on a crisp

autumn afternoon, the kind of day that should have been beautiful, peaceful.

The gazebo in the town square had been draped with flowers, most of them in soft shades of white and pink. Framed photos of Erica and Vanessa sat side by side on a small table, surrounded by flickering candles. It was a strange pairing, and everyone knew it.

Vanessa Caldwell—the queen of perfection, the embodiment of grace and elegance. Erica Miller—messy, flawed, broken.

And yet, here they were, sharing a memorial service.

The crowd gathered slowly, filling the square with a mix of familiar faces and curious outsiders. Women in tailored coats clutched tissues in one hand and their purses in the other, as though even here they weren't entirely safe. Men stood stiffly, their hands jammed into their pockets, speaking in low murmurs that carried the weight of discomfort.

The pastor, a balding man with a kind but weary face, stood on the steps of the gazebo, his hands clasped tightly around a worn leather Bible. He looked as though the weight of this town's grief had settled directly onto his shoulders.

He began his speech with a soft clearing of his throat.

"We gather here today," he said, his voice steady but solemn, "to remember two women who were taken from us far too soon. Vanessa Caldwell, who touched so many lives with her generosity and grace, and Erica Miller, whose kindness and wit brought light to those who knew her best."

The crowd murmured softly, shifting uncomfortably.

Miriam caught the subtle glances exchanged between some of the book club members. Jilly's lips tightened into a thin line. Her arms were crossed protectively over her chest. Pam stared at the ground, while Dani and Tiffany exchanged pointed looks. Bee stood locked to her children as though they were life rafts.

The pastor continued, oblivious to the tension. "We may never understand why such tragedies occurred in our community. But we must remember that even in the face of darkness, we are called to forgive, to love, and to find hope in one another."

His words hung in the air, but they felt hollow. The people of Willow Creek weren't ready to forgive. They weren't ready for hope.

The remaining members of the book club stood together near the back of the crowd. Not by choice. None of them had spoken much since Charlotte's arrest.

Miriam simply watched. Watched the way the town clung to Vanessa's image, the way they whispered about how tragic it was, how beautiful she had been, how much of a loss her death was for the community. Perfect Vanessa.

"Give me a break," Pam muttered under her breath.

Miriam turned to her, raising an eyebrow. "What?"

Pam gestured toward the table with the photos and candles, her lips curled in irritation. "Look at this."

Dani leaned in slightly. "What's wrong with it?"

Pam scoffed. "All these flowers. All this fuss. You'd think she was a saint."

Dani's voice was low, cautious. "She's dead, Pam."

"So is Erica," Pam shot back. "And look at how they're treating her. Like she's an afterthought."

Miriam's eyes flicked toward the photos again.

She couldn't argue with that.

The flowers were mostly arranged around Vanessa's photo, a perfectly lit portrait of her with her flawless blonde hair and dazzling smile. Erica's photo was smaller, tucked slightly to the side, a candid shot where she wasn't even looking directly at the camera.

"Pam's right," Jilly muttered, her voice shaking with anger.

"Vanessa was a bully. She blackmailed me. She blackmailed Charlotte. God knows what else she did to people in this town. And now she's being treated like some kind of tragic hero."

Miriam placed a hand on Jilly's arm, her grip gentle but firm. "Let it go."

Jilly turned to her, her eyes blazing. "How can you *stand* this?"

Miriam's voice was calm, steady. "Because it's not about Vanessa. Not really. It's about the town. They need to believe she was perfect. It makes them feel safe. Like what happened can't happen again."

Jilly shook her head, tears welling in her eyes. "But it's a lie."

"Most things are," Miriam said quietly.

As the service ended and the crowd began to disperse, the book club members remained standing together, their presence an awkward reminder of the cracks in the town's polished surface.

Pam broke the silence first, letting out a shaky laugh. "Well, I guess this is it. The last time we'll all be in the same place."

Dani nodded but her expression was grim. "The book club's officially over."

"No kidding," Tiffany muttered.

Bee hesitated, then said softly, "Do you think we'll ever get past this?"

Miriam didn't answer. She looked out over the square, watching the last of the crowd drift away. Watching the flowers and candles flicker in the soft breeze. Watching as the town tried, and failed, to bury its secrets. Because no matter how many flowers they laid, no matter how many whispered prayers they offered, Willow Creek would never forget. And neither would Miriam. Not ever.

As the crowd at the memorial began to thin, Jilly found

herself standing at the edge of the square, staring at the flickering candles on the table.

So many lives ruined. Vanessa, Erica, Charlotte. Gone. But the damage didn't stop with them.

Vanessa's husband, Simon, now a shell of a man, wandering the town like a ghost, unable to shake the weight of his own guilt.

Charlotte's children, ripped from their home, forced to carry the shame of their mother's crimes.

Bobby, once the mild-mannered man who stood awkwardly on the edges of every book club event, now the punchline of cruel jokes whispered in every corner of Willow Creek.

And what about the rest of them?

Jilly looked at Bee, fidgeting with her purse strap, her eyes darting nervously from side to side. Dani and Tiffany, once so close, and now they could barely stand to be near each other after weeks of tension and suspicion.

And Miriam. Jilly watched her from a distance, standing perfectly still, her sharp eyes taking in everything. They were all scarred, fractured, holding onto the pieces of what had once been normal lives. All because of poor choices. Secrets. Lies.

The book club had started as a place for connection, for friendship. Now, it was a graveyard.

Jilly tightened her arms around herself, a bitter laugh catching in her throat.

She had always thought herself the quiet one, the harmless one. But even she had made choices that had led her here, to this moment, to this mess.

The book club wasn't just Charlotte's downfall. It was everyone's.

Miriam's voice broke through her thoughts.

"Ready to go?"

Jilly turned, blinking back the tears she hadn't realized were there. She nodded. As they walked away from the square, Jilly cast one last look over her shoulder. The candles flickered in the soft breeze, the flowers beginning to wilt. It was a beautiful display. But it couldn't hide the truth. The town wasn't grieving for the people they had lost. They were grieving for the illusion they had shattered.

30

A NEW START

The bookstore smelled of fresh paper, the way it always did after a new delivery. Stacks of cardboard boxes were piled in the back corner, their contents waiting to be shelved, cataloged, and arranged into neat rows.

Jilly stood behind the counter, carefully slicing through packing tape with a box cutter. Her movements were slow, almost mechanical, as though the act of unpacking books was the only thing keeping her grounded.

Miriam knelt by a lower shelf, sliding hardcovers into their places. She worked methodically, her fingers brushing against the crisp spines, her thoughts elsewhere.

The store felt quiet, peaceful even, but there was an underlying tension between the two women, the unspoken weight of everything they'd been through.

Jilly glanced at Miriam, her brow furrowing. She couldn't help but notice how Miriam had changed over the past few weeks—her sharp eyes seemed even sharper now, her movements more deliberate, her presence more commanding.

Finally, Jilly broke the silence.

"Do you ever stop thinking about it?" she asked quietly, her voice almost hesitant.

Miriam didn't look up. "About what?"

"You know what."

Miriam slid another book into place, pausing for a moment. She exhaled softly.

"No," she admitted. "I don't."

Jilly let out a sigh, setting a stack of books on the counter. "I just can't wrap my head around how you figured it all out. How you pieced everything together."

Miriam straightened, dusting her hands off on her jeans.

"It wasn't easy," she said, her tone calm but thoughtful.

Jilly leaned against the counter, crossing her arms. "Start from the beginning."

"At first," Miriam said, "I didn't suspect Charlotte at all. She didn't seem the type. Too careful. Too composed."

Jilly nodded. "She was good at hiding things."

"Too good," Miriam agreed. "But that's what tipped me off. The way she always seemed... perfect. Too perfect."

She moved to the counter, picking up a small stack of hardcovers.

"But it wasn't until I started digging into Vanessa that I found the first crack," she continued. "Vanessa wasn't as careful as Charlotte. She left pieces behind."

Jilly frowned. "Pieces?"

Miriam gave a small, knowing smile.

"Emails," she said. "Vanessa's husband, Simon, wasn't exactly discreet. He forwarded certain conversations to himself, probably as some kind of insurance. When Vanessa found out about his affair with Erica, she made sure to get copies of those emails. And let's just say, Simon wasn't her only target."

Jilly's eyes widened. "You found those?"

"Not at first," Miriam admitted. "But I overheard Simon

arguing with a lawyer at the memorial planning meeting. He mentioned Vanessa's habit of documenting 'sensitive' information. That's when I started asking questions."

Jilly set her box cutter down, her hands trembling slightly. "You were asking questions about Vanessa?"

Miriam nodded. "Quietly. I didn't want to draw attention to myself. But the more I asked, the more I found out. Vanessa had a reputation for keeping files. Emails, photos, texts—she kept dirt on people to hold over them."

Jilly paled. "You mean she really had...?"

"Yes," Miriam said, her voice soft. "She had a folder. On you. On Charlotte. On Erica. She kept it in her office at home, locked away in a drawer."

Charlotte was desperate to protect her secrets. Vanessa and Erica both knew too much."

Jilly sighed, running a hand through her hair. "You know, Simon came by the store a few days ago."

Miriam raised an eyebrow. "What did he want?"

Jilly hesitated, then let out a bitter laugh. "He told me I don't have to repay the loan Vanessa gave me. Said he wanted to make things right."

Miriam frowned. "That's generous of him."

"Oh, please," Jilly snapped. "He's just trying to save face. He's probably hoping I'll feel sorry for him. As if cheating on his wife with two women in our book club wasn't bad enough."

Miriam smirked. "Classic Simon."

Jilly shook her head, her expression softening slightly. "It's just sad, you know? All of it. The book club, the friendships, everything. It's all gone now. And for what?"

Miriam was silent for a moment, her gaze drifting to the shelves around them.

The book club had started as something simple, innocent. A

way to connect, to escape the monotony of suburban life. But now it was nothing but ashes.

"Everyone wanted something," Miriam said finally. "Vanessa wanted power. Charlotte wanted control. Erica wanted revenge. And the rest of us, we wanted to belong."

Jilly nodded slowly, her eyes glistening with unshed tears. "But it didn't matter, did it? It all fell apart anyway."

Miriam placed a gentle hand on Jilly's shoulder. "Sometimes, things have to fall apart to show us what they really were."

Jilly let out a shaky breath, brushing away a tear. "Do you think we'll ever be normal again?"

Miriam didn't answer right away. She simply turned back to the shelves, picking up another stack of books.

"No," she said softly. "But maybe that's not such a bad thing."

The store fell silent again, the only sound the faint rustle of pages and the soft patter of rain against the windows.

Outside, the world kept turning. But inside the bookstore, two women stood among the ruins of something they had once believed in, trying to make sense of it all.

"Do you know what?" Miriam said turning, holding a copy of Colleen Hoover's latest bestseller in her hand, "I have an idea." Her eyes twinkled with youthful excitement. "I think we've all lost enough over the last few weeks. I think that we need to breath some new life back into this town and I know just where to begin."

31

SECOND CHANCES

The scent of freshly brewed tea and lemon cake filled the bookstore, mingling with the earthy aroma of books and polished wood. Sunlight streamed through the large windows at the front, casting warm golden pools across the floor and shelves.

Jilly stood near the counter, carefully arranging a tray of pastries. Her movements were precise but quick, a quiet energy buzzing beneath her usually cautious demeanor. A soft hum escaped her lips as she worked, a tune Miriam couldn't quite place but found soothing, nonetheless.

At the back of the store, Miriam straightened a row of mismatched chairs around a collection of small round tables. Each table held a stack of books—their first read for the new book club, carefully chosen for its lighthearted tone and uplifting story.

Everything was perfect.

"Well," Miriam said, stepping back to inspect her work, her hands on her hips. "What do you think?"

Jilly glanced up from the pastries, a small smile tugging at the corners of her mouth. "It looks good," she said softly. "Really good."

Miriam smirked. "Just good?"

Jilly rolled her eyes, but her smile widened. "Okay, fine. It looks amazing. Are you happy?"

"Very," Miriam said, brushing her hands together. She tilted her head toward the tray Jilly was fussing over. "And the cakes?"

"Perfect," Jilly replied, giving the tray one last nudge to center it. "Do you think we'll have enough?"

"We've got three trays of pastries, two cakes, and more tea than we'll ever need," Miriam said with a laugh. "If they're still hungry after that, we'll point them to the bakery down the street."

The two women paused for a moment, taking in the scene they had created. The bookstore felt warm, inviting, a stark contrast to how it had felt just weeks ago, heavy with secrets and tension.

Jilly fiddled with the hem of her sweater, her eyes scanning the room. "Do you think people will actually show up?"

Miriam shot her a look. "You're joking, right? Have you seen how many people signed up online? Half the town wants to be part of this."

Jilly bit her lip. "Yeah, but after everything that happened, do you think they'll really want to be here? With us?"

Miriam softened, stepping closer.

"Look at it like this," she said gently, resting a hand on Jilly's arm. "This is a fresh start. For both of us. For the store. For the book club. What happened before, it doesn't have to define us."

Jilly hesitated, then nodded. "You're right. It's just weird, you know? Starting over like this."

"It is," Miriam admitted. "But weird isn't always bad."

They went back to their tasks, tidying the last few details. Miriam rearranged a small sign near the front door that read:

Willow Creek Book Club – Meeting Today at 6 PM

The letters were bold and inviting, a promise of something new, something better.

Jilly placed a vase of fresh flowers on the main table, their vibrant colors adding a touch of life and cheerfulness to the space. She glanced at the clock on the wall and took a deep breath.

"Ten minutes," she said. "It's almost time."

Miriam smiled, reaching for a stack of coasters. "Ready?"

"As ready as I'll ever be," Jilly replied, her voice steady but tinged with anticipation.

The bell above the door jingled softly, signaling the first arrival.

A young woman stepped inside. Her expression was curious but shy. She clutched a tote bag to her chest, the faintest hint of nervousness flickering in her eyes.

"Hi," she said, her voice warm but tentative. "I'm here for the book club."

Miriam's smile widened. "Welcome. Come on in. Help yourself to some tea and cake. We'll get started in a few minutes."

The woman nodded, relaxing slightly as she moved toward the refreshments.

The door jingled again, and this time, two women entered together, chatting softly. Then another, and another. Within minutes, the room began to fill with new faces, new voices, and an energy that felt fresh and full of possibility.

Jilly stood by the counter, watching as the newcomers settled into the chairs and introduced themselves to one another. She glanced at Miriam, who was moving confidently through the room, offering smiles and small talk like she'd been doing it her whole life.

For the first time in weeks, Jilly felt a flicker of hope.

"This might actually work," she murmured to herself.

Miriam caught her eye and gave her a knowing smile, as though she'd heard her. And as the chatter grew louder, as the smell of tea and cake mingled with the soft rustle of books and laughter, Jilly realized something.

The book club wasn't just a new chapter for the town. It was a new chapter for her. For Miriam. For all of them. And for the first time in a long time, she felt ready to turn the page.

The door jingled again, and a tall woman with short auburn hair and a confident stride walked in. She wore a crisp blazer over jeans, her presence radiating calm authority. She glanced around the room with a slight smile before heading toward Miriam and Jilly.

"Hi, I'm Denise," she said, her voice warm but self-assured. "I just moved to Willow Creek last month. Thought joining a book club would be a good way to meet people."

"Welcome, Denise," Miriam said, extending a hand. "I'm Miriam, and this is Jilly. We're so glad you could join us."

Denise smiled, her green eyes crinkling at the corners. "Thanks. It looks cozy here. I was worried it'd be too formal, but this is perfect."

"We're aiming for fun and relaxed," Jilly said with a small smile. "Help yourself to some tea and cake. We'll start soon."

Denise nodded and moved toward the refreshment table, pausing to introduce herself to the women already seated.

Next came a petite woman in her late thirties with a bright, cheerful expression and curly blonde hair pulled into a loose bun. She was juggling a diaper bag and a small stack of books, clearly frazzled but determined.

"Hi, I'm Elsie," she said breathlessly as she reached the counter. "Sorry I'm late—I had to drop my youngest off with my husband. He promised he could handle bedtime tonight, but, well..." She rolled her eyes playfully. "We'll see."

Jilly laughed softly. "Don't worry, Elsie. You're right on time."

Elsie beamed. "This is my first book club ever. I've been meaning to join one for years, but, you know, kids."

Miriam handed her a cup of tea. "Well, you're here now, and that's what matters."

Elsie took the cup gratefully and headed to an open seat, chatting with the women nearby as she settled in.

Behind her came a woman in her fifties with silver-streaked hair and a colorful scarf wrapped around her neck. She had a kind, serene air about her and carried a notebook tucked under her arm.

"Hello, I'm Patty," she said, her voice soft but melodic. "I'm so happy to see a new book club forming. I've lived here for years but never found one that felt quite right."

"Well, Patty," Miriam said with a smile. "This one is all about starting fresh. We're glad you're here."

Patty nodded, her smile widening. "Fresh starts are exactly what I need."

As Patty found a seat, another newcomer walked in—a young woman in her early twenties with long dark hair and a nervous but eager expression. She wore a hoodie and jeans, her hands stuffed into her pockets.

"Hi," she said quietly. "I'm Katie. I, uh, just graduated college and moved back in with my parents. Thought this might be a good way to... you know, get out of the house."

"Of course," Jilly said warmly. "We're happy to have you, Katie. There's tea and cake over there, please help yourself."

Katie nodded quickly and her cheeks flushed pink as she headed to the refreshment table.

As the room filled, the atmosphere grew warm and lively. Laughter bubbled up from different corners of the space as introductions were made and conversations blossomed.

Unlike the old book club, where tension and competition had lingered beneath the surface, this group felt open, inviting.

Elsie was already swapping bedtime horror stories with Denise, who offered advice on managing three kids while working full-time. Patty sat with Katie, gently encouraging her to talk about her college experiences.

Miriam stood near the counter, watching it all unfold with a quiet smile.

"This feels... different," Jilly said softly, stepping up beside her.

"It is," Miriam replied, her voice calm but satisfied.

Jilly glanced at her. "Do you think it'll last?"

Miriam took a moment, her gaze sweeping across the room. The new members were chatting easily, their voices rising and falling in a comforting rhythm. The soft clink of teacups and the hum of friendly conversation filled the store, creating an atmosphere of genuine warmth.

"I think it's off to a good start," Miriam said finally.

Jilly nodded, a small smile breaking through her uncertainty. "Maybe we're not as broken as we thought."

Miriam turned to her, her expression thoughtful. "Or maybe we're just learning how to rebuild."

Jilly didn't reply, but the relief on her face spoke volumes. And as the evening unfolded, as the women settled into their chairs and the first book discussion began, the bookstore felt like it had finally found its purpose again.

The sing song of conversation filled the bookstore, a gentle rhythm of laughter and soft chatter that felt worlds away from the tension that had defined the old book club. The women, each with their own unique energy, had settled into their seats, teacups in hand, small plates of cake balanced on their laps.

Miriam stood near the head of the table, a quiet smile playing on her lips as she watched the group. She felt something she hadn't expected to feel again after everything that had happened.

Hope.

Clearing her throat softly, Miriam drew the group's attention. The conversations fell away, the women turning their gazes toward her.

"Thank you all for coming tonight," Miriam began, her voice warm and steady. "I know some of you might be nervous, especially after everything this town has been through. But this is a fresh start—for all of us. A chance to leave the past behind and focus on what brought us here in the first place: our love of books."

The women nodded, their expressions ranging from eager to reflective.

Miriam reached down and lifted a hardcover book from the table, holding it up so everyone could see.

It was an old classic mystery novel, the cover worn but elegant, the title embossed in gold letters.

"For our first read," she said, a small smile tugging at her lips, "I thought we'd start with something light but gripping. This is a story about secrets, lies, and, of course, a murder or two. But don't worry, this one is purely fictional."

A ripple of laughter ran through the group, easing the last traces of tension that lingered in the room.

Denise leaned forward and Miriam noticed her green eyes sparkling. "A mystery? Bold choice for a fresh start."

Miriam shrugged playfully. "It felt appropriate."

Elsie raised her hand, a bright grin on her face. "Do we get hints about the ending?"

"Absolutely not," Miriam said firmly, but her smile widened. "That's the fun of it. You'll just have to read and find out."

Miriam placed the book back on the table, resting her hands on the edges as she looked around the room.

"I know the last book club in this town didn't exactly end well," she said, her tone soft but serious. "But this time, we're starting fresh. No secrets. No tension. Just a group of women coming together to share stories, thoughts, and maybe a little cake."

Another ripple of laughter followed, and Jilly, standing near the counter, raised her teacup in a silent toast. Miriam reached for her own teacup, holding it up as she looked at the women gathered before her.

"This time," she said, her voice steady but filled with quiet determination, "let's leave the crime to the mystery writers."

The room erupted in laughter and a chorus of hear-hears, the women clinking their cups together in a toast. For the first time in months, the bookstore felt alive and as Miriam sipped her tea, she couldn't help but think that maybe, just maybe, the worst was finally behind them.

This wasn't just a new chapter. It was a whole new story.

EPILOGUE

Prison is quieter than I expected. At least, at night it is.

During the day, it's filled with the sounds of metal doors slamming, guards barking orders, women arguing in corners of the yard. There's always something happening. Someone crying in their bunk, someone sneaking contraband under a table, someone making threats they may or may not follow through on.

But at night, when the lights dim and the whispers die down, that's when I do my best thinking.

Because here, in this concrete box, surrounded by women I have nothing in common with, my thoughts are the only thing that belong to me.

So, I think about them.

The ones who walked away. The ones who get to pretend that they were just innocent bystanders in all of this. The ones who will never admit how much they enjoyed watching me fall.

No one cares who you were before you got here.

Wealth, status, beauty, none of it matters when you're stripped down to the same beige jumpsuit as everyone else.

Some of the other women watch me, waiting to see how I'll break.

The first few weeks, a few tried to intimidate me, bumping into me in the corridors, "accidentally" knocking my food tray onto the floor. One woman, a gang leader, from what I've gathered, cornered me in the laundry room, waiting for me to cower.

I smiled instead. And she backed off. Because the thing about predators? They recognize their own.

I don't make friends, but I don't make enemies either. I'm too cold for the weak and too unpredictable for the strong. And so, I walk through this place like a ghost, ignored by some, watched carefully by others.

The guards don't trust me. They never say it, but I see it in their eyes. They're used to women who fight, who scream, who break down. Not women like me. Women who wait. Women who watch. Women who never look sorry.

Most of the women here have someone waiting for them.

A sister who visits. A boyfriend who writes letters. A mother who still believes they're good at heart. I have no one.

Bobby took the boys and left Willow Creek. I don't know where they are, and I know I should care. But I don't.

They were never mine, anyway. Not really. They belonged to the life I built. And now, that life is gone. All I have left is the town I burned to the ground.

I do sometimes wonder about them, the ones who survived.

Miriam made herself the town's moral compass, the great detective, the one who uncovered the truth.

People eat that shit up. They like knowing there was a villain to blame. A monster to point at. A name to whisper in hushed tones over morning coffee.

Miriam came out of this untouched. Stronger, even.

And Jilly? Sweet, shaky Jilly with her secondhand cardigans and nervous little smiles? She finally grew a spine.

I read an article someone sent me, about how she expanded the bookstore, turned it into a community hub. Oh, the irony.

It took a few murders for her to finally find her voice.

Pam and Bee were never built for the spotlight. I heard Bee sold her house and moved upstate. She couldn't take the whispers, and the pitying looks in the grocery store. She never wanted to be involved in any of this, and yet there she was, front and center for the fallout.

Pam didn't leave, but she shrank. Stopped going to the club. Stopped socializing as much. Some people just aren't made for carrying the weight of things like this. They retreat. And the town lets them. Because as much as people love gossip, they also love forgetting.

Oh, Willow Creek pretends it's changed.

They installed new streetlights, started a community watch program. They shake their heads and sigh dramatically when my name is brought up, talking about how they never saw it coming.

But the truth is nothing really changes.

The women still whisper at brunch. The men still carry their secrets in crisp, monogrammed pockets. The houses are still clean, the lawns are still trimmed, and underneath it all, the same old darkness still lingers.

They just learned to hide it better. For now.

But I hope they never recover. I hope every time they pass my old house, they feel a chill in their bones. I hope they wonder if they ever really knew the women who sat beside them at dinner parties. Because here's the thing. I was not the first monster in Willow Creek. And I won't be the last.

People like Miriam think they won. They think because I'm

behind bars, because my nails are chipped and my hair has lost its shine, that I've been defeated.

They think the worst is over. That light has returned. But the thing about light, is it doesn't erase the monsters. It just casts longer shadows.

And if there's one thing I know for certain, monsters always lurk in the shadows. Even in Willow Creek. Especially in Willow Creek.

The town just hasn't met the next one yet. But it will.

Printed in Dunstable, United Kingdom

78240869R00151